The
Invisible
Girl

D0257380

Northamptonshire Libraries & Information Service	
80 002 714 037	
Peters	13-Sep-07
CF	£5.99

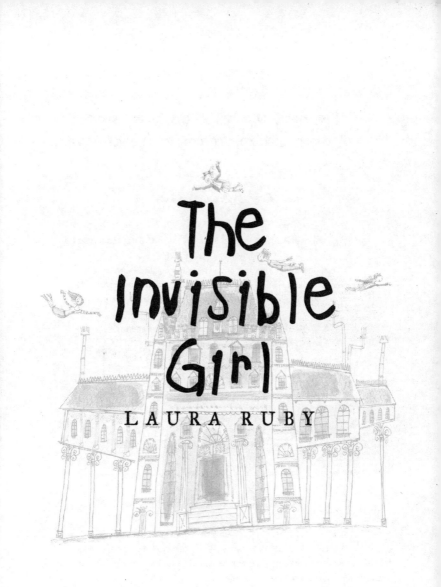

The Invisible Girl

LAURA RUBY

For Anne, who has kittens in her pockets
And for Gretchen, the original Answer Hand

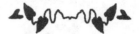

First published in Hardback in Great Britain by HarperCollins *Children's Books* as
The Wall and The Wing 2006
This edition published in Great Britain by HarperCollins *Children's Books* 2007
HarperCollins *Children's Books* is a division of HarperCollins*Publishers* Ltd
77-85 Fulham Palace Road, Hammersmith, London W6 8JB

The HarperCollins *Children's Books* website address is
www.harpercollinschildrensbooks.co.uk

1

Copyright © Laura Ruby 2006

ISBN-13: 978-0-00-721008-4
ISBN-10: 0-00-721008-6

Laura Ruby reserves the right to be identified as the author of the work.

Printed and bound in England by Clays Ltd, St Ives plc

Conditions of Sale
This book is sold subject to the condition that it shall not, by way of trade or
otherwise, be lent, re-sold, hired out or otherwise circulated without the publisher's prior
consent in any form, binding or cover other than that in which it is published and without
a similar condition including this condition being imposed on the subsequent publisher.

This book is proudly printed on paper which contains wood
from well managed forests, certified in accordance with
the rules of the Forest Stewardship Council.
For more information about FSC,
please visit www.fsc-uk.org

Mixed Sources
Product group from well managed
forests and other controlled sources
www.fsc.org Cert no. SW-COC-1806
© 1996 Forest Stewardship Council
FSC

THE CHAPTER BEFORE THE FIRST

The Professor Remembers

IN A VAST AND SPARKLING city, a city at the centre of the universe, one little man remembered something big.

He was very old, this little man, his full name forgotten over the years. He called himself The Professor. His specialities were numerous and included psychology, criminology, mathematics, history, aerodynamics, zoology and gardening. He also collected beer cans.

Other than the delivery boy who left his groceries at the back door, The Professor hadn't seen anyone in at least ten years. It was just as well, since a hair-growing experiment had left him with a head full of long green grass. Also, he didn't like clothing, so he wore ladies' snap-front housedresses and rubber flip-flops with white socks. He spent much of his time fiddling in his workshop, feeding the many kittens that popped out of his pockets and looking things up on eBay.

Today he stood in front of his blackboard – which was covered with mathematical equations – tugging at a dandelion that had poked up through the lawn on his scalp. Suddenly, his eyes widened. He scrawled a few more equations. Yes! He saw it. Right there, in his many calculations.

A child.

He stared at the figures dancing across the board, his forehead creased with annoyance. How on earth he could have forgotten that such a thing, such a *person*, existed, was beyond him. But The Professor simply didn't like people. Not their company, not their conversation, *nada*. Anything having to do with people made the roots of his teeth pulse with irritation. And here on his blackboard was proof that a very particular sort of person had been born into a cruel and stupid world filled with cruel and stupid people.

Frankly, The Professor wanted nothing to do with any of them.

But facts are facts and The Professor liked to keep his straight. Shaking his head at himself, he sat down at his lab table, pulled his notebook from underneath a large tabby cat and made a few notes. "Approx. once every century or so," he wrote. "Wall. Usually, but not always, female."

After scribbling these notes, The Professor smoothed out a rumpled map. "One lived here," he muttered to himself, putting a dot on the map, "another here. This one was born there and moved here." When he finished plotting points, he connected the dots, then took out a protractor to measure the angles between. Lost in thought, he tapped his teeth with his pencil. Something wasn't quite adding up. Where could this girl be?

After working for two frustrating hours, he walked over to a filing cabinet, unlocked the bottom drawer and pulled from it what looked like a human hand mounted upright on a black marble stand. The Answer Hand. He did not like to consult The Answer Hand and very rarely did. The Hand, being a hand, could not speak and was therefore difficult to comprehend. (It knew the sign language alphabet but had to spell everything out. And then it talked in circles.) The Professor could not deny, however, that The Answer Hand often had the answers to perplexing questions, which was exactly why The Professor had purchased it (on eBay of course, from some guy in Okinawa).

He put the mounted Hand on top of the table, pointed at the equations on the blackboard and then to the map. "Where?" he asked.

The Answer Hand's fingers drummed thoughtfully on its marble base. After a few moments, The Hand began rambling about a number of irrelevant topics: the average rainfall in

Borneo, the merits of California wine, the fat content of hot dogs.

"Focus!" barked The Professor, pointing again at the blackboard.

Insulted, The Answer Hand made a waving gesture at the map. When The Professor still didn't understand, The Hand bent at the wrist and finger and crawled across the table, dragging its heavy base behind it. It grabbed the pencil from The Professor, scrawled a star on the map and gave the pencil back.

There, that's where, The Hand signed. *Happy now?*

"I've got to hand it to you," grumbled The Professor sarcastically. He had the distinct feeling that this recent discovery was only going to cause him trouble. Plus there was the fact that one of his cats, Laverna – strong willed, even for a cat – had somehow escaped the safety of his apartment and, despite the flyers he had paid a company to hang around the city, no one had called. In his book, wandering girls and wayward cats added up to a whole lot of unhappiness.

Someone knocked on the door. The Professor scowled, as there hadn't been a knock on the door since, well, the last time there was a knock, possibly months before, years even. The Professor ignored it.

The knock came again, louder. "I only take deliveries Tuesdays and Sundays. Go away," grumbled The Professor. "Go, go, go."

There was a crash as somebody kicked in the door, splintering the jamb. The Professor, always peeved when he was disturbed, was especially rankled. He liked the door the way it was.

Two men strolled down the steps leading to The Professor's rooms. One was handsome, with thick gold hair and a rosy complexion. The other was impossibly tall and dark, a vicious and terrible scar like a huge zipper running diagonally across his face. Both looked familiar, but The Professor couldn't remember where he'd seen them before. A book? A newspaper? And there was something odd about the way the scarred man moved. Not walking so much as drifting or floating.

"Professor," said the handsome one cheerfully. "I hope you don't mind the intrusion."

They were, now that he'd had a few moments to consider it, rather intimidating. "I have important work to do," said The Professor, sounding not the least bit frightened, though his knobby knees had gone as weak as egg noodles.

The handsome man stared pointedly at his head. "I see that you have some dandelion issues." He patted the pockets of his overcoat. "I might have a Weedwhacker around here somewhere."

"What do you want?" The Professor made more notes in his book: "Two scary men. Need weapon. Sharpen pencil?"

The handsome man hesitated, as if waiting for The Professor to say something else. "I'm being rude," he said. "I'm Sy Grabowski."

How do you do, Sweetcheeks? The Answer Hand signed politely.

The Professor dropped his pencil to the floor. "Sweetcheeks Grabowski?"

"In the flesh," said the man, obviously proud that his reputation had preceded him. "This is my associate, Mr John."

"Odd John," said the Professor. Odd John grinned. The Professor could see his teeth were tiny, like a child's. And he could also see that the scar was not *like* a zipper, it *was* a zipper. The silver tab on his forehead glittered when he moved. The Professor decided he would not like Mr John to unzip his face. No. That wouldn't be pleasant; he was sure of it.

Sweetcheeks reached out and plucked the dandelion from the top of The Professor's head, making the little man wince. "We're a little curious."

"Yes, you are. I mean, what about?" said The Professor. He was trying not to focus on The Answer Hand, which was busily erasing the star it had marked on the map and putting another star somewhere in Brooklyn.

"About your research, of course." Sweetcheeks eyed the cats warily, his lip curling up with disgust. "I thought these animals were rare."

"They are," The Professor said and pulled a rambunctious marmalade kitten out of the pocket of his housedress. "Just not here." He placed the kitten directly on top of the map, obscuring what had been drawn on it.

"Hmmm..." said Sweetcheeks, before turning the notebook around to read what The Professor had scribbled there. He smiled when he came to the last bit about the scary men.

"I do lots of research," said The Professor. "What are you interested in? Zoology? Psychology?"

"Oh, a scrap of this, a shred of that," Sweetcheeks said. "I'm especially interested in this curious little thing that happens once every century or more. This very odd thing. Do you know the thing I'm talking about?"

"Yes," said The Professor, wondering how the man had found out about it. He sighed. "You want to know when it happened, I suppose."

"I already know when it happened. I need to know where and I need to know who. And," he said, turning the notebook back to face The Professor, "I need to know now."

"*Who?* I don't know *who* it is," said The Professor. "How would I know that until she shows herself? Er, I mean, until she doesn't show herself rather. As for where, I can't be sure..."

"You can't?" said Sweetcheeks. Using his thumb and forefinger, he lifted the tiny kitten from The Professor's map. "Look on this map, John. A star!"

"Oh, that?" said The Professor. "You mustn't pay attention to that. That map marks the sites of vampire nests around the city, that's all."

"Vampires? Tsk, tsk, Professor. I would think that you would be able to come up with something more creative than that." Sweetcheeks took the map, folded it and slipped it into his breast pocket. "That takes care of where. Now I need to know who."

"I'm telling you, that map is meaningless to you."

"I think The Professor needs a little encouragement, don't you, Mr John?"

Uh-oh, signed The Answer Hand.

"But..." stammered The Professor.

"Please," said Sweetcheeks. "I know that you're a genius. Everyone knows that. I also know that given the proper motivation, you'll find a way to get the information I need, won't he, Mr John?"

The big man smiled with his baby teeth and clasped the silver tab of his zipper, drawing downwards ever so slowly.

The Professor had been correct.

Not pleasant. Not pleasant at all.

CHAPTER 1

The Girl Who Wasn't There

GURL HAD NO IDEA WHAT made her do it. One minute she was surrounded by a sea of snoring girls, staring at the broken lock on the dirty window. The next minute she was racing through the city like an ostrich on fire.

She ran many blocks before she stopped, shocked at herself. She – Gurl the gutless, Gurl the helpless, Gurl the useless – had escaped from Hope House for the Homeless and Hopeless, even if it was only for the night. In front of her, the city snaked out like an amusement park. Gurl drank in as much as she could: the glittering lights of the buildings, the laughter of the people floating by, the bleating horns of the taxis, the scent of car exhaust tinged with tomato sauce.

It was this last that drew her to the section of the city called Little Italy, to Luigi's Restaurant. She loitered in front of it, catching her breath as she watched the diners inside sip wine and twirl spaghetti on to their forks. People-watching was her favourite thing to do and she was very good at it. It seemed to Gurl that everyone was either a watcher or a doer and the watchers were greatly outnumbered. However, there were benefits to watching. For example, inside Luigi's a couple drifted from their table, forgetting a package of leftovers, which was then scooped up by the young waiter.

Gurl ran around the restaurant to the alley behind, crouched next to the garbage cans and waited for the waiter to come out with the evening's trash. Someone kicked a can down a nearby sidewalk and its tinny clang echoed in the alley. "You wanna mess? You wanna mess?" she heard. "Yeah, *boyee*, let's mess!" The voices got louder as a bunch of teenagers flew by the alleyway, throwing long shadows on the greasy pavement. Gurl smiled to herself. The noise was a part of the music of the city and she could listen to it all night long if she wanted.

She leaned her head back against the brick and looked up at the sky, plush and grey like a dome of fur, brightened by the lights from the skyscrapers and billboards. An occasional Wing darted high overhead, looping and weaving around the buildings, but it was nothing like daytime. In the daytime people hopped and bounced and flew all over the place, even if they could only get an inch or two off the ground. Just one more reason to enjoy the dark. Only a few showy Wings rather than thousands of them, thrilled with their own stupid tricks.

Airheads, the whole bunch. She was not jealous of them. Not one little bit.

The metal door of the restaurant opened and the young waiter hopped out, swinging two garbage bags. Even with the garbage bags, the waiter was trying to fly. He jumped straight up, but the weight of the bags and his obvious lack of talent ensured that his feet lifted no more than a yard from the ground. Gurl muffled a giggle with the back of her hand as the waiter jumped his way over to the Dumpster, looking very much like a giant, ungainly frog. He opened the Dumpster and tossed the trash bags inside. Then he turned and leaped into the air, this time clearing the top of the Dumpster before landing. Gurl was sure the waiter – only a few years older than Gurl herself – had hopes of being a great Wing, dreams of joining a Wing team or maybe competing in the citywide festival and taking home the Golden Eagle. She wondered when he would realize that his dream was just that, a dream. When he would see that most of his life would be spent scuttling closer to the earth.

The waiter dropped in a crouch, panting. He looked around, to the left and to the right. Gurl stiffened, keeping herself completely still behind the garbage cans that hid her. He squinted, staring at something. A mouse, running alongside the brick. The waiter jumped up again, crashing to the ground in front of the mouse. It gave a tiny squeal and ran the other way. The waiter did it again, jumping and crashing, terrifying the little animal, laughing as he did so. Gurl waited until he sprang up a third time before reaching out from her hiding place, snatching up the mouse and tucking it into her sleeve.

The waiter landed, his grin turning to a frown, wondering where his victim had gone. Then, shrugging, he veered around and went back into the restaurant, slamming the door behind him.

Gurl rested her hand on the pavement. The mouse crawled out from the safety of her sleeve and ran into the darkness. "Bye," said Gurl, watching as it disappeared through a hole in the brick. She supposed she was lucky that the waiter hadn't seen her, but then again, she was not the type of girl that people noticed – she was too thin, too pale, too quiet. Sometimes people looked right through her as if she weren't there at all, their eyes sliding off her as if she were made of something too slippery to see. *Nobody, nowhere.* When she was little, it made her feel lonely. Now she only felt grateful.

She stretched and walked over to the Dumpster. After throwing open the lid, she dug around until she found what she was looking for: *four* foil-wrapped packages of leftovers. Ravioli, lasagne, salad and a huge hunk of gooey chocolate cake.

If only the other kids from Hope House for the Homeless and Hopeless were here, watching, maybe they wouldn't think so little of her. But they, like everyone else, believed flying was their ticket to fame and fortune, and thought Gurl was horribly afflicted, maybe even contagious. Mrs Terwiliger, the matron of Hope House, had taken her to a specialist once. First he thumped at her knees with a rubber mallet to check her reflexes. He had her breathe in and out very quickly, hyperventilating, to see if the added oxygen might lift her off the floor like a soap bubble. Then he strapped her into a white quilted jacket with huge feather wings and had her run around the office flapping her arms. Finally, he said: "Not everyone can, you know, and most don't do it well. In any case, it's nothing to be ashamed of." As a consolation, he gave Gurl a red and white beanie with a propeller on the top. Mrs Terwiliger told the other kids that people had different talents and they should celebrate them all. "Leadfoot!" the kids yelled as soon as Mrs Terwiliger left the room. "Freak!"

Gurl smiled bitterly to herself. If they were such big deals, why hadn't they noticed the broken lock? Why hadn't they thought to sneak out of Hope House at night? Why weren't they having dinner at Luigi's? No, this was hers and hers alone. "No man is an island," Mrs Terwiliger had told her. "One must learn to get along." But this sparkling city was an island and it got along fine, didn't it?

Just as she plucked up a pocket of ravioli with her fingers, she heard a sound, one she had heard only on TV.

"Meow."

She turned, sure that someone was playing a trick on her. But it was no trick. A cat, as plush and grey as the sky above, padded down the alleyway and sat a few feet from her.

Gurl dropped her ravioli, gaping. She'd seen pictures of cats in books and magazines, of course, but Gurl couldn't imagine where this one came from. Perhaps it was lost? But how could it be? Nobody let a cat outside; they could get hurt or sick or worse. Plus, there was the matter of people's regular pets: birds. If people saw a cat, especially without a leash, they'd call the police. What if it attacked an old lady's budgie or a businessman's parrot?

The cat regarded her with queer green eyes that glowed in the dark of the alley. "Who belongs to you?" Gurl murmured. Cats chose their owners rather than the other way round; everyone knew that. This cat surely had an owner, someone who liked exotic animals, someone who worked in a zoo maybe. Gurl glanced around at the buildings that rose along either side of the alley. There were lights in some of the windows, but Gurl saw no worried faces in them, heard no frantic calls.

"Meow," the cat said and took a few steps closer.

"Hey," said Gurl. "Are you hungry?" She looked at the food in the packages and nudged the one with the lasagne. The cat sniffed, then began to eat in big gulps.

"You *are* hungry, aren't you?" Gurl said. "Well, you and me both." Keeping her eyes on the cat, she reached out and grabbed the package containing cake. Gurl ate like the cat did, in huge greedy bites.

The cat finished everything, right down to the noodles. Then it did something totally unexpected. It walked over to Gurl, reached up with a grey paw and patted Gurl's cheek, once, twice, three times. Gurl's eyes opened wide. "No, no, no!" she said. "I can't take care of you! I'm just an orphan."

"Meow," said the cat. It yawned, climbed into her lap and began to make an odd rumbling sound. *She's purring*, thought Gurl, who had read about it but never experienced it.

Gurl stared down at the cat. What was she supposed to do now? Where would she keep it? What would she feed it? She shifted her weight and her arm brushed against the cat's leg. So soft. Hesitantly, Gurl ran a gentle finger between the cat's ears, the way she would pet a friendly bird. The cat closed its eyes and sighed, pressing its head into her palm.

Just then, the back door of the restaurant flew open and the cat sprang from Gurl's lap. The waiter marched out the open door carrying another bag of garbage.

"Whoa!" he said. Gurl froze, wishing with all her being that she was nothing more than one of the bricks in the wall. A queer shiver went through her.

But the waiter didn't even glance in her direction. With his foot, he prodded the opened packages of food. Then he saw the cat standing there, back arched and tail spiked. "What the heck? Where did you come from?"

"Meow," the cat said.

"Meow is right," said the waiter. "Here, kitty."

Since she was so close to him, Gurl could see that his brown eyes were hard and shiny, his smile cold. But why wasn't he looking at her? Why was he acting as if he couldn't see her? She was sitting right in front of him, right out in the open! But maybe he was just ignoring her like everyone else. The thought made her angry and she reached out for the cat.

What was wrong with her hands?

She could see them, but just barely. It was as if she were wearing gloves exactly the colours and textures of the alley itself: the black of the pavement, the red of the brick, the pink and white of the graffiti. And when she moved them, they changed to match the background. She touched her face, feeling the heat of her skin beneath her fingertips. If her hands looked like this, what did her face look like?

The waiter bent towards the cat. "Come on now," he said. "I know someone who'd pay a lot of money to get a load of you." He lunged for the cat, grabbing it by its front paws. The cat howled. "Shut up, you stupid thing," the waiter said. The animal hissed, clawing with its back legs.

"Ow!" the waiter yelled, but didn't let go. Carrying the wildly gyrating cat, he took one huge leap over to a garbage can on the other side of the alley and threw the cat inside. He quickly slammed the cover down and held it. The garbage can bucked and bounced, and the waiter kicked it. "Shut up!" he yelled.

Gurl was furious, but she didn't know what to do. The waiter wasn't big, but he was probably stronger than she was. And he could fly, even if he couldn't do it that well. She unfolded her legs and saw they were exactly like her hands, nearly invisible. If he couldn't see her, then...

The waiter kicked the garbage can again and the terrified mewls of the cat were too much for Gurl to bear. Though she had never done anything like it before, though she thought her heart would burst like a water balloon, she crept behind the waiter. Grabbing the waistband of his trousers, she yanked upward as hard as she could.

The waiter never flew higher than he did that moment and never would again. Gurl popped the lid off the garbage can. The cat vaulted into her arms, instantly becoming the colour of the air, the colour of nothing. The two of them, Gurl and cat, raced from the alley, just as if they had wings of their own.

CHAPTER 2

Blue Foot, Blue Foot

RUNNING, RUNNING. SHE WAS RUNNING, the cat curled in her arms, running so hard that her lungs hurt, running until she didn't feel the pavement beneath her feet any more, until the ground below dropped away and she rose up into the air...

Gurl sat up in bed, clutching her chest. A dream. But not all of it. Not Luigi's chocolate cake, which she could still smell on her fingertips. Not the cat, who slept across her feet under the threadbare blanket. But what about the rest?

She looked at her hands. They were thin and pale, but they were *there*, plainly visible. Gurl pulled the covers off her legs. Hands, check. Legs, check. She pulled the covers back up and shivered. The clock on the wall read 5.36am and pinkish sunlight marbled the iron sky outside the windows. The alley had been so much darker. Maybe that was why her hands had looked so strange, why the waiter hadn't seen her. She had been hidden in dark shadows, odd shadows that mottled her skin.

Yes, she thought. *That had to be it.*

The cat mewled softly from beneath the blankets and crawled up to sit at Gurl's side. She wasn't much to look at. Cats in books had impish black faces and blue eyes, or smushed noses and fur the colour of butterscotch. With a wide, plain face and fur the grey of morning fog, this cat seemed unremarkable in comparison. Except for her eyes, the acid-green eyes that blinked so slowly as Gurl scratched one ear, then the other. The cat rolled over and exposed a white, tufted belly. She put her forepaws in the air and flexed them, clutching at something only she could see.

Gurl scratched the cat's belly and a strange feeling came over her, a sleepiness, a peacefulness. A musical sort of purring filled Gurl's ears, erasing the frown that had pulled at her lips. *If a tree falls in the forest and there is nobody around,* she thought, *does it make a sound? If a tree falls... if a tree falls... if a tree falls...*

If anyone in the dorm had awakened, they would have thought Gurl had gone into a trance. Time passed, syrup slow, as Gurl scratched and scratched and scratched. Finally, the cat turned her little face to the clock and mewled softly. Gurl shook herself awake and checked the time: 5.57! In three minutes the alarm would ring and all the kids would wake up. What was she going to do with the cat? She couldn't let anyone see it or else they would take it. Gurl was not very brave, not as brave as she wanted to be, but she was responsible. And if the cat had really chosen her, well then, the cat was Gurl's responsibility.

Gurl climbed from her bed and pulled a box from underneath it, a box with a couple of old sweaters in the bottom. She reached into her bed, lifted the sleepy animal and laid it gently in the box. The cat peered at Gurl. "I'm sorry," whispered Gurl, "but I can't let anyone see you. Can you stay in this box until I can come back?"

The cat circled the box, kneading the sweaters. After curling up in a ball, she reached out with a white paw and rested it on top of Gurl's hand. "You understand, don't you?" Gurl breathed. Gurl knew that was a silly thing to think, that the cat was just an animal and couldn't possibly understand what Gurl was saying. But cats were rare and special, Gurl told herself. Maybe the cat did understand. Gurl gave the cat one last pat and then she closed the box again, hoping that cats liked small spaces and sleeping for hours.

She didn't have a lot of time to worry about it because soon the alarm rang and the kids climbed from their beds. As usual, no one greeted Gurl, no one asked her if she wanted to sit with them at breakfast. She ate as she always did, in the very back corner of the cafeteria, watching as all the others laughed and talked and shoved one another. It was just as well. Gurl had nothing to say to them anyway. A piece of toast fell lard-side down in front of her, but she ignored it.

"What's up, Leadfoot?" said a voice. Gurl didn't have to look to know who it was: Digger.

"Nothing," Gurl muttered. It was what she always said.

"What? I can't hear you!" Digger bellowed, getting up from her own table to lumber over to Gurl's. She was huge, bigger than most of the boys even, with a great square head like a block of wood. She wasn't much of a flyer, but she didn't need to be. Once a brick had come loose from the second storey of the dormitory building. It had fallen on Digger's foot while she was playing killer ball in the yard. She'd turned and proceeded to kick the wall so hard that some of the other bricks came loose. "Nobody messes with me," she said. "Not even the buildings."

Digger was tough, the toughest actually. The only thing that wasn't tough was the way she picked her nose: delicately, with the tip of her pinky extended like she was sipping tea from fine china.

Gurl pushed her eggs around her plate, wondering if Digger would flip them on the floor or in her lap. Not that it mattered, for the eggs smelled like sweaty socks stuffed with day-old fish and were the last things in the world Gurl wanted to eat.

Digger snatched the fork from her hand and smacked Gurl's plate to the floor, the eggs pellets scattering. "I said, I can't hear you! Speak, Freak!"

Gurl finally looked up into that big blockhead face. Digger's expression was the same as the waiter's had been: smug and triumphant. It was like she knew that Gurl was beaten already, doomed before she began. Gurl thought of what she had done to the waiter, and a tiny smile made her lips curl up at the corners.

Digger's nostrils flared. "Look at you," she said. "You're pathetic. All you do is sit there like a lump and stare at everyone." With her knuckles, Digger rapped painfully on Gurl's skull. "Hello, Lump. Is anyone in there?"

For a moment, Gurl wished she could disappear. Wouldn't that be amazing? Then what would Digger do?

But her hands and legs and the rest of her stayed exactly the way they were and even Digger grew bored. "Freak," she muttered and went to find someone more interesting to torment.

A word about Hope House: there are places in the world where so many desperate people have lived and so many bad things have happened that the places themselves have become desperately bad. They're damp and weird and smell like foot fungus. The windows are never clean and the lino curls up at the edges because it can't stand the floor. Every corner is sprayed with cobwebs and quivering shadows. When you walk into these bad places, you can feel a headache brewing between your eyebrows, a churning in your gut, a cold prickle at the back of your neck. You feel sad and angry and helpless, all at the same time. These bad places seem to hate you, but they also seem to want to keep you there very, *very* much.

Hope House for the Homeless and Hopeless was one of these places. But, as Gurl had learned in her history lessons, Hope House for the Homeless and Hopeless had not always been called Hope House for the Homeless and Hopeless. Back in the early 1800s, when it was first built, it was called The Asylum For The Poor, The Lazy and The Wretched, and its mission was "to teach idle, wild and disobedient children self-discipline of the body and soul". After that the name was changed again, to The Home of the Friendless – "for unprotected children whose only crime is poverty". And then for a while it was called The Institute of the Destitute, which offered orphans job training in such occupations as sheep shearing, basket weaving and flower arranging.

Despite the various name changes, the mission was generally the same: keep homeless kids out of trouble and try to teach them something useful. To that end, in literature class the orphans of Hope House were again composing business letters to rich people urging them to join the Hope House "Adopt-an-Orphan" programme, in which a donation of just $7.50 a day – only the price of a double latte! – would keep an orphan fed for a year. In art they made Hope House oven gloves and place mats, which were sold for $14.95 plus $5.99 shipping and handling on the orphanage website. In computer class they learned how to send emails to thousands of people at a time, with subject lines like "Don't let hope die at Hope House!" or "The truest heart gives until it hurts!"

As always, Gurl finished her work quickly and then stared out of the window or watched the other students. Preoccupied by the fact that she might have disappeared like a phantom the night before, and by the cat that she hoped was still sleeping in a box underneath her bed, she didn't notice the new boy until biology. Gurl was particularly bored in biology because they never learned about any animals except birds (with the occasional bat or flying squirrel thrown in). And while Gurl liked birds well enough, she hated it that everyone else worshipped them just because they could fly. Just once Gurl wanted to learn about a wolf or a salmon or a salamander or an ant. "An ant can lift ten times its own body weight," Gurl had once timidly told her teacher, Miss Dimwiddie, hoping that maybe she might do a lesson on something else. Miss Dimwiddie had barked, "Birds *eat* ants for lunch."

This morning Miss Dimwiddie began with the same question she always began with: "Who wants to tell me about the bumblebees?"

"Bumblebees!" echoed Fagin, Miss Dimwiddie's parrot, who perched on Miss Dimwiddie's shoulder.

Persnickety's hand shot into the air. Since it was the only hand to shoot into the air, Miss Dimwiddie said, "Yes, Persnickety."

"Bumblebees shouldn't be able to fly," Persnickety said, knotting her hands on the top of her desk. "Their bodies are too big and their wings are too small."

"Yes, Persnickety, that's absolutely right."

"Absolutely right," croaked Fagin.

"Now, children, I want you all to remember that. Bumblebees look as if they'd be too heavy to fly and yet scientists have discovered that they beat their wings in circles to create lift. Now, none of you look like you can fly either, but you must all be like the bee. You children can use the bumblebee to inspire you to great heights. All right?"

She smiled, waiting for the students to agree, but the room was silent. Miss Dimwiddie cleared her throat. "Well then. Today we're going to talk about the blue-footed booby."

"Blue-footed booby," parroted Fagin.

The class sniggered and Miss Dimwiddie put her hands on her ample hips. "Does someone want to tell me what's so funny?" Ruckus, always the first to cause a ruckus, shouted, "You said 'booby'."

"You're the booby," said Fagin.

Ruckus's tiny black braids, sticking up from his head like caterpillars reaching for a leaf, shook. "Shut up, you dumb bird."

Fagin flapped his wings. "Booby head. Worm head."

Miss Dimwiddie continued as if she hadn't heard. "I want you all to turn to page eighty-nine in your textbooks. You will see a photograph of the blue-footed booby. Note its distinctive powder-blue feet."

"Powder-blue feet," Fagin crowed.

"The blue-footed booby lives on the Galapagos Islands," said Miss Dimwiddie. "The blue feet play an important part in their mating rituals." Again she had to ignore a lot of snickering. "The male booby initiates the mating dance by raising one foot and then the other. Like this..." Miss Dimwiddie raised one foot then the other, delicately pointing her toes as they touched the ground. On her shoulder, Fagin did the same.

"See?" said Miss Dimwiddie. "Blue foot, blue foot. Blue foot, blue foot."

The class bit their knuckles to stifle their laughter. Except for one person, who laughed out loud. Gurl turned to look. In the back of the room was a new boy that Gurl hadn't noticed before. This was unusual, the not noticing, and because of it Gurl watched him all the more closely. He was broad-cheeked and broad-shouldered, with large, wide-set blue eyes that made him look a bit like a praying mantis. He noticed Gurl noticing him and he raised his eyebrows. She looked away, feeling her face grow hot. (She hated to be noticed noticing.)

Miss Dimwiddie stopped blue-footing about. "That's enough!" she said sternly. "These are birds we are talking about and they deserve your respect. Birds can fly. Now, correct me if I'm wrong, but none of you can fly as well as a bird, can you?" She cast her icy eyes around the room. "Can any of you fly as well as a bird? And isn't that why we learn about birds, to learn about flying?"

Fagin squawked. "No feathers. No wings. No crackers for you."

"There there, Fagin," said Miss Dimwiddie, patting the bird on the head. "I'll have you know that the blue-footed booby is one of the most spectacular hunters in the bird kingdom. These birds actually stop in mid-flight and drop into a headlong dive into the ocean from heights of eighty feet."

The praying mantis boy snorted. "Nathan Johnson has flown higher than that and he isn't a bird."

Miss Dimwiddie narrowed her eyes. "Excuse me?"

"Nathan Johnson," said the boy. "He's the Wing who won

the Flyfest three years running. He can fly ten storeys in the air, go into a free fall and stop two feet before he hits the ground."

"Really?" said Miss Dimwiddie. "How informative."

"Ugly boy," Fagin crowed. "Stupid boy."

Miss Dimwiddie smiled. "You're new. Have you gotten your name yet?"

"No," said the boy. "But I like to call myself—"

Miss Dimwiddie cut him off. "So you admire Nathan Johnson?"

"Yeah," said the boy. "Doesn't everyone?"

The students started whispering, much to Miss Dimwiddie's annoyance. "I admire birds," said Miss Dimwiddie. "They are the *true* Wings."

Mantis Boy scowled. "I still think Nathan Johnson is the best Wing we've ever had."

"Let me guess," said Miss Dimwiddie. "You're going to be just like him one day."

The boy's scowl got even deeper. "So what if I am?"

"We'll see about that," Miss Dimwiddie told him. "At Wing practice you can show everyone at Hope House that you're better than birds. I'm sure you'll put on a spectacular show." She clapped her hands together. "Now let's turn to the next chapter. Can anyone tell me why crows like shiny objects so much?"

The boy crossed his arms across his chest and stared at Miss Dimwiddie as if he wanted to take a shiny object and thwack her in the head with it. Gurl wished he would, as it could keep them both from talking about birds and about flying. Gurl was so sick of hearing about flying. What was so great about it anyway? What was the point?

She looked down at her hands and tried to convince herself that she was more special because she *couldn't* fly. Being a leadfoot made her watchful and patient. It had got her out of Hope House. It had got her a fabulous dinner. And, most importantly, it had got her the cat.

The cat!

After class, Gurl rushed back to the girls' dorm. She got down on her knees and pulled the box out from under her bed – just enough so that she could see inside, but not far enough that any of the other girls could. The little cat was still there, curled in a tight ball. Gurl breathed a sigh of relief, thankful that the cat hadn't disappeared.

No, you're the one who disappears, she thought. But of course that couldn't be true.

The cat rolled over and stretched, letting Gurl scratch its belly. She didn't even know this cat and it wasn't hers, but she already loved it more than she had ever loved anything else. *If a tree falls in a forest, and no one is around, she thought, does it make a sound?*

And then she thought: *Yes. It purrs.*

CHAPTER 3

The Chickens of Hope House

DAYS PASSED AND GURL WAS more and more convinced that though the cat was real, vanishing had been a trick of the light or of her imagination. Every morning, Gurl got up, put the little cat in the box under her bed and warned her to stay put. Remarkably, she did stay, sleeping all day only to wake up to the bits of food Gurl had saved from that night's dinner. (For some reason, the cat never seemed to need a litterbox and never left a mess. Gurl was too grateful to think about it.) Every night, the little cat sprawled across Gurl's feet, purring strongly enough that Gurl felt the vibrations all the way up into her heart. Though she felt guilty that the cat was trapped under the bed all day, Gurl told herself that it was only for a while and that eventually she would let the cat go.

Eventually.

Meanwhile, she daydreamed and people-watched through her classes, trying very hard not to be noticed – especially at Wingwork practice. There Coach Bob led the children in their flying exercises, walking back and forth between the rows of kids, his whistle bouncing up and down on his big round belly. "Crouch!" he shouted with his great trapdoor mouth. "Spring! Up!" He watched the kids attempt to get themselves into the air, then took his hat off and threw it to the ground. "Ruckus!" he said. "Do you call that a spring? I call that a *wobble*. Hogwash, when I told you to use your arms as levers, I meant use them as levers. Are you an orphan or an air traffic controller? And Blush! This is *not* a game! This is Wingwork! You kids will never be Wings with all this goofing around! Now, all of you, again!" He pointed at two kids who were jumping up and deliberately crashing into each other. "Lunchmeat and Dillydally, see me after practice!"

Gurl followed Coach Bob with a yardstick and a notepad. After the specialist had declared her hopelessly landlocked, Mrs Terwiliger and Coach Bob had excused her from Wingwork and given her a job: record the heights of everyone's practice leaps. It wasn't much of a job because the children of Hope House could fly about as well as chickens could, which is to say not very well at all.

Gurl stopped next to Ruckus and measured his next leap. Though he did everything that Coach told him to do – crouched as low as he could go, used his arms for levers – Gurl got a measurement of two feet. Ruckus always got a measurement of two feet.

Ruckus dropped to the ground. Beads of sweat gave him a frosty moustache that gleamed against his chocolate skin. "What was it?" he asked her, breathing hard.

"Two," she said.

"It was more than two!"

"No, it was two."

"It was at least *three*." His squinty eyes darted left and right, and he dragged a hand through his crazy caterpillar hair.

Gurl sighed and wrote "2" on her notepad.

Ruckus did what he usually did: grabbed the notebook from her hand, tore off the top page and stuffed it into his mouth, chewing defiantly. After he swallowed, he said, "Who'd believe you? You can't even get your toes off the ground."

"Neither can you," said Gurl, under her breath.

"Leadfoot!" Ruckus yelled.

"Ruckus, stop making such a ruckus!" said Coach Bob. "And

Gurl..." he began, then trailed off. Coach Bob didn't like to shout at her. Coach Bob felt bad for her. At least the other kids *might* fly one day.

She didn't hope to fly. In her daydreams, no one could. The whole city was rooted as firmly as she was. She imagined a life for herself in her non-flying world, a nice life – not amazing, but nice. *A girl who lives with her parents in a tidy brownstone walks to her after-school job as an ice-cream taster. She says the rum banana is good, but the huckleberry swirl needs more swirl. "You can never have enough swirl," she tells Mr Eiscrememann, the manager of the ice-cream store. "You're right," Mr Eiscrememann says. "What a smart girl! What an observant girl! Here, have a sundae!"*

Just then, Mrs Terwiliger, the matron of Hope House, flew out of the main building, her skirt so tight in the knees that she looked like an airborne eggwhisk. For a long terrible moment Gurl worried that the cat had been discovered in the box under her bed.

"Coach Bob? Is there trouble? I heard shouting from my office." She noticed Gurl and smiled. "Oh, hello, Gurl. I didn't see you standing there."

Gurl frowned. Mrs Terwiliger had been saying that ever since Gurl could remember, but she'd never thought about it before.

"Gurl, I said 'hello'."

"Hello, Mrs Terwiliger," Gurl said.

"That's better," said Mrs Terwiliger, while Coach Bob inspected the brim of his Wing cap. Mrs Terwiliger had been the matron of Hope House for more years than anyone could count. With her tight skirts, poofy blonde hair, drawn-on eyebrows and facelifts that stretched her toffee apple-red lips so wide that the corners nearly grazed her ears, nobody knew how old she was. Somewhere between forty and eighty went the guesses. It was she who started the tradition of naming the children who came to Hope House after their personal characteristics and temperaments. Thus, the baby boy who threw tantrums became Ruckus, the boy with the slick, ruddy skin became Lunchmeat, the boy who was full of excuses became Hogwash and the girl who couldn't keep her fingers out of her nose became Digger. "It's just like how the Indians used to name their children. Those Indians were so colourful! Running Bear, Clucking with Turkeys, Little Pee Pee."

Gurl thought it was lousy to blame the poor Indians for the dumb stuff Mrs Terwiliger called the kids of Hope House. Gurl got her own name because Mrs Terwiliger kept losing her as a baby. "I would turn around and poof! You were gone! And I would say to myself: Self, where *is* that GURL? Where has that GURL gotten to? And then I'd open the linen closet, looking for some towels, and there you'd be. I suppose I should be grateful that you have no talent for flight. You would have just floated away and no one would have been the wiser. Like a little cloud. Hmmm... Little Cloud would have been a nice name too, wouldn't it? No?"

Now Gurl wondered about her name, about getting lost all the time. Was it possible that what happened in the alley had happened before? And would it happen again?

Mrs Terwiliger lowered her voice. "How are the children doing today, Bob?" Each syllable uttered by Mrs Terwiliger was enunciated in the most exaggerated fashion, as if the world were populated entirely with lip-readers. "How are they flying?"

Coach Bob shoved the cap back on his head. "What do you think? It's like they've got bowling balls stuffed in their underwear."

"Oh, dear. I *had* hoped..." said Mrs Terwiliger. She always hoped that the kids would do better, maybe one day make their way on to a Wing team and make Hope House the talk of the town, but they never did. Gurl looked through the chain-link fence, out on to the street. The people buzzed by, on foot, on flycycles, on rocket boards, in cars, flitting off to wherever they had to be. Some wore business suits, others wore chains and nose rings, but most didn't notice the kids of Hope House jumping, straining, failing. If they did happen to look, they frowned in concern and pity or giggled in amusement. Even the crows that gathered in the single tree on the grounds seemed to laugh at them: "Ha! Ha! Ha!"

Gurl wondered if that was why Mrs Terwiliger made them practise outside. She kept a metal donation box bolted to the gate, which was often stuffed to the brim with dollar bills. *What*, thought Gurl, *did she spend all that money on?* She certainly didn't spend it on the kids at Hope House. The clothes were tattered, the shoes too small, the food inedible and the dorms freezing. The few times that they got to go out on field trips, Mrs Terwiliger took them to Times Square, gave them each a can full of Hope House pencils and told them to sell the pencils to passersby for a dollar each. She said that it was a character-building exercise.

"Hey!" bellowed a voice. "What are *you* looking at?"

Mrs Terwiliger, Coach Bob and Gurl turned, expecting to see Ruckus causing a ruckus again. But it wasn't Ruckus; it was the nameless new boy. He was shouting at a woman who had stopped her flycycle long enough to tape some sort of notice to the front gate. "I said, what are you looking at?"

The woman, dressed in a neon-pink sweatshirt that fell off one shoulder, glanced behind her, as if she assumed he was talking to someone else.

"Yeah, I mean you!" shouted the boy. "What are you looking at?"

The woman held up a hand. "Are you talking to me? I don't think you're talking to me, ya little snot."

Bug Boy laughed. "I think I am tawkin' to ya," he said, imitating her thick city accent.

Mrs Terwiliger egg-whisked over to the boy. "Stop that! Since when do we accost people who are walking down the street?" She pursed red lips. "Never, that's when. Now apologise to the young lady."

The boy crossed his arms. "She was staring. She was watching me fly."

"Ya call that flying?" shouted the woman. "I seen better lift on a block of cement!" She got on her flycycle and took off.

"I'll show you!" the boy yelled. He turned away from the woman and from Mrs Terwiliger. He crouched, then jumped. Gurl winced, seeing that he barely made it a foot off the ground. He tried again, his face twisted with the effort, and got about six inches off the ground. Then four. Then two. It seemed that the angrier he got, the heavier he got. Soon he looked as if someone had glued the bottoms of his sneakers to the pavement. The other kids, whom you might expect to make fun of the boy, said nothing. His failure reminded them of their own and who wanted to think about that?

Mrs Terwiliger put her hand on the boy's shoulder. "I

think that's about enough for today. We'll try again tomorrow, Chicken."

"What did you call me?"

Mrs Terwiliger sighed and brushed a bleached strand of hair from her thick, fake eyelashes. "You can't fly. Neither can chickens. In ancient times the Indians who used to roam these lands liked to name—"

The boy cut her off. "Nobody calls me 'Chicken'." Red-cheeked, his light brown hair lank with sweat, the boy shook free of her and shuffled from the tarmac, kicking rocks so hard that they rang against the chain-link fence.

"ZOOT!" Dillydally said. "Boy needs to pop a pill and chill."

"Right on," said Coach Bob, who knew that Dillydally was obsessed with old TV shows and his speech was littered with peculiar slang.

"Chicken is having a bad day. We all have bad days, don't we, Ruckus? Lunchmeat? Dillydally? We have to be understanding at times like these." Mrs Terwiliger looked thoughtfully at the gate, where the notice the woman had hung flapped in the wind. "Gurl, be a dear and fetch that notice for me, would you?"

"I'll get it," cried Ruckus, preparing to leap.

"I asked Gurl to do it, Ruckus."

"Awww," said Dillydally. "That's so *establishment*."

Gurl walked over and pulled the notice off the fence. She nearly tripped and fell when she saw what it said:

MISSING CAT!

Very rare! Grey, with white belly. Green eyes.
Answers to the name "Laverna"
(but only when she feels like it).
Owner frantic! Reward offered!
No questions asked!
Call 555-1919!

"Gurl," said Mrs Terwiliger. "Bring it over here, dear."

Gurl reluctantly handed the paper to the matron.

"A missing cat!" said Mrs Terwiliger. "My stars! I haven't seen a cat in years!" Her eyes scanned the notice. "Nasty animals."

"They're not nasty!" said Gurl before she could think about it.

Mrs Terwiliger patted Gurl on the head. "I know you children fancy yourselves worldly and sophisticated, but I daresay I know a bit more about wild animals than you do. Cats are bird-killers." She tapped a long red fingernail on her teeth. "Though I wouldn't mind finding this one. I wonder how big this reward is."

"Can I go to my room? I'm not feeling too well," said Gurl, doing her best to sound ill. She had to get inside the dorm; she had to check on the cat.

"Oh, of course, Gurl," Mrs Terwiliger enunciated, her plump lips shining like slugs. "I know how hard these Wing practices must be for you, with your condition. Fly along, then. Oh! I mean, *run* along."

Gurl turned and walked slowly to the main building, holding her stomach, sick for real with the thought of having stolen someone else's pet. Gurl could not bring herself to give the cat back, not yet. For the first time in her life, she felt as if she had made a friend (even if it was a fuzzy, nonhuman friend). *Just a little while*, she thought. *I'll just keep her a little while. That's not so bad, is it?*

Once she got inside, however, she ran down the hallway to the girls' dormitory and raced to her bed. "Please be here, please be here," she whispered, pulling out the old sweater box and opening the flaps.

But she knew what she'd find even before she opened the box because it was what she expected each and every day.

Nothing.

CHAPTER 4

Bugged

THE BOY BOUNCED DOWN THE corridor, punching the wall every few feet or so. Feline Face. Bug Eye. Lizard Man. Any of those names would have been all right with him; he knew his eyes were so big and far apart they were practically on the sides of his head. So, fine. Bug. Bugs were cool. Bugs could fly. Some, like praying mantises, even had those sweet backward scythes for arms. He wondered why grown-ups had operations to have their eyebrows pasted up on their foreheads or fat vacuumed from their butts but never got anything practical. Like antennae. Or fangs. Or scythes for arms. The boy would have enjoyed having scythes for arms because then he could slash through the fence around Hope House for the Homeless and Hopeless and fly away for ever. Instead, he was stuck here with Mrs Terwiliger. Mrs Terwiliger looked like a flying Pez sweet dispenser.

He stopped and jumped as high as he could, but his feet were so heavy. It was like he had been chained to the ground. *Wham!* He punched the wall so hard he bloodied his knuckles and had to stuff his fist in his mouth.

She named him Chicken. Chicken! Chickens couldn't fly. Why chickens were even considered birds was a mystery. They were more like walking cushions or fat clucking possums or something.

He tried to jump again, his feet sticking to the floor. *Wham! Wham! Wham!* He didn't cry out at the pain in his hands; he welcomed it. It kept his mind off everything else. This stupid place. His stupid new name. The stupid food, worse than monkey chow. The fact that he could hardly get his feet off the ground when in his mind and in his dreams, he could soar.

If only he knew who he was. Who he really was. The other kids said that no one ever remembered much about who they were when they came to Hope House, not even their own names, that your memories faded as soon as you crossed the threshold. Bug did remember crossing the threshold, sitting in Mrs Terwiliger's office and being snarky when she asked for his name: "Mary Poppins! Harry Potter! Stanley Yelnats!" He also remembered hearing music – maracas or cymbals or something – and whispering in someone's ear. But whispering in *whose* ear? And whispering *what*? His real name? His address? His favourite colour? He just didn't know. But it was better that way, the other kids told him. Otherwise, you'd spend all day crying over the fact that your parents died or your Aunt Lucy gave you away like a pet parrot who talks too much and poops all over the floor. And who'd want to know that? Better to forget. Better to jump up and down like an idiot in the playground at Hope House, wishing that one day you'd make it more than a couple of feet.

"Meeow."

Bug – if he had to have a name, that was the one he wanted, thank you very much – swung around, bloody fists high. Something small and fuzzy was sitting at the end of the hallway, near the entrance to the girls' dormitory. *What the heck was that*, he thought. *A rat?* City rats could grow big, he knew. The subways were overrun with them. Hairy, dog-sized things with long yellow teeth, all the better to gnaw you with, my dear.

He walked cautiously towards the animal, whatever it was, ready to kick. (He wasn't about to get gnawed on by an overgrown rodent. Nuh-uh.)

But it wasn't a rat. It was a cat. He'd never seen one before. Not a real one.

Bug lowered his fists and stared at the cat. The cat stared back. Then it dropped to the floor and rolled around in what

Bug thought was a sort of happy way. A friendly way. A hello, how-are-you-I'm-fine kind of way. It looked like fun, or at least distracting. Since no one was around, since flying was futile and since he'd probably break his knuckles if he kept punching the walls, Bug dropped to the floor too and rolled from one side to the other. Encouraged, the cat rolled back the other way, and soon they were both rolling at the same time and in the same direction, back and forth, back and forth. Bug could have sworn the cat was smiling.

A girl ran out of the dormitory and into the hallway, almost tripping over Bug and the happily rolling cat. The cat got to its feet and wound itself around the girl's ankles. After scooping up the cat, she glared down at Bug as if he were... a bug.

He was embarrassed to have been caught rolling around on the floor, but not too embarrassed to notice how tightly the girl was holding on to the cat. As if she thought it belonged to her. "What's your problem?" Bug asked her.

The girl bit her lip. She was that weird girl, the one just called Gurl. The one who watched everyone. The other kids said that since she didn't look like any particular thing and couldn't seem to do any particular thing, Mrs Terwiliger chose the obvious name. Bug himself might have tried to be a little bit more creative. *Pasty Face would work*, he thought. *Or Ghost. Spooky! Now that was a good name for her*. Her skin was white and her long dishevelled hair was almost the same. Her eyes were grey and almost as big as his own, but you could hardly see them through the curtain of hair. They were like headlights glaring through fog. Even her lips were colourless. Bug wondered if she had any blood at all.

Gurl clutched the cat close. "She's not your cat." Her voice was low and sort of scratchy, as if she didn't use it much.

"Sure she is," said Bug, getting to his feet. "I found her."

She tried again. "This is the girls' dorm."

"No, this is the hallway."

"This is the entrance to the girls' dorm. You have to leave."

Bug laughed. "You gonna make me?"

She gripped the cat tighter in her arms. "You can't tell anyone," she said.

"About what?" He looked down at his mangled knuckles, red and scraped from punching the walls. She saw them too and took a step back.

"You can't tell anyone about the cat."

"Why not?"

"Because!" the girl blurted. She looked as if she might burst into sloppy tears, which just made Bug think of an even better name for her: Dishwater. Weepy Dishwater Pasty Face.

"She's mine," said Bug. "She chose me."

"She did not!"

"She did too! She was rolling around with me. You saw her."

"That's doesn't mean she chose you," said Gurl. She seemed to think a minute and then she said, "Listen, Chicken—"

But Bug cut her off. "Don't call me Chicken!" he shouted, punching the wall. "That's not my name!" *Wham!* "I have a real name." *Wham!*

The girl took another step away from him. "OK, OK," she said. "Sorry, what's your name?"

"What do you think?" he said, opening his eyes as wide as he could. "It's Bug."

The cat began to wriggle and struggle in the girl's arms until she was forced to let it go. "See?" Bug told her. "She wants to come back to me. She plays a mean game of rolling pin."

But the cat trotted past both children and strode into the bathroom at the other end of the hallway. Bug followed, the pasty girl on his heels, but the cat ran behind the door and pushed it shut.

"What's she doing?" Bug said, pressing an ear to the door.

"She's fine," the girl told him. But she seemed just as confused as Bug was.

After a few minutes, they heard the toilet flush.

"Come on!" said Bug. "Cats use toilets?"

"Of course they do," the girl said, obviously surprised as well. Soon they heard the sound of water splashing in the sink. "Anyway, you can go now. I'll catch her when she comes out."

"No, how about *you* can go and I'll catch her when she comes out," Bug said. Not only was the cat rare, it was some sort of super-genius, toilet-flushing cat. Maybe she could fetch! Maybe she could balance pineapples on her nose! Maybe she could juggle chipmunks! He wasn't going anywhere.

"She's not yours!" the girl hissed. Suddenly, she got paler – if that was even possible – and her grey eyes went all silvery, like two nickels. Quickly, she pulled the sleeves of her red sweatshirt over her hands.

The girl was weirder than everyone said she was. "What's wrong with you?" Bug said.

"What's wrong with who?" said a voice. Mrs Terwiliger glided down the hallway. "Chicken! I've been looking for you. What are you two doing loitering near the girls' dormitory?"

"Nothing," Gurl and Bug said at once.

Mrs Terwiliger's eyes narrowed, staring down at them both. "Gurl, you look pale," she said, sounding more accusatory than compassionate. (And she enunciated the word "pale" with so much force that she spat.)

"I'm just tired," croaked the girl. "I think I need a nap." She tugged at the sleeve of her sweatshirt again. Was it Bug's imagination or did the sweatshirt seem to be fading somehow? It had been red, but now it looked pink. And there was a faint pattern in it that he hadn't noticed before, like the lines in a brick wall. Just like the painted brick of the hallway.

Mrs Terwiliger's overwide lips turned down at the corners and Bug wondered if she had noticed the same strange things. But all she said was, "A nap is a wonderful idea. Go." She waved her bony hand and Gurl practically ran into the girls' dorm.

Then Mrs Terwiliger crooked a finger at Bug, the fluorescent lights shining off her tight, waxy skin. "Come, Chicken. Instead of punching the walls, I'd like you to help me move a filing cabinet. There's a good boy!"

She turned and floated off. Bug started to follow, peeking inside the open door of the girls' dormitory as he passed. And that's when he saw her. Uh, *didn't* see her. Because the girl wasn't there. The room was empty.

Bug opened his mouth to shout – because what else do you do when a weird, weepy girl ups and totally disappears? – but then he thought better of it. Something *extremely* funky was going on with Pasty Gurl, but he'd keep his mouth shut.

That is, he would keep it shut in exchange for a certain toilet-flushing, rolling pin-playing, very rare, genius cat.

"Chicken!" said Mrs Terwiliger. "Move it along!"

"Yes, ma'am," he said, a sly grin on his buggy face. "I'm moving it as fast as I can."

CHAPTER 5

Attack of the Umbrella Man

GURL HURRIED ALONG THE CITY streets, the cat peeking out from an old backpack. She'd had to wait nearly an hour for the other orphans to fall asleep. (Digger kept untucking the sheets on Persnickety's bed, just to make *her* cry, and stealing Tot's doll, just to make *her* cry.) When Gurl finally slipped from the window and out of the front gate of Hope House, it was close to eleven.

The air outside was crisp and fresh, and Gurl welcomed it. Inside the orphanage everything seemed confused and difficult to figure out, so much so that she rarely tried. Outside the orphanage, however, her thoughts were clear. Something was happening to her, something weird and scary and important, and she needed to understand it, control it. For that, she'd go back to the place it first happened: the alley behind Luigi's. She needed to see if it would happen again.

Plus, she needed a snack.

Luigi's Dumpster yielded a feast. Tangy Italian meat loaf, delicate squash ravioli, fettucini with peas, prosciutto and cream sauce. Gurl offered the meat loaf to the cat, who ate a few bites before turning her attention to the fettucini. Gurl munched on the meat loaf as she watched the cat drag a long noodle from the packet and proceed to shorten it, bite by bite. "You know, I've been doing the same thing Mrs Terwiliger does," Gurl said. "I've been calling you 'cat', the most obvious thing, even in my own head!" She smacked her forehead to demonstrate the foolishness of this. The cat stopped nibbling on the noodle to stare. "I could call you Laverna, like that flyer said. Hey, Laverna!" The cat blinked, bored. "Maybe not," said Gurl. "So, instead of calling you what you are, which is easy, or calling you something that describes you, which is boring, why don't I call you something that you like?" The cat blinked slowly in the way of cats, the way that said they were listening carefully and you had better say something interesting for a change. "Why don't I call you Noodle?"

The newly named Noodle uttered a short mew, which Gurl took as an OK, before getting back to her fettucini. "Noodle it is, then," Gurl said, feeling immensely pleased with herself. She had never named anything before. No wonder Mrs Terwiliger liked it so much, even though she was awful at it.

Gurl finished the meat loaf and polished off the ravioli in a couple of swift bites, eyeing her own hand as she did. She wondered what triggered it, what exactly made her fade. She could feel the tingling in her skin that afternoon, knew it was happening and was terrified that Mrs Terwiliger or that crazy boy – Bug or Chicken or whatever his name was – would notice. They didn't seem to, or at least neither of them said anything. But she didn't like the look on Bug Boy's face as he turned to follow Mrs Terwiliger. It was a smug, self-satisfied look, the one everyone seemed to give her. A look that said Gurl was doomed, beaten before she even started.

"No, I'm not," she said and her words echoed in the dark alley. Noodle's whiskers twitched in disapproval. "Sorry," she said, softer now. If she had to choose between being noticed and being ignored, she would take ignored any day. Bad things happened when she was noticed.

Noodle curled up in Gurl's lap and Gurl leaned back against the brick, just as she did that first night, and stared up at the sky and the buildings that reached ecstatically towards it. A newspaper wafted on the wind, looking beautiful and fluttering and alive. Gurl felt a thousand things at once. Small and big. Safe and free. Invisible and yet exposed. In her mind, she rifled through her daydreams and found a favourite: a girl stands ankle-deep on a beach with the ocean roaring in front of her. Behind her, a boy shuffles out of a cozy cottage and calls out to the girl: "Mom and Dad say it's time to come inside now."

Noodle shifted in Gurl's lap and mewled softly. "I know," said Gurl. "We have to do what we came to do." She held up her hands. "They look the same, Noodle. Just regular old hands." With her nose, Noodle nudged her fingers. "Yes, concentrate. That's a good idea." Gurl focused all her attention on her hands, willing them to fade. She tried harder, squinting with the effort. After a while, her right wrist seemed to look a bit nubby like the pavement beneath her, but it hadn't changed colour and nothing else seemed different at all. Her hands dropped to nestle in Noodle's fur. "This is not going to work," she said. "I didn't even think about it both times it happened before. It just happened. Maybe it was because I was scared?"

Gurl sat in the alley until her butt and the cat fell asleep. Now what should she do? Would she just keep blinking on and off like a light bulb, never knowing when it was going to happen next? But she couldn't sit here all night. Though it was only September, the temperature had dropped a few degrees and she was getting a little cold. She tapped the cat to wake her and helped her into the backpack. Gurl would have to try again on another night, maybe in another place.

Gurl slipped the pack on, careful not to jostle Noodle. At least the ravioli was good, she told herself. The trip was not a total waste. She paused at the entrance to the street and looked right and left. It was so late that the city seemed deserted and Gurl felt a flutter of nervousness in her stomach, a flutter that matched the trash dancing in the wind. Even Noodle seemed to sense Gurl's anxiety and pulled her head inside the bag.

Nothing to worry about, Gurl thought. *You'll be fine.* She straightened the straps of the pack before heading out on to the street. Walking briskly, Gurl glanced behind her every so often. Wan light pooled beneath the street lamps, giving the air a sickly, yellowish hue, while the bulbs themselves issued a low, eerie buzz.

Plink!

Gurl whirled around, scanning the street. The trash danced, slick puddles glistened, but no one followed her. *This is the city and it never sleeps*, she thought. *Probably someone kicking a stone down the sidewalk blocks away.* She told herself that she was being paranoid. And then she told herself to walk faster. For about the billionth time in her life, she wished she could fly.

Pssst!

Again, Gurl turned to face an empty street. But wait: there, in the darkened doorway of a shuttered shop, was someone lurking in the shadows? She stared, straining to see. On the opposite side of the street, a black dome rose from the subway entrance and Gurl's stomach clenched. But the black dome turned out to be an umbrella, an overcoat-clad person beneath it. Gurl sighed with relief. Some businessman coming home late from the office. Well, if he thought it was OK to be out this late at night, then she was probably fine. She glanced back at the businessman, who held the umbrella so low that she couldn't see his face. Like Gurl, he didn't fly, but walked in a swaying lurch that favoured one leg. She felt a little sorry for him, not only unable to fly but also barely limping along. Imagine if the weather were bad. If it were stormy? It would take him for ever to walk a few blocks!

Gurl frowned. But if it wasn't stormy, why was he carrying an umbrella?

She turned and started to walk again, a little faster than before. So the guy was a little strange; it didn't mean he was dangerous. Maybe he just liked to be prepared.

From the backpack, a paw batted her ear. "Yeah," Gurl whispered. Noodle tapped her again. "What is it?" The cat growled low in her throat, reared up from the backpack and nipped Gurl on the earlobe. "Ouch!" Gurl yelped.

Behind her, a gurgling voice said, "Ouch!"

Gurl whirled around so fast that Noodle almost fell from the pack. The man, who had been at least a block and a half away, now stood just a few feet from her. His overcoat, which had looked fine from a distance, was torn and stained with food and mud and things that Gurl didn't want to think about. He wore two different shoes, one black, one brown, both slashed at the top to make room for long horny toenails. The umbrella, which he still held low over his face, was lacy with holes, as if someone had sprayed acid on it.

The man giggled, lifting the umbrella just a little, so that she could see the fine grey down that covered his cheeks, the teeth that he had filed to points. "Nice kitty," he whispered. "Nice, *nice* kitty."

And then he said: "Run."

Gurl took off, running faster than she ever thought she could, Noodle bouncing in the pack on her back. But she could hear the man-thing panting and giggling, the slap-drag of his worn shoes on the sidewalk as he lurched after her. Frantic now, her heart pounding so hard that she thought it would pop out of her mouth, she feinted left but ran right. She could feel something tug at the backpack and heard Noodle's hiss. "No!" she screamed and stumbled as the pack was wrenched from her shoulders. Reaching back to grab it, she fell to the ground, hitting her funny bone on the pavement and badly bruising her hip. She flipped to her back and squeezed her eyes shut, waiting for the giggling toothy thing to attack. She could smell his hot breath, stinking of trash and bones and rot.

"Nice?" said the thing. She opened her eyes to see him

standing over her, cradling the backpack in one arm. He lifted the umbrella and sniffed the air with a nose that seemed unusually long and mobile, like the nose of a rat. And that's when she felt the tingling in her hands, in her face, across her whole body, and knew that it had happened again. That the thing couldn't see her any more.

Slowly and as quietly as she could, Gurl got to her feet. Noodle poked her face from the top of the pack and mewled. Burbling absently, the thing pulled the flap down, sniffing the air. Then he started to shamble back the way he came. Slap-drag, slap-drag. Gurl tiptoed behind him and gave his overcoat a rough tug. The thing grunted and twirled on its short leg, almost stumbling itself. "Bad," he said. "Bad, bad, bad."

He clutched the cat tighter and Gurl could hear Noodle's plaintive mews through the canvas.

"Give me my *cat*!" said Gurl and she ripped the umbrella out of his hand.

The thing gasped and covered his red eyes with his forearm, as if against a strong light. Gurl dropped the umbrella and grabbed the backpack, which promptly disappeared in her grip. The thing gibbered and wailed, "Kitty! Kitty! *Kitteeeee*!" She could still hear him wailing two, three, five blocks away. And then she was standing at the gates of Hope House, chest heaving like a bellows, and she couldn't hear him any more. But she could see herself again, her own arms and legs plainly visible in the dim light. She hugged Noodle close and the animal's low purr filled her with joy.

"It was you," she whispered in Noodle's ear. "Every time I changed it was because I was afraid – not for me, but for you."

Armed with this realisation, she opened the gate and crossed the yard. She had just slipped around the side of the dormitory when a hot white light blinded her. Someone snatched the backpack and then grabbed the lapel of her jacket.

"Hello, my dear," Mrs Terwiliger said, reeling Gurl in close.

CHAPTER 6

Mrs Terwiliger's Monkeys

MRS TERWILIGER HAD ONE HAND on the strap of the backpack and one hand on Gurl's arm in a death grip as she half flew, half dragged Gurl across the yard to the main building. "I don't know what gets into you children. After all I do for you, to just run off like that! And you can stop struggling," she said. "I might lose sight of you, but I won't lose you altogether." She lifted the backpack so that Gurl could see it. "I won't lose your little friend either."

More worried for Noodle than herself, Gurl stopped struggling. "Where are you taking us?" Gurl squeaked.

"Where do you think?" snapped Mrs Terwiliger.

Another orphanage? The animal shelter? Jail? Gurl couldn't imagine. Because of her fear, she tingled all over. It seemed that her body was as confused as her head and flashed an alarming array of colours and textures. One arm was striped like Mrs Terwiliger's coat, the other arm seemed to be made of red brick. Both her legs somehow mimicked the shadows behind them, so that it appeared she had four instead of two. She kept silent until they reached the front door of the main building.

"Open the door and be quiet about it," Mrs Terwiliger said. "We don't want to wake anyone else now, do we? Children need their rest."

Gurl clutched the brass door handle, noticing that her hand immediately turned the same bright yellow colour. Mrs Terwiliger noticed too. "That's quite a talent. Better than flying, that talent is," she said, not talking as much as muttering to herself as she led Gurl down a long dark hallway. At the end of it was a black door, upon which were five separate locks and the words *Matron Geraldine Terwiliger* in looping golden script.

"Reach into my right pocket," said Mrs Terwiliger, "and remove the keyring." Gurl did as she was told, the keys making a faint jingling noise as she pulled them from Mrs Terwiliger's jacket.

"The silver key opens the top lock," Mrs Terwiliger told her. "The red key opens the second, the blue key unlocks the third, the gold key opens the fourth and the tiny little key you use on the doorknob."

Gurl fumbled with the keys, not because it was too dark to see, but because sometimes her hand would turn the colour of the key or the key would turn the colour of her hand.

"I'm waiting," said Mrs Terwiliger, tapping her high-heeled shoe impatiently. Noodle mewled and Gurl's hands shook.

Gurl finally managed to unlock the five locks and open the door. "Now," said Mrs Terwiliger as they stepped inside, "close the door and return the keys to my pocket. Good. Use the chain to turn on the lamp. Ahhh, that's better, isn't it?"

The small lamp cast an eerie glow around the office and Gurl gasped when she saw a hundred pairs of eyes gaping at her from all around the room. "What are they?" Gurl asked. Mrs Terwiliger's overlarge teeth flashed in a wicked smile, but she didn't answer the question. "Have a seat," she said, pushing Gurl into a chair next to a huge marble desk. She set the backpack on the desk and produced a set of handcuffs from her left pocket. As soon as she saw them, Gurl tried to rip her arm from Mrs Terwiliger's grasp, but because of the bruised hip and elbow, she couldn't move fast enough. One click and Gurl was cuffed to the chair, unable to get away. Mrs Terwiliger sighed, walked around to the other side of the desk, and sat in her own chair, a red velvet one the size and shape of a throne.

"Well," she said. "Here we are. At least, here I am. If I didn't know what you were capable of, I might think I was the only one here. I saw that you were starting to... er... *fade* this afternoon in the hallway. I got curious, so I kept an eye on you. I saw you sneaking in and out of the dorm to bring this animal" – she gestured to the backpack on the desk – "some of your dinner. And then I watched you sneak out this evening, and I waited for you to come back. Did you know that you simply appeared out of nowhere, right in front of the orphanage gate? Astonishing! And you're nearly invisible right now. You blend right in with that chair. You're like a chameleon. Or a stick insect. Have you ever heard of a stick insect?"

Gurl didn't respond to this speech. Her eyes had adjusted to the light, so now she could see that every shelf, every filing cabinet and every surface was covered with monkeys. Hundreds of mechanical monkeys. Some of them were no bigger than a fist; others were as high as a foot. On the end of the marble desk, facing her, sat a monkey wearing a little gold fez and holding tiny gold cymbals. Gurl wondered if its fur was real, and worried all the more for the fate of Noodle.

"A stick insect is a type of insect that appears to be a stick, yet is not a stick but an insect," Mrs Terwiliger was saying. "Isn't that fascinating, dear? Gurl? Are you admiring my monkeys? They're beautiful, aren't they?"

Beautiful was not the word that Gurl had been thinking of. Creepy, bizarre, freakish – those were the words that she had been thinking of. And now that she was thinking of it, those words sort of summed up the whole night. What *was* that thing that chased her down the street? And here, all these ugly monkeys, some with hats and waistcoats, some with bugles or drums, some grinning very unmonkeylike grins – no, they were not beautiful. Noodle was beautiful, but how would Gurl ever get her back? How could she get them out of here? And then, even if she could get them out of here, where would they go?

Mrs Terwiliger reached across the desk, plucked up the fez-wearing monkey and wound a key in its back. She set it down on the desk and it promptly began clapping its cymbals, its mouth opening and closing. Noodle, still in the backpack on the desk, peered out at the clanging thing with her ears flat to her head.

The monkey kept banging away, and the sound went right up Gurl's spine and into her brain, ringing there like a fire alarm. She wanted to shut it up somehow, to tell it something to make it quiet. A secret. She felt something inside her opening up, yearning to spill her innermost thoughts. Yes, it wanted her secrets: her secrets would make it happy. Monkeys *loved* to hear secrets.

But she didn't know any secrets. It was obvious she was as changeable as a chameleon. That was no secret, at least not to Mrs Terwiliger. And Noodle was sitting right there, peeking her head out of the backpack, so she wasn't a secret either. Wasn't there anything she could give to this noisy, banging monkey to shut it up? *There's the umbrella man that came out of the subway*, a little voice in the back of her head whispered. *You could tell that secret. Why don't you? If you do, it will be quiet and then you can relax, maybe even take a nap...*

Noodle howled, snapping Gurl out of her reverie, and the monkey stopped clanging. Feeling slightly dazed, Gurl looked at Mrs Terwiliger. She could have sworn that the matron was disappointed, but about what she had no idea.

The monkey seemed to have another effect on Gurl; she was visible. "Ha, there you are," said Mrs Terwiliger. She pulled another monkey from the shelf behind her, this one with a purple waistcoat and a pair of maracas. "This monkey is one of my favourites," said Mrs Terwiliger, her rubbery lips twisting like licorice. "They talk too, you know."

"They talk?" said Gurl, too startled to keep her mouth shut.

"If you give them a penny they do. Do you have a penny? Oh, silly me! Orphans don't have extra pennies, do they, dear? I'll lend you one, how about that?" Mrs Terwiliger opened the top drawer of her desk and pulled out a penny. She tucked the penny into the purple waistcoat. Then she sat down and set the monkey in front of Gurl.

The monkey's eyes rolled until they focused in on Gurl. It opened its mouth and yelled: "MONKEY CHOW!"

Gurl was so surprised that she jumped. The chair fell over backwards and she went with it.

"Oops!" said Mrs Terwiliger, rushing out from behind the desk to help Gurl right herself. "I should have warned you that they can be a bit... er... vehement about what they have to say." And then she added, "Although I do wish that when they talked, they would have something of substance to offer." She glared at the monkey. The monkey shook its maracas over its head before going completely still.

Gurl rubbed the back of her head where it had connected with the floor. The umbrella man, the talking monkey – she was having some kind of nightmare, but she was too tired to wake herself up.

On the wall next to the desk, the only space not taken up with shelves of monkeys, there was a full-length mirror. Gurl imagined Mrs Terwiliger spent many hours twirling around in her chair, gazing at herself. "What do you want?" Gurl asked wearily.

Mrs Terwiliger leaned her liposuctioned posterior on the desk. "What do you think! What's best for you, of course. What's best for Hope House. And I think that there's a way for you to help me to do what's best."

"There is?" said Gurl.

"Absolutely!" said Mrs Terwiliger. "We're going to have to start small, I think. With some shoes."

"Shoes?"

Mrs Terwiliger frowned (as much as a woman who'd had weekly Botox shots to paralyse the muscles in her forehead could frown). "Gurl, I'm surprised I have to explain this to you. I am the matron of Hope House, yes?"

"Yes."

"And as the matron, I represent the children wherever I go, correct?"

"Uh. I guess."

"So I can't walk around looking like last season, can I? I have a certain responsibility, a certain image to maintain. For the sake of Hope House. And your sake. So I'd like you to pick me up a few things."

"Besides the shoes?"

"I did see some gorgeous new scarves at Harvey's."

Gurl was more dazed than ever. "You want me to go shopping?"

"Tomorrow afternoon you'll go to Harvey's an hour before closing," said Mrs Terwiliger. "Then you'll hide in one of the changing rooms until you hear the workers lock up. Then you can turn on the stick insect act and fetch me some of those scarves. You can't miss them. Silk scarves in the display case at the back of the store. Oh, I wouldn't mind some new gloves. Shoes, the highest heels you can find. Size six. And a coat. Make it a fur coat. Fox, if they have it."

Go to Harvey's? Hide in the dressing room? Make like a stick insect? "Wait a minute. You want me to *steal* for you?"

"Steal? Who said anything about stealing? It sounds so harsh."

"But that's what it is!" Gurl said. "I can't do that! What if someone sees me?"

Mrs Terwiliger looked at her as if she were as dumb as one of the mechanical monkeys. "You're invisible. Who's going to see you, silly?"

"But it just happens!" Gurl said. "I can't control it!"

"Oh, you'll learn," said Mrs Terwiliger.

"I don't want to learn. I don't *want* to become a thief."

"What does it matter what you want?" Mrs Terwiliger said sharply, then caught herself. "You're an orphan, Gurl. I'm offering you an opportunity. You act as if I'm asking you to commit a crime!"

"You *are* asking me to commit a crime," said Gurl.

"Just a little one. It barely even counts. It's not like robbing a bank."

"I won't do it!" said Gurl.

"You will," said Mrs Terwiliger. From behind her chair, she hauled out a large birdcage, which she put on top of the desk. Then she opened the clasp on the backpack, deftly scooped Noodle from the interior and tossed her into the cage.

"Don't hurt her!" said Gurl, skin tingling.

"You're invisible again. Now, see how easy that was?" said Mrs Terwiliger as she latched the cage. "I'm going to keep your pet in a safe place and you'll do a couple of things for me. Just to prove that I can trust you again. You do want me to trust you, right? And when you're done with your errands, a few teeny-tiny errands, then you can have the cat back. What do you say?"

Gurl watched as Noodle pawed at the latch on the cage and meowed forlornly. "What if I don't?" Gurl said, pulling at the handcuff that held her, even though she could no longer see the wrist that it chained. "What if I *can't*?"

"That would be terribly unfortunate," said Mrs Terwiliger. She opened the top drawer of her desk and pulled out the notice that had been tacked to the gates of Hope House. "Because then I would be forced to call the number on this notice. I'd have to return, uh, Laverna here to her rightful owner. How could I leave her in the hands of such an irresponsible, ill-behaved, untrustworthy girl? I just couldn't. I couldn't live with myself." Mrs Terwiliger shrugged and stood. "The choice is really up to you," she said. She dangled the huge birdcage over Gurl's head and swung it like a pendulum. "But children often like to learn the hard way."

CHAPTER 7

What Not to Wear

SICK WITH APPREHENSION, GURL TOOK the long walk uptown to Harvey's, wishing that she could melt into the sidewalk. She tried to see some way out of her predicament, but what? Mrs Terwiliger had hidden the cat. And even if Gurl knew where to find her, she didn't know *how* to get her away or where to take her. She felt as helpless and useless as when Digger was knocking on her head.

But, despite the sick feeling in her gut, she did as Mrs Terwiliger had told her to; Gurl entered Harvey's an hour before closing, pretending to browse among the $100 belts and $250 ties. Her normally straight, long hair was curled in stiff but frizzy corkscrews and she was wearing clothes that Mrs Terwiliger had given her: a lacy yellow dress, a lime-green velvet jacket, tights and white vinyl boots. She also carried an overlarge vinyl tote bag. Gurl thought the outfit made her look like a reject from the Radio City Music Hall's annual Christmas show, but Mrs Terwiliger had insisted that the hair and clothes would allow Gurl to fit in with Harvey's wealthy clientele until she could slip into the changing room and disappear. *If this is what rich people wear*, Gurl thought, *then I'd rather be an orphan.*

Instead of helping her blend in, however, the outfit made Gurl stick out like a frog among peacocks. Other girls her age – and Gurl couldn't believe there were other girls her age with a need for $250 dollar ties – wore everything *but* yellow dresses, lime green velvet jackets, tights and vinyl boots. These girls eyed Gurl over the racks, smirking and snickering.

Totally humiliated – and totally itchy under all that lace and nylon – Gurl meandered back to the changing rooms with the intention of hiding until closing time. But the rooms were locked. All of them. For the plan to work, she would have to act as if she really intended to buy something.

She milled around for ten minutes before pulling several sherbet-coloured designer dresses from the racks. Finally, she walked over to a saleswoman who was stacking $1,000 cashmere sweaters on a shelf. She took a deep breath to calm herself; she had lived her whole life in an orphanage and had only rarely talked to strangers. "Um... excuse me?" she asked the woman timidly. "Can I try these on?"

The woman – silver haired, silver eyehadowed, silver suited and thin as a greyhound – turned and gasped, dropping all the sweaters to the floor.

"I'm sorry," Gurl stammered, "I just wanted—"

"Jules," whispered the woman, staring. And then she shouted, "Jules! Get over here! Now!"

A man with short dark hair, tiny rectangular glasses and purple leather trousers flew out from the back room. "What are you caterwauling about, Bea? Oh. My. God." He too stared at Gurl, his jaw hanging open.

Gurl had no idea what they were so upset about. "I didn't mean to interrupt your work, but I need to try—"

"Bea," said the man, Jules, tipping his head at Gurl meaningfully. "I think she represents the Lullaby League." His voice was deep and yet sort of raspy-squeaky, as if he had borrowed it from an old woman with a bad smoking habit. "Or maybe," he continued, "she represents the Lollypop Guild." Gurl thought she detected a British accent, but then again, a lot of people in the city had British accents, though most of them weren't British.

Bea looked down her sharp nose at Gurl and then at the dresses she held. "She's obviously in the theatre."

"Please tell us you're in the theatre," said Jules, clasping his hands together as if in prayer.

"No," said Gurl miserably. "I just wanted to try these on. Uh... I need something for... uh... my cousin's wedding."

"Your cousin's wedding," said Bea, her lips curling. Her eyes slid down Gurl's green jacket.

Gurl's palms began to sweat. These people didn't believe her. Maybe it was the huge tote bag, she thought. Maybe they suspected she was there to steal something. They would throw Gurl out and Mrs Terwiliger would send Noodle away. Gurl couldn't bear the thought of it. "Please," said Gurl. "The wedding's this weekend and my... my... grandmother will kill me if I don't get a dress. I just need some help with a changing room."

"You need more help than that, young lady," Bea said. She pursed her lips, took the dresses from Gurl's hand and returned them to the rack. She pointed to Gurl's jacket. "Where did you get that outfit?"

"Uh... my grandmother bought it for me."

"Well, she should be brought up on charges," Jules barked.

Gurl didn't disagree.

"Do you understand what we're saying?" asked Bea.

Gurl burned with embarrassment and horror under the disapproving stares of the two salespeople. "I think so."

"Do your other clothes look like this?" said Bea in a grave

tone of voice that one might normally use when discussing funeral arrangements.

"And what," said Jules, "is going on with your hair?"

Bea tried to fan herself with one of the cashmere sweaters. "Is that *green* eyeshadow you're wearing?"

"Your fingernails are all broken!" said Jules. "Were you buried alive somewhere? Were you forced to dig yourself out with your bare hands? Should we call the police?"

Bea collapsed in the pile of sweaters. "I think I need to sit down."

"This is no time for hysterics, Bea," said Jules. "Is Paulo still upstairs in the salon?"

"Yes, I think so."

"Tell him that he has one more client today."

Gurl's eyes widened. "Oh, please, no. I just came in to buy a dress for—"

Despite his disgust with Gurl's outfit, Jules's eyes were warm and kind. He took both Gurl's hands in his own. "Darling, don't look so upset," he said. "We like *you*; we just *hate* your clothes. What's your name?"

"Gurl."

"Gurl?" said Jules. "How... obvious." He turned back to Bea. "Take her to Paulo. I'll round up some respectable clothing and set up changing room five."

With those orders given, Jules buzzed around, pulling

items off the racks, while Bea pushed Gurl towards the staircase at the back of the store. Intent on their tasks, none of the staff responded to Gurl's feeble protests. Paulo, the head stylist for Harvey's salon, fainted at the sight of Gurl's hair and had to be revived with smelling salts while Gurl was being shampooed with beer and honey. An Asian woman who smelled of lilies daubed at Gurl's face with cucumber lotion, scowling at the eyeshadow that came away on the cloth.

After two bracing cups of green tea, Paulo was ready to work. He hovered like a hummingbird about Gurl's head, scissors snapping so fast and furiously that they were a silvery blur. When he was through with the cut, Gurl's hair was gelled, blow-dried, sprayed, fluffed and gelled again. The Asian woman – "Call me Miss Coco," she said – brushed blusher on Gurl's cheeks and gloss on her lips. Another woman came and filed her nails with a "natural sea stone". Then Jules returned to take her back downstairs.

"You. Look. Gorgeous," said Jules, pushing her into the changing room. "Don't you think you look gorgeous?"

Gurl felt as if she had just been on a very fast merry-go-round. "I... I don't know."

"What do you mean, you don't know?" cried Jules.

Gurl peered into the mirror. She had never spent much time looking at herself and no one ever seemed to notice her anyway. While she wasn't exactly gorgeous, she did look better than before. Sort of. Her wild, silvery hair now poured softly over her shoulders like a waterfall and she didn't have to push her fringe from her eyes to see. Her normally pale, dull skin and bloodless lips were fresh and rosy. "I don't recognise me."

Jules clicked his tongue on the roof of his mouth and smiled. "I guess I wouldn't either. Anyway, start trying on these clothes and let us know if you need any help."

Gurl nodded and Jules shut the door. Gingerly touching her new hair, and then the rack of expensive jeans, dresses and skirts, Gurl swallowed back tears. She hadn't had this much attention since, well, never. No one had ever told her she looked gorgeous (even if she didn't); no one had ever picked out clothes especially for her. For a minute she could imagine what it might be like to live someone else's life – a rich person's life, a happy person's life – and instead of making her feel better, like her daydreams always did, it made her feel terribly alone. But she didn't have time to feel sorry for herself. It was true: she was an orphan, she was hungry, she had been chased by a babbling rat man with an umbrella. She was not a rich person and she was not a happy person. She also was not alone. She had Noodle, didn't she?

At least, she would have Noodle if she got Mrs Terwiliger those scarves and shoes. But how would she do that now that the salespeople knew she was here? She couldn't just hide in another changing room; they would look for her. She would have to make herself fade or blend in or become invisible, or whatever it was that she'd been doing inadvertently for days. But this time she'd have to figure out a way to it on purpose and that's all there was to it.

Someone rapped on the door and Gurl jumped higher than any of Ruckus's practice leaps. "How are you doing in there?" said Jules. "Is everything fabulous?"

"Yeah," said Gurl. "I'll be out in a second to show you."

"I can't wait," Jules rasped with his odd, deep voice, sounding as if he really couldn't wait. Gurl felt a stab of guilt at the thought of tricking them, of stealing even more than she already had. But she couldn't worry about that now.

She stared at herself in the mirror, trying to concentrate, but the lime-green jacket glowed under the fluorescent lights, distracting her. She shrugged it off and tried again, but this time the yellow dress diverted her attention.

"Excuse me!" said Bea. "I don't hear any hideous clothes being kicked to the floor!"

Gurl unzipped the dress – it really was ugly – and tossed it over the changing room door. Bea cheered. "I'm going to fly over to the staffroom to burn this on the stove," she said. "I'll be right back."

Gurl turned to the rack, grabbed a pair of jeans and a shirt and quickly pulled them on. Staring at her own unrecognisable face, she took a deep shuddering breath. *OK, OK*, she thought. *Now. Blend in.*

She concentrated as hard as she could, watching her face for any signs of change. Then she remembered how it was Noodle who had seemed to cause her to become invisible, so she closed her eyes and thought of the cat. The way her fur felt. The way she purred. How, when Gurl petted her, time seemed to stop and strange riddles filled her head.

But that didn't do it either. Bea and Jules would be back at any moment and Gurl was becoming desperate. Why couldn't she do this? Why, why, why? She needed to do this; she *had* to do it. At this moment it was the most important thing in the world. And yet, here was her face in the mirror, her dumb face, all dressed up like it was someone else's. She was supposed to blend in, be like the walls and the clothes and the rug. Be like the mirror. Be like everything but herself.

And that's when she saw it, the way the skin on her face began to take on a slightly bluish cast like the dress hanging behind her. Was that it? "I am the wall," she whispered and her skin got even bluer, and she could see stitching marching across her forehead. *I am the wall and the ground and the air.* The mantra echoed in her mind. Her skin tingled and she could feel the change in her whole body. Soon she couldn't see herself in the mirror; she could only see the vague outline of herself, her skin the colour of the wall and the clothes that hung behind her.

"It's official; I burned the dress!" said Bea. "It gave off the most foul odour. Synthetic fabric, you know."

Quickly, Gurl sat in the corner of the changing room and pulled her legs in close.

"Gurl!" said Bea. "How are you doing on those outfits?"

"Tasty, aren't they?" added Jules. "I'll bet your favourite is the foil T-shirt. What do you think?"

"Gurl?" said Bea.

Gurl's heart pounded as Bea and Jules started rapping on the door.

"I think she's locked herself in there," murmured Bea. "Do you think we came down on her too hard?"

"Too hard!" said Jules. "That outfit was a crime!"

"Shhh!"

"Gurl, are you all right?" Bea said. "I'm unlocking the door."

Gurl heard the key in the lock and willed herself to think, *I am the wall and the ground and the air, I am the wall and the ground and the air.* The door swung open.

"What is going on here?" said Bea.

For a minute Gurl thought she had failed until Jules said, "Where did she go?"

"I swear," said Bea, "she was just in here a minute ago. She gave me that yellow dress to burn."

Jules looked at Bea. "Did she actually tell you that you could burn it?"

"Come to think of it, no."

"Well, what if she gets in trouble if she comes home without the dress?" said Jules, using his index fingers to jam his glasses up the bridge of his nose.

"I didn't think of that," said Bea. "I was just trying to get her to loosen up a bit. She was a little sad sack, wasn't she? It was like she'd never been in a store before."

"Oh, I don't know," said Jules. "She wasn't Miss Cheery Cheerleader, but those people make me want to fling myself out of a window. She was a serious person. I happen to like serious people. I myself am often very serious."

"Paulo's going to get serious himself when he finds out that he gave a free haircut and style," said Bea.

But Jules looked at her scornfully. "It was obvious the girl didn't have the money. He's an artist. He did it for art's sake."

"Which means that you're going to pay the bill, aren't you?"

"Never mind about that," said Jules. He leafed through the clothes left on the rack. "Looks like she took some jeans and a shirt with her. I guess I'll put those on the tab as well."

"We can use our discounts," said Bea. "I feel better that there's one less badly dressed, badly coiffed girl in the world, don't you?"

"Absolutely," said Jules. "We should be on television, you know. Giving makeovers to sad people."

Bea rose up to the ceiling, doing a balletic kick through the air. "That is a marvellous idea!"

"Come down and help me get these clothes back on the racks," said Jules. "We've had a long, exciting day."

Gurl held her breath as the two salespeople gathered the discarded clothes around her. Bea swept out of the changing room with armloads of outfits, while Jules picked up the stray hangers from the floor. Just as he was about to close the door behind him, he looked straight at Gurl.

And winked.

CHAPTER 8

Sweetcheeks: A History

IN A CITY WITH ITS fair share of swindlers and con men, gangsters and thieves, Sylvester "Sweetcheeks" Grabowski was perhaps the most famous (and absolutely the best looking, or so he liked to think). And yet, despite the city's rich criminal history, and despite his own pedigree – Sweetcheeks was the son of Tommy "The Trigger" Grabowski and Lurlene "Lightfinger" Looney – Sweetcheeks had always been a disappointment to his father.

"Where's the pretty boy off to today?" Tommy would grumble as Lurlene brushed the golden hair from her young son's brow.

"A modelling shoot for Luvvie's No-Pee Pull-Up Pants."

"Gangsters don't pose for diaper ads."

"There will be plenty of time for crime when he's older," Lurlene would reply.

"How's my hair, Mama?" the wee Sweetcheeks would ask. He didn't much care for his father, who reeked of warm beer and stale cheese curls.

"See!" said Tommy, shouting. "You're turning my son into a pansy!"

"A pansy who makes a thousand dollars a day."

"There's no talking to you, woman. I'm gonna go out and shoot something."

Tommy's wife shrugged. "If it will make you feel better."

Lurlene was right, however, in saying that there was plenty of time for crime. Her son's modelling career was cut short by the fact that Sweetcheeks himself came up short – only five feet eight inches in a world that favoured six footers. But that didn't bother Sweetcheeks. By the time he was fifteen, he knew that someday he'd be much bigger than his dad, a criminal mastermind of epic proportions.

That is, if he lived long enough.

Day after day and night after night, he was forced to sit at his father's side, practically dying of boredom while Tommy The Trigger entertained his own rather scruffy gang with stories of his exploits (which, in Sweetcheeks's opinion, were decidedly less than epic). They usually involved stealing Social Security checks from little old ladies, convenience store robberies and a little backroom poker.

Even worse was when Tommy The Trigger babbled on about "the olden days" when gangs ruled the entire downtown area. Gangs like The Daybreak Boyz, schoolkids who robbed drunken sailors lost in the twisting maze of streets. The Mashed Potato Men, known to stomp their victims into stupors. The Plug Uglies – huge, monstrous souls who wore bowler hats like tiny toilets and clubbed anyone who dared to laugh. And let's not forget The Dead Rabbits, The Cranky Babies, The Whyos, The Whosits, The Weepy Pinkies, The Meat Grinders, The Slug Salters, The Sewer Rats of Satan, yadda yadda yadda.

The most fearsome of these downtown gangsters, Tommy claimed, was Sweetcheeks's own great-great-great-great-grandfather, Mose The Giant. Mose was eight-and-a-half-feet tall and had fists the size of Thanksgiving turkeys hanging past his knees. Mose barrelled through the throng of bodies that poured from the downtown bars, bashing heads and picking pockets as he went. He stole steaming yellow ears from hot corn-on-the-cob girls and robbed all their pennies while he was at it. Mose was so big and so fierce he could rip up a lamp-post and whip up a good brawl whenever he wanted. Mose punched this, Mose stomped that, Mose Mose Mose. As far as Sweetcheeks was concerned, it was all a bunch of hooey.

On a snowy winter day in 1845 – as if anyone cared what happened more than 150 years ago – Mose was beating up a Sewer Rat in an alley when a lone little man stumbled down Mulberry Street. The little man didn't look that rich, but his wool coat was thick, his umbrella straight and his spectacles unbroken. Carrying a notebook in one hand, he read as he walked, while a tiny brown monkey perching on his shoulder picked snowflakes from the man's hair. Most of the eyes peeking from the windows and alleys saw the coat and the spectacles and decided he looked rich enough. A few others noticed the monkey and wondered what sort of loony bin he had escaped from. But, Tommy said, only Mose saw what went unseen: footprints in the thin layer of new snow behind the little man. Not the prints made by the little man himself, but a second set made by no one, as if a ghost followed on the little man's heels.

The little man stopped walking and removed a silver pen from his coat – perhaps to make a note in his book. But that shining silver pen was all the encouragement the gangs needed. Billy Goat Barbie, leader of The Dead Rabbits, did what she did best; she ran out into the street, head-butted the little man in the gut, and grabbed the first thing she laid her hands on: the monkey. A dozen Sewer Rats of Satan swarmed from their underground tunnels to rip the umbrella from the man's hand and the coat from the man's back. Dandy Bill, a notorious Cranky Baby, swiped the silver pen and the notebook before anyone else could think to take it.

But that wasn't the end of the story, Tommy said. For Mose The Giant strode from an alley where he'd been waiting, instantly scattering The Sewer Rats of Satan. Ignoring the little man, Mose crouched as low to the ground as his huge frame would allow, staring at the trampled snow. Suddenly, he lunged, snatching at something only he could see. And then, just as suddenly, Mose The Giant – all turkey-fisted, hobnail booted, eight-and-a-half feet of him – vanished. "Just like that," Tommy said. "Can you believe it?"

No, Sweetcheeks didn't, thank you very much.

Every night that Tommy The Trigger gathered his men around him for the evening, Sweetcheeks had to endure these sentimental ramblings. And when Tommy "The Trigger" Grabowski wasn't waxing poetic about Mose The Giant, he was waxing poetic about the failings of his own son. On that particular topic, Tommy The Trigger was a master of association. His son was not only a pansy, he was a wimp. A wimp and a coward. A coward and a spineless jellyfish. A jellyfish and a sticky lump of tapioca. A sticky lump of tapioca and a great big bogey. A bogey head. A bogey face. A bogey butt. A bogey brain. He had the brains of a sheep and the guts of a rabbit. He had the speed of a snail and the strength of a tissue (bargain brand). He was a blood-sucking, money-grubbing, opera-loving, quiche-eating, greedy little snot-nosed pretty boy, and he wouldn't ever amount to anything but a sweet-cheeked diaper model.

And then Tommy would laugh. Laugh so hard that his cheeks would turn red. So hard that he would cry. Soon the rest of the scruffy, moth-eaten gang would be laughing too, and Sweetcheeks would have to sit there, biting his tongue and biding his time.

Until one day, when he was twenty-three, when he couldn't stand it any more. His father was doubled over, laughing so hard that he'd shot beer right out of his nose (which made him laugh harder because that was just the sort of thing that he found amusing). Sweetcheeks stood up and swept the cards and poker chips off the table. He ran his hand through his golden hair, tossed his head and, in a low, ominous voice, said, "That's enough."

Tommy The Trigger stopped laughing. "What did you say?"

"I said, that's *enough*."

Tommy The Trigger's trigger finger itched, just as it always did when someone challenged him. "Sit down, Sweetcheeks."

Sweetcheeks's cheeks burned. "*You* sit down."

"What are you talking about, you dumb bunny? I *am* sitting."

"Yeah, well, shut up."

"What did you say to me?" Tommy The Trigger growled, standing to tower over his son.

Sweetcheeks poked his father in the chest. "I said shut up. You big moron."

"Big...?" sputtered Tommy The Trigger, the veins on his forehead standing out like cables.

"Moron," said Sweetcheeks.

Tommy The Trigger shook his head, as if he couldn't understand what was happening. But then he seemed to relax. He sat, a slow smile spreading across his face. "So," he said. "I'm a moron."

"Yes."

"And you're the big man now, am I right?"

Sweetcheeks drew himself to his not-all-that-tall-but-tall-enough height. "Yes."

"What do you say, boys, is he the big man now or what?"

"Or what!" one of boys said, sniggering.

"Yeah, you're the big man. So what are you going to do now, big man?"

"Do?" said Sweetcheeks. Well, he hadn't thought of that yet.

Tommy The Trigger began to laugh again. "Get a load of you. You're not going to do nothing, Sweetcheeks," he spat. "You're just a stupid kid. You're a zero. You're less than a zero. You're just *less*, how about that?"

Sweetcheeks lifted his chin. "I'll show you," he said.

"Yeah, yeah, sure you will. Get outta here."

Sweetcheeks Grabowski turned on his heel, walked out of his father's dusty apartment and kept walking. He walked across the Brooklyn Bridge into the heart of the island city and did not stop walking until he reached Chinatown. With the money from his childhood modelling jobs (and a few quickie but rather skilled burglaries), he bought his own place and started up his own gang. A *classy* gang. No backroom poker for Sweetcheeks and his men. No two-bit muggings or cheesy swindles. No, they only took on big jobs: jewellery and bank robberies, money laundering and high-stakes gambling. He got himself a wife – Donatella Arribiata Conchetta Schiavoni, daughter of one of the city's premier crime bosses – and a kid. He was ruthless, but refined. Elegant, but understated. Blood-thirsty, but tasteful.

The years passed and everything was settling nicely. Sweetcheeks was certain that eventually he would have enough clout to crush his beer-sneezing father beneath his boot. And he would have, if Donatella hadn't taken up with the plumber and run off to Boise, if the kid hadn't turned out to be a whiner who had to be pawned off on a bunch of nannies, and if Sweetcheeks hadn't got bored with robbing banks. No, Sweetcheeks wanted something bigger.

And then he remembered the story of his great-great-great-great-grandfather Mose The Giant. What if that stupid story was true? What if, as Tommy said, Mose The Giant really *had* managed to capture an invisible girl? And what if

Sweetcheeks could do the same thing and catch an invisible girl for himself? Why, an invisible girl could turn everything around. An invisible girl could help change a better-than-average thief with marital problems into the greatest gangster of all time. Imagine what you could steal if you were invisible. You could steal the most powerful weapon in the world!

He had to find her.

How was the question. Sweetcheeks thought he'd conceived the perfect plot, but so far it hadn't produced satisfactory results. And grabbing that map from that batty old man and his vicious band of cats hadn't worked either. Some genius that guy turned out to be! The star on the map had marked the location of Kakusaki's House of Sushi and the very polite, very frightened and very cooperative Mr. Kakusaki hadn't heard of any invisible girl. (But he did make a luscious California roll.)

Despite some serious evil-planning issues, Sweetcheeks gathered his men in the Armoury, a large round room deep in Sweetcheeks's basement lair. Circling the room were a dozen suits of English and French armour, each of them positioned at the ready, as if they were about to race off into battle. (Sweetcheeks swore the suits of armour liked to march around at night, and that when he woke up in the morning they had all switched places.) Display cases filled with antique swords, guns and bullets graced the walls. The oval meeting table was clear glass, so that the eighteenth-century cannon that formed its base was visible. The finishing touch was Odd John, standing in the corner with an enormous battle-axe slung casually over one shoulder. (Sweetcheeks thought he looked fabulously menacing that way, and often made John stand there when Sweetcheeks was negotiating with rival gangs.)

Sweetcheeks leaned forward as he finished telling the story of Mose The Giant. "No one knew what had happened, not even my great-great-great-great-grandfather Mose himself. But at that moment, he'd grabbed the ankle of the biggest prize of all. The Wall. The one who wasn't there, the invisible girl, whatever you want to call her. And together the two of them went on to perform the biggest bank and jewellery robberies of the nineteenth century, all of them unsolved to this day." Sweetcheeks' famous cheeks were flushed and a single lock of golden hair fell attractively over one blue eye – the very same way it did in the ads for Luvvie's No-Pee Pull-Up Pants – as he leaned back in his seat once more and looked around at the men. "Now, have you ever heard a more fascinating story?"

In their collective opinion, his men had heard more fascinating nursery rhymes. But they knew that if they didn't show the right level of excitement, Sweetcheeks would go back to the beginning and tell it all over again, just like he'd told it 4,000 times before. And if that wasn't enough to stir up some enthusiasm, he might start chopping off random ears, noses and little toes. It was only with a great effort that the men managed to say, "Wow," or "Gee whiz," or "Who'd a thunk?" before tossing back their whiskies and pouring out more.

"So, Boss," said one of the men, Bobby The Boy, too new at this gangster gig to know when to speak up and when to cork it. "The little guy... uh... the one who was robbed. He had a monkey?"

"Yes, he did."

"Why?"

"Well, Bobby, I really couldn't say."

"I don't like monkeys," one of the other men said. "Too noisy. And all that swinging makes me dizzy."

"Yeah," said another guy, "and they have those creepy little faces, you know? Like... uh... little monkey faces. Mean ones."

The group nodded in agreement at these slights against the monkey population. "They smell, too."

"The monkey is beside the point though, isn't it?" said Sweetcheeks, sighing in annoyance. "The monkey was just a minor detail."

"And what about the notebook?" said Bobby. "What do you think he was going to write in it?"

Sweetcheeks was blunt: "Who cares?"

"I mean," Bobby said. "Could have been something important, you know? Like a secret formula."

"A secret formula *for what*?" Sweetcheeks snapped.

"I don't know," Bobby said. "Something secret. And the pen. You said it was silver?"

"The pen," said Sweetcheeks. "Now that's a totally different story. The pen was something special. And still is."

But Bobby wasn't finished with his questions. "Was she ugly or something?"

Sweetcheeks raised one of his delicately arched eyebrows. "Excuse me? Was *who* ugly?"

The other men stared into their glasses as Bobby The Boy continued. "The Wall. Was she ugly or something? Is that why she, you know... uh... was invisible and stuff? Or maybe Mose never saw her or nothing?"

"Ugly? *Ugly?*" said Sweetcheeks. "The Wall was beautiful. The most beautiful girl in the world. And my great-great-great-great-grandfather loved her. He loved her *dearly*. And she loved him. It was the romance of the century! They were like Bonnie and Clyde!" The truth was that The Wall had been no great beauty and Sweetcheeks's great-great-great-great-grandfather Mose was no romantic. Unless he needed her help for some shady criminal activity, Mose kept The Wall locked in the chicken coop in the backyard of his mother's house in New Jersey, where she survived on only the eggs the chickens saw fit to give her.

But Sweetcheeks hated to be reminded of annoying things like truth or justice or unwilling invisible accomplices left to suck eggs in chicken coops. "Let's not get sidetracked here," he said, glaring at Bobby. "My point is that we need to get our hands on our own Wall. There's one born every hundred years or so. This new one would be about twelve now. I know that because she and I have... uh... met once before, when she was quite a bit younger."

"What do we need her for?" said Bobby The Boy.

"What do we need her for? Were you paying attention to my story? Do I need to tell it all over again?"

The other men started to grumble and one them waved a salad fork at Bobby menacingly.

"What I mean is," said Bobby, "you already pulled off some of the biggest bank robberies, right?"

"Some," said Sweetcheeks, mollified.

"And some of the biggest jewellery robberies."

"Go on."

"And some of the biggest cons."

"It's true."

"With all that, Boss, why do you need some invisible girl?"

"Oh," said Sweetcheeks. "Well, my young friend, one can't rest on one's laurels, can one?"

Bobby The Boy bunched his eyebrows together. "What's a laurel?"

But Sweetcheeks wasn't listening. "You have to have a goal, you have to keep moving on to bigger and better things, otherwise you grow old and stale. I've got some plans – big plans – that require The Wall's special talents." He looked around the room meaningfully. "Some plans that involve The Richest Man in the Universe."

One of the men gasped, and several others poured themselves double and triple shots of whiskey.

"I hope that satisfies your curiosity," said Sweetcheeks. "Now let's move on to the next item on the agenda. I want to know what's going on with The Punks. I haven't received my cut of their take, I've gotten no word and I'm becoming quite irritated about the whole thing. Unless I get some news from them soon, I'm thinking about gassing the whole subway system just to get rid of them."

But Bobby The Boy, unfortunately for him, still wasn't *quite* done asking questions. "Boss, I thought you said last time that you had some kind of spy looking for The Wall."

"Yes, yes, I did say that. What about it?"

"How come he ain't reported in yet?"

"Ain't?" said Sweetcheeks. "What language are you speaking?"

"And," said Bobby The Boy, oblivious to the growing hostility of the group and to the purpling of Sweetcheeks's cheeks, "how do you know that once you catch this Wall girl, she won't get away from you like she did when she was a baby?"

Sweetcheeks lost his patience and nudged the man to his right. "Lefty, who hired this idiot? I want him fed to the dogs."

"You don't have any dogs," Lefty said, twirling his dark handlebar moustache. "And you're the one who hired him."

"Ah. Well, that was clearly a bad call," said Sweetcheeks. "Mr John, I am in need of some toes for my charm bracelet. You pick the foot. And use a floor cloth, will you? Last time you made such a mess that the cleaning crew charged me extra."

Thick as he was, Bobby The Boy finally realised the kind of trouble his big mouth had got him into. He leaped up from his chair and flew around and around the table, chased by a cheerful but persistent John and his handy battle-axe. Sweetcheeks and his men were just settling in for a bloody bit of entertainment when one of the guards burst into the room.

"Boss!" he said. "A Sewer Rat!"

"What?" said Sweetcheeks. "Where?"

"Here!" yelled the man. "Now!"

Before the guard could say any more, he was clubbed from behind and shoved to the floor. Standing in his place was a man – or at least someone the general shape and height of a man – wearing a stained and ragged wool coat and holding an umbrella like a baseball bat. The man-thing dropped his umbrella and fell to his knees. He took a deep, shuddering breath, threw back his sloping, rodentlike head and shrieked: "KITTY!"

CHAPTER 9

Outsides and Insides

HER FIRST BURGLARY LEFT GURL triumphant. Then shaken. Then exhausted. Then ashamed. But whatever she felt, she knew she did not want to go back to the orphanage. Not yet. She walked (numbly and invisibly) for too many blocks to count until she found herself at one of the many mouths of Central Park.

She entered the park, found a restroom, and – after many unsuccessful and nerve-racking attempts – made herself visible again. She left the bathroom to search for a place to rest. A patch of soft grass, a bench, a rock – it didn't matter. She tried to ignore the ice-cream and hot-dog vendors, the rumbling of her own gut, and the many people who floated and bounced along the path.

As she passed a pretzel vendor, her stomach growled loudly and the vendor laughed, calling, "*¿Hola, cómo está usted?*" She didn't understand Spanish and was embarrassed when he pointed to the pretzels and then to her belly. She shook her head and pulled out an empty pocket. The kindly vendor smiled, dressed a fat pretzel with a yellow ribbon of mustard and held it out to her. Even more embarrassed, she shook her head again, but he would not take no for an answer. Gratefully, she took the pretzel and thanked the vendor as best she could. She found a soft patch of grass at the edge of an open field. She leaned up against her tote bag, now stuffed with stolen items, and took a bite of her pretzel.

A particularly spectacular macaw, swishing a two-foot-long tail, ambled over to where she sat. It wore a red velvet collar with the name *Darla Jean* scrawled in rhinestones. "One bite?" it said. "Pretty please?"

Gurl glanced around at the people who reclined on blankets and benches all around her, but no one seemed to be paying any special attention; no one seemed to care that the bird was bothering her.

Gurl held the pretzel over her head so that the huge bird couldn't reach it. "Piggy!" it said, angry. "Oink, oink, oink!"

A cockatoo — his name appeared to be Reginald, if you

believed the writing on his tiny T-shirt – wandered by. He preened for a taste of the pretzel and squealed like an infant when Gurl said, "No!"

"Mean!" said the cockatoo.

"Piggy," corrected the macaw.

But that wasn't the worst of it. Soon waves of pigeons washed the ground around her, peering at her with one eye, then the other. Loons and gulls and pied-bellied grebes stopped by, as did black crows that gleamed purple in the dimming light. She was mocked by the mockingbirds and taunted by the bobolinks. The only bird that didn't make an appearance was the dancing blue-footed booby.

On top of that, dozens of Wings and wannabes darted around and above her. She watched as a pear-shaped man in a shiny warm-up suit bounced along the path in front of her, his loose flesh shaking like half-set gelatin. An older woman with hair dyed an unnatural shade of red held her arms out aeroplane style as she zoomed through the air in weird, shuddering spurts, as if she were having trouble switching internal gears.

Gurl gave up. The birds were right. She was officially a thief, so who was she to deserve a reward, even one as small as a pretzel? Squeezing back the tears that welled up, she broke the pretzel into pieces and watched as the birds fought for the crumbs. She wondered about the salesman, Jules. Perhaps he never saw Gurl at all – the wink another figment of her imagination – or maybe he *had* seen her somehow and didn't care enough to get her in trouble. But then again, what if he were just waiting for her to actually leave the store to call the police? Gurl tensed with alarm, looking around wildly. They could be searching for her right now! Here she was, just sitting around, waiting to be caught!

She scooped up the tote bag and ran, scattering the birds like a toddler on the beach.

But no one ever came searching for her. Once Gurl got away with that first burglary, Mrs Terwiliger sent her out almost every night. Fourteen pairs of high-heeled shoes, fifty-seven silk scarves, thirty-nine hats, twenty-two sweaters, ten bottles of French perfume, seven lipsticks and five fur coats (fake, but Mrs Terwiliger didn't seem to notice the difference) – that was what Gurl stole for Mrs Terwiliger in the month that followed the first outing, and still Mrs Terwiliger had produced Noodle only once a week and then for only a few minutes. Every time Gurl brought back more scarves, hats, shoes and perfume, she asked for Noodle. And every time Mrs Terwiliger told her, "Just a few more errands, Gurl, dear and then you can have your little friend back."

Gurl was beginning to think that Mrs Terwiliger intended to use her to steal expensive junk for the rest of her life, and that Noodle would die alone and lonely in that horrible birdcage. But Mrs Terwiliger wouldn't tell her where she was keeping Noodle, and just because people couldn't see her didn't mean that Gurl could see through walls or locked doors. Plus, Mrs Terwiliger seemed to know that with every "errand", Gurl got better at controlling her talent. She had installed brand-new locks on all the doors and windows and rigged the main building with some sort of motion detector. So Gurl was forced to keep doing Mrs Terwiliger's bidding, hoping that one day, some day, the matron would get careless and leave her alone with Noodle long enough for Gurl to get them both out of Hope House.

Besides her frustration with Mrs Terwiliger, there were her feelings about the stealing itself – the fact that sometimes, she was proud of what she had been able to get away with and yet, at the same time, ashamed of it. How could that be possible? And what did that say about her? Was she a bad person? Was she born that way?

There was one good thing about stealing for Mrs Terwiliger, Gurl thought, as she trudged back to the orphanage after an errand to nab some Russian caviar. She could experience the city in a way she never had before, from the outside in. Sure, she had gone out alone a few times late at night to get some food in Luigi's alley. But she had never been able to walk undetected into Luigi's kitchen and see how the food was made, the chef murmuring lovingly to his dishes as if they were alive. She had never been able to go to boutiques so expensive and exclusive that they catered only to supermodels and pop stars (who often whined about the prices, threw tantrums in the changing rooms, and left lipstick stains all over the $500 T-shirts they tried on). There was the pet shop where a parakeet turned to a lorikeet and said, "So, who is this Polly and why does she want a cracker so bad? I'd take a Mexican tamale any day." Even the public library was a surprise; the great stone lions that guarded the steps turned out to be two pale and sweaty actors in lion suits, paid to stand still.

And in this city you *would* have to be paid to stand still because everything else moved so fast! The streets were a blur of glittering eyes, windswept hair, billowing overcoats and shining boots, all gliding and hopping and floating and flying along in a dizzy, colourful confusion. *Perhaps*, thought Gurl, *the city dwellers came to fly because walking wasn't fast enough to get them to where they needed to be.*

Gurl also saw things that weren't so wonderful: sweatshops where hundreds of women pieced together clothes, homeless people curled up in doorways, the flashing lights of police cars, fire trucks and ambulances. (She also saw Laverna flyers posted on every block, each of them begging for the return of a certain grey cat.) Despite these things, she came to view this sparkling island city as a great buzzing hive, with every single person doing his or her part to make it the place it was, the place where everything and anything could happen, a city of endless possibilities. She often felt as if she couldn't keep her eyes open wide enough or long enough to take it all in.

If you were to ask Mrs Terwiliger, she'd say Gurl *never* took in enough. As usual, Gurl met Mrs Terwiliger at the door to the main building after everyone else had gone to sleep. Mrs Terwiliger grabbed Gurl's hand firmly while she unlocked the main door and then the door to her office. She watched silently, still holding Gurl's hand, as Gurl pulled jars of caviar from her tote bag.

"A dozen jars?" Mrs Terwiliger said. "Is that all you could get?"

"That's all they had." It wasn't, but Gurl didn't like to steal more than she absolutely had to. Plus, it made her feel less like a slave to defy Mrs Terwiliger in this small way.

Mrs Terwiliger pursed her lips, freakishly large now that she'd had them plumped with collagen. "Then you'll have to forgo this week's visit with your friend."

"What?" said Gurl. "But I've been doing everything you asked!"

"I asked for *two* dozen jars, not one. If you're going to hold out on me, dear, then I'm going to hold out on you," she said sweetly. "This is a two-way street. We have to learn to trust each other." She looked past Gurl, fluffing her hair in her full-length mirror.

But Gurl saw nothing two-way about it. She twisted her wrist in Mrs Terwiliger's hand. "No," she said, so quietly that even she could barely hear it.

"Excuse me? Did you say something?"

Gurl looked into Mrs Terwiliger's surgery-enhanced face and wondered where her courage was coming from. "I said no. If you don't let me see Noodle now, I'm not doing anything else for you."

"Don't be silly, dear. Now, I was eyeing this gorgeous little antique shop the other day and I saw an exquisite vase that would look perfect in my office. When visiting dignitaries come to see Hope House, it will make them feel welcome. Here, I have a photo—"

"I said I'm not doing it."

Mrs Terwiliger pushed Gurl back into the chair and snapped the handcuffs on her. "I don't see why you have to be so stubborn."

In response, Gurl vanished, blending in neatly with the chair behind her.

"Stop that," said Mrs Terwiliger. "I'll leave you here, I mean it. I'll lock you where no one will ever find you!" She stamped her foot.

"Then I guess you won't be getting that perfect vase you want so badly." Gurl was glad that Mrs Terwiliger couldn't see her trembling. She had never in her life spoken this way. But her travels outside had begun to change her inside. She felt stronger somehow. Braver. And more than that, she was angry. Angrier than she'd ever been. All Gurl had ever tried to do was get along, to stay out of everyone's way, and not call attention to herself. And the only reward she'd got for it was one tiny cat who chose to be her friend. And this woman had turned her into a thief! It wasn't fair! It wasn't right!

Mrs Terwiliger looked at the photograph she held and then at the chair, longing and rage etched on her face. "All right," she said. "If you are going to be so difficult about it, I suppose I could appease you this once. But don't expect me to do this all the time! You've been getting snippier and snippier ever since you got that haircut, if you'll pardon the pun. I expect to be rewarded for my generosity." She flicked the handcuff with a fingertip and said, "Don't go anywhere. I'll be right back."

Gurl sat in the chair, waiting for her to return with Noodle. The fez-wearing monkey still perched on the desk where it had been the first time Mrs Terwiliger dragged her to this office. "Hey, monkey," she said. "Did you hear? The matron's doing an errand for *me*. What do you think about that?"

The monkey clapped its cymbals twice and then stopped, its eyes seeming to stare right back at her. *So?* its eyes said.

That's no secret. Tell me something I don't know. Gurl picked it up to examine it more closely. It was cheap, like something a street vendor would sell for a few bucks. She fingered the little waistcoat and saw the gold velvet was worn and threadbare, the fur sparse and thin. Idly, she flipped the monkey over. On a white sticker pasted to the monkey's butt was a name: GURL.

"What?" said Gurl out loud. The monkey's cymbals clapped weakly and Gurl threw the thing back up on the desk.

Why did a stupid mechanical monkey have her name on its butt? What did it mean? She glanced around at the other monkeys. Did they all have names? Forgetting the handcuffs, she got up and shuffled to the closest shelf, dragging the chair along with her. She snatched up a yellow monkey with a red chapeau and searched its backside for a sticker. JESSAMYN JACOBSON. She put that monkey down and plucked up the one next to it. MICHAEL O'KEEBLE. The next said SHERMAN PERLMUTTER. Who were these people? Why were their names on the monkeys?

What was going on here?

Just then Gurl heard the familiar creak of Noodle's birdcage. She put down the monkey she was holding and dragged the chair to its original position in front of the desk. Mrs Terwiliger pushed open the door. "What were you doing?" she said. "I heard noises."

"Not much," Gurl told her. "Looking at the monkeys."

"Were you now?" said Mrs Terwiliger, placing the birdcage on the desk next to the fez-wearing monkey. Noodle thrust her nose between the bars of the cage and meowed.

"Can't you take her out?" Gurl pleaded, barely able to get a little finger inside the cage to pet the cat. "It's so small in there."

"No, I can't take her out," said Mrs Terwiliger. "She gets bathroom breaks twice a day and that's quite enough trouble. Strange little animal. Refused to use a litterbox."

"Wouldn't you?" said Gurl.

Mrs Terwiliger harrumphed but didn't comment further. And she let Gurl have five minutes more than she normally did, enough time for Noodle's purr to get so loud that it filled Mrs Terwiliger's head and made her sleepy, made her peaceful, made her wonder about trees falling in the woods and the sounds that they made when they did.

Mrs Terwiliger didn't know how long she had been napping, but when she came to, Gurl was still petting the cat, a dazed and dreamy expression on her face. "Snap out of it!" Mrs Terwiliger shouted, more for her own sake than Gurl's.

Gurl blinked and said, "What is it? What's going on?" The fez-wearing monkey clapped its cymbals until the cat mewled.

"What's going on is that we're going to talk about your next errand," said Mrs Terwiliger, pulling the birdcage off the desk and putting it on the floor.

Gurl felt another surge of anger – how long could this possibly go on? – but she swallowed it. "The vase. I remember."

"No, I've changed my mind. Forget the vase. I want you to do something bigger and more important."

Gurl, suddenly worried that Mrs Terwiliger wanted to branch out into bank robbery, said, "What could be more important than a vase?"

"I'll tell you what's more important," said Mrs Terwiliger. "What's important to any girl. My face."

"Your face," repeated Gurl.

"You might be surprised to hear this," Mrs Terwiliger told her, "but I've had a few things done to... er... spruce up a bit. A few minor surgical procedures."

"Really?" said Gurl, trying to keep the sarcasm from her voice.

"I *am* the face of Hope House," Mrs Terwiliger said. "And if I don't look good, then the orphanage doesn't either. I'm scheduled for a few more procedures, but there's a bit of a problem with my credit card. And until I get it straightened out, my doctor has refused to do them."

"Can't you just pay your bills?" said Gurl.

"Well, yes. I plan to do that as soon as I can. But I need the procedures now. Some things can't wait."

Gurl was confused. "What can I do about your bills?"

"The bills are generated at the doctor's office by the

computer." She handed Gurl a slip of paper with an address. "You'll go uptown. Sneak into the building, boot up the computer and mark the balance as paid. I trust that you've had enough experience in computer class?"

"Uh... sure, I can do that," said Gurl. "Can I pet Noodle again, just for a few more minutes?"

"Not so fast, dear. You should know one more thing. In the daytime that office has more staff and more patients going in and out of it than Grand Central Station. Even if you're invisible, I don't see how you can get to the computers then. You'll have to go at night."

"I've gone out at night before," Gurl said. "Can I please pet Noodle?"

"But at night," Mrs Terwiliger continued, "there's a rather elaborate alarm system. You'll have to find a way to get past it."

"What?" said Gurl. "How? I don't know anything about alarms!"

"Oh, you'll manage. I have complete faith in you. And Noodle does too." Mrs Terwiliger sighed, her face a mask of sadness. "I don't really know what's going to happen to her."

"What do you mean?"

"Look at her. She's obviously an old cat. I don't know how many days she has left."

Noodle didn't seem that old, but Gurl couldn't tell a young cat from an old one. "Noodle's fine."

"*Now* she's fine. But what happens if I forget to feed her?"

"Why would you do that?"

"I'm very busy, Gurl. I have a lot of people depending on me. One day I could forget." She smiled at Gurl. "You wouldn't *want* me to forget, would you?"

Mrs Terwiliger wouldn't do anything to Noodle, thought Gurl after a sleepless night spent tossing and turning, *she couldn't do anything*. But then maybe she would. Maybe Mrs Terwiliger already had enough scarves and hats and perfume to last her a lifetime. Maybe Gurl had pushed her too far.

It seemed that she was pushing everyone too far. On her way back from the cafeteria line, she bumped someone with her shoulder. "Sorry," she said.

"Hey!" Bug said, the front of his shirt dripping with orange juice she'd made him spill, his huge wide eyes darkening with anger. "Why don't you watch where you're going?"

She barely glanced his way. "Whatever."

Dillydally whistled. "Far out! The leadfoot's getting a bit of a 'tude, bro!"

Bug looked as if he wanted to say something more, but Gurl swept past him and sat in her usual place in the cafeteria, stirring her eggs but unable to eat a bite. She was so preoccupied that she didn't hear Digger until Digger was right up in her face.

"Whatcha eating, Freak?" Digger took Gurl's carton of milk and downed the contents.

Milk for the cow, Gurl thought. *Eggs for the chicken*. How was she going to get past an alarm? It was impossible!

"I'm talking to you," said Digger, her little finger flirting with her nostril.

"Mmm-hmmm," said Gurl absently. Maybe the alarm was one of those kinds with a card key. If she could steal one, that might work. Or if there was some sort of code, she could sneak up behind some people and see what numbers they punched in.

"Hey!" snarled Digger, furious that her mere bulky, blocky presence wasn't enough to set Gurl trembling as usual. But Gurl was tired and anxious, so much so that she was impatient.

"Oh, sorry," said Gurl, "did you want something?" She picked up her breakfast plate and offered it to Digger. "Go ahead. Get it over with."

"Huh?" said Digger.

"No, wait, on second thought I'll do it for you."

Two hundred orphans' mouths grew slack and round with shock as Gurl threw her own plate to the floor, where it smashed into a million pieces.

CHAPTER 10

Two Little Mice

WHISTLING A NONSENSE TUNE, BUG sidled over to the door to the main building, the unbent paper clip hidden behind his back. When he thought no one was looking, he jiggled the clip in the doorknob until he felt the lock give and the knob turn. Then he opened the door and slid inside.

Finally, he thought. *Elvis is in the building.* He started to take a step when he heard a beeping sound and noticed something hinky: faint red laser beams crosshatching the hallway. An alarm system! Motion detectors! The moronic matron strikes again! Well, he could take care of that.

He turned and scanned the wall for the alarm panel. He

pulled the cover off the panel and inspected the wiring: blue, red, yellow, white. No problem. Snip the red wire, splice together the blue and white, tie the yellow in a knot, put back the cover. The beeping stopped and the lasers disappeared.

Bug crept down the darkened hallway, peeking in offices, bathrooms and broom closets, exploring every nook and cranny. When he got to Mrs Terwiliger's office, he smiled at the five locks. *So paranoid*, he thought. Then he thought: *for good reason*. He pulled out the handy paper clip and a few more from his pockets and soon he had all five locks picked and the door open. Cruising the office, he sneered back at the monkeys who sneered at him from their perches on the shelves. *Geez*, he thought. *Look at them all. What kind of wacko would collect stuff like this?*

A wacko who stole people's cats, that's who.

Frustrated, he punched the wall. *Wham!* That stupid Gurl. *Wham!* Lost his cat. *Wham!* He'd been having flying dreams again, ones where he'd been so high he'd cleared the top of the Empire State and then doubled back to dart around the needle on the roof. Strange sounds interrupted the dream and he'd woken up, at first just disoriented, then so disappointed he nearly cried (but he did *not* cry). He'd punched his pillow a few times, then got up and crept to the window. Gurl stood outside, lurking by the door of the main building. Soon Mrs Terwiliger floated across the yard. He'd watched them go inside and decided he would follow. He'd heard the whole thing, or at least the last part of the whole thing, while eavesdropping outside Mrs Terwiliger's door. Gurl was going out at night, doing stuff for the matron, some kind of secret stuff because the matron was keeping the cat prisoner to make her do it.

And here he'd searched every inch of this place for the last couple of weeks and the cat – *his* toilet-flushing genius cat! – was nowhere to be found. And if Gurl didn't go to that doctor's office and do something about Mrs Terwiliger's bills, well, he didn't want to think about it.

Why he didn't want to think about it is another story. The truth was, he'd only seen the cat once, and while it was a cool cat, and cats were rare and everything, it was still just an animal. All he knew was that the idea of not seeing the cat again, the idea that Mrs Terwiliger was keeping it in some cage somewhere and it couldn't get out, made him, well, want to punch the walls.

Wham!

If only he had something to blackmail Mrs Terwiliger with, something that would force her to give him the cat. He started searching the desk. He found disciplinary files on Digger (fighting), disciplinary files on Lunchmeat (loafing), disciplinary files on Dillydally (dillydallying). In his opinion there should have been a disciplinary folder on Gurl, for showing up one day with movie star hair like she'd had it her whole dumb life, for spilling orange juice all over him and barely saying she was sorry, for throwing her plate on the floor and freaking out the whole orphanage, and for generally acting like a whole different person than the weepy dishwater pasty face he thought she was.

He kicked the chair. It slid backwards and bumped the shelf behind it, and a monkey – a shoddy-looking thing with a waistcoat, maracas and a stupid grin – fell to the floor. He remembered that monkey. It was on Mrs Terwiliger's desk the first time he came to see her. She said it was...? He had to try hard to remember. His friend. She said it was his friend. He nudged the toy with his sneaker. There was something on the bottom of the monkey, a white sticker with writing. Bug picked it up to see. WHAT'S IT TO YOU? Well, no clues there, but if this monkey was Bug's friend, then Bug was just going to keep ole What's It To You? for a while. He slid the small monkey into his pocket.

Apart from all the monkeys, there was nothing weird on Mrs Terwiliger's desk, say a letter that admitted to holding a cat hostage to force a minor to commit fraud. Bug sat down behind the desk with his head in his hands, wondering what he should do now. Well, there was a computer. He could boot it up and see what's what. And if there wasn't anything on it, well, he could still surf the Net. When he pulled his hands away from his eyes, however, he saw the business card taped to the computer, the one with a surgeon's name and address.

He pulled the monkey from his pocket. "What do you think?" he said, turning to the mirror on the wall next to the desk. "Could I use a couple of emergency cheek implants or what?"

The monkey kept on grinning.

"That's what I thought. I better get to the doctor."

Wham!

Bug waited until after lights-out before throwing off the covers and slipping from his bed. All around him, orphans sighed and orphans snored, orphans wheezed and orphans whistled. Now that was the good thing about boys, he thought, they could sleep through fireworks. He tiptoed across the dormitory, even though he didn't have to, and slipped from the room. It took him just a few minutes to pick the lock to the door that let him outside.

It was dark, of course, but not that dark; the city napped, but it was never out cold. Bug skipped down the long avenues, occasionally trying to fly. After finding that he couldn't fly any better outside the orphanage than inside, he mostly ran the dozens of blocks until he was close to Central Park. He found the building he was looking for and through the glass door saw Gurl standing in the darkened, deserted lobby, staring at the keypad of some sort of alarm system. Her face was crumpled up like a napkin and he knew she was about to cry any second.

That, he didn't need. Quickly, he picked the flimsy lock on the door and let himself inside. "What are you doing here?" he said.

She gasped, whirling around to stare at him. "How did you get in?"

"I picked the lock. How did you get in?" he said, figuring that she just followed someone inside.

"Me?" she stammered. "I'm just... um... visiting. A friend."

"Really," he said. "A friend." He pointed to the list of the building's occupants. "Is your friend with the insurance agency? Or the day spa? Or maybe with the chiropodist's office?"

He thought that she might start babbling again, but her grey eyes got a flinty look. "The chiropodist. I have bad feet. They have this awful tendency to kick nosy, stupid people in the head."

Snap! He was impressed. "That's a problem."

"For the nosy people," she said. "OK, it was nice to see you. You can go now. To wherever you're supposed to be." She was looking at him in the same way she looked at him in the cafeteria after she spilled juice all over him. The way that told him that on a scale of important things she had to worry about, Bug rated a minus 40. Her eyes were on the keypad of the alarm. It wasn't very high-tech for a nice building, just a plain old numerical code that you had to punch in. Easy stuff.

No reason to tell her that.

"You'll never get it," he said.

"What?"

"The alarm system."

"What are you talking about?" she said. "Are you crazy?"

"I'd have to pull the cover off the panel, but it looks pretty tough. They probably have motion detectors, cameras, you know."

She opened her mouth as if she might argue with him, but instead of speaking, she slid down the wall and sat on the floor.

"Are you resting for your chiropodist appointment?"

"Oh, shut up," she said. "Just shut up." Then she really did start to cry, sobs that she muffled in the crook of her arm. That made him feel kind of mean and stupid. So he pulled the cover off the alarm and scrutinised the wiring. He took a tiny pair of scissors from his pocket and made a few artful snips. Then he punched in some numbers and replaced the cover. "OK," he said.

"OK, what?"

"OK, OK," he told her. "Alarm's off."

She lifted her head. "What?"

"It's off."

"It is? The whole thing? Cameras and stuff?"

"Didn't I just say that?"

She blinked at him. "But how?"

"What do you mean, how?"

"Where did you learn how to do it?"

He frowned. Something itched at the back of his mind, but for the life of him, he didn't know what it was. How did he know how to pick locks and disarm alarms? It seemed as if he had always known it, that there was never a time in his life that he didn't know it. But that couldn't be true. A person isn't born knowing how to pick locks! "Never mind that," he said. "Let's go."

"Go?" she said. "Go where?"

"Look," he said. "I heard the whole thing, OK? I was listening at the office door when you were in there with the monkey queen. You have to get up to the doc's office and erase Mrs Terwiliger's bills from the computer. And you have to do it because she's got my cat."

"You mean she has *my* cat," Gurl said.

"That's what I said," replied Bug. "So are we going or what?"

"No, I'm going. You're staying here."

Wham! "Don't think so."

She looked at him for a minute or two, then said, "It's on the thirty-first floor. We'll have to take the elevator. And we still have to be careful. You don't know if people are working late."

"Right," he said.

"Just don't punch the walls any more?"

Wham!

"You have an anger problem, do you know that?"

Wham!

Once they got off the elevator, they saw that Dr Lucre's medical practice took up the entire floor. Doors with etched glass led directly into the large reception area, doors that Bug opened in just a few moments of paper-clip wriggling. "Wow," he said. "Tight security."

"Lucky for us. Now we just have to find the right computer," said Gurl.

"Maybe the billing stuff isn't on any one computer, but on a network," Bug said.

"Maybe. Let's try one behind the reception desk. Most people pay before they leave, right?"

They climbed over the top of the desk and settled in a couple of the chairs. While they were waiting for the computer to boot up, Gurl said, "What if it has a password?"

"Mrs Terwiliger doesn't find out that kind of stuff for you?"

"No. She doesn't care how I get what she wants, just as long as I get it."

"What does she make you do?"

"Steal. Clothes, perfume, whatever."

"Don't you feel bad about it?"

He got an icy glare for that one. "Don't *you* feel bad about breaking into places?"

"*I've* never stolen anything," he said.

"What do you want me to do? I don't know where she keeps Noodle and until I find her I can't stop."

Gurl's face screwed up and Bug worried that she might cry again – why were girls always crying? He tried to distract her. "Noodle? My cat isn't named *Noodle*."

"It's better than 'Bug'," she said.

"It's way better than 'Gurl'. OK, computer's up." He used the mouse to open folders and look inside. "Doesn't look like it's got a password."

"Try the one that says 'Patient Financials'."

He clicked open the folder and found a database. He scrolled through the names, whistling when he saw some of the famous people who visited Dr Lucre. "Whoa! I knew those were fake."

"Come on, scroll down to the *T*'s."

"We've got a few minutes," Bug told her. "I want to see who else is on here." He stopped when he got to the *J*'s.

"What?" said Gurl.

"John," he said.

"Who?"

Bug stared at the screen. John. O. John. He knew that name. But who was it? "Odd," he said.

"Hey," said Gurl. "What's wrong with you?"

"Nothing, nothing." He continued to scroll through the names until he got to the *T*'s. "Here it is: 'Terwiliger,

Geraldine.'" He clicked on the name and got to her file. "Man! She owes more than $20,000!" Gurl grabbed the mouse from his hand and deleted the balance. "Not any more she doesn't. Now let's get out of here."

"Are you sure you don't want to stay a little while? We can look through some more of these files. I think every star in Hollywood is on—"

Gurl grabbed his arm. "Shhh! Did you hear that?"

"What?"

A squeaking sound echoed through the empty offices.

"That!" hissed Gurl. "Shut it down, shut it down."

Bug powered off the computer, and both he and Gurl dived underneath the desk.

The squeaking sound was followed by a man's voice, singing. "There was a fine lady who swallowed a pie. I don't know why she swallowed a pie. Perhaps she'll die." The squeaking sound stopped, and there was a lot of banging, and then the sound of papers falling.

Bug and Gurl looked at each other underneath the desk. "The janitor," Bug whispered.

The squeaking started up again and now they both knew what it was. The janitor's cart, rolling towards them. The cart stopped right next to the reception desk. The janitor sprayed some sort of sickly sweet, orange-smelling cleaner around and began to wipe down the top of the desk.

"There was a fine lady who swallowed some cheese. Quick as you please she swallowed some cheese. She swallowed the cheese to chase back the pie. And I don't know why she swallowed the pie. Perhaps she'll die!"

He finished wiping down the counter and then walked behind the reception desk. He pulled out the chairs behind the desk and reached underneath for the trash can, catching hold of Bug's woolly sleeve instead. "Hey!" the janitor yelled, stumbling back a step. "Who's under there?"

Bug tensed to run, but Gurl grabbed his hand and held it hard enough to break the bones. A queer shiver went through his body, as if he had got a brief electric shock. The janitor dropped to his knees to look under the desk. "Looks like I caught a big rat!" he said.

His mind whirling a thousand miles a minute, Bug tried to come up with an explanation. *OK*, he thought, *we're orphans, and we were just looking for a place to hang out for a while. We weren't going to steal anything, we swear, Mister.* He opened his mouth, but Gurl clapped her other hand over it.

The janitor shook his head, his bald white scalp gleaming. "Or a mouse. Damn mice! Doctor's head's gonna pop off. Ain't my fault he got mice. Needs an owl, that doctor. Owl'll take care of the mice nice and quick." He grabbed the trash can, got to his feet and walked away singing. "There was an old doctor who swallowed a mouse, what a louse, he swallowed a mouse!"

Was the guy blind? thought Bug. He turned towards Gurl to peel her hand from his face but stopped, utterly shocked. He could feel her hand in his, and he could feel her palm on his lips, *but he couldn't see her*!

What? What? His mind babbled. But it got worse. When he looked down, he couldn't see himself! It was like his legs were the same colour and pattern as the rug beneath him. He thrashed and kicked, but the girl managed to hold on till they couldn't hear the janitor's song any longer. Then she let him go, her face and body appearing before him as if he'd just opened his eyes after a brief nap.

"You're fine," she whispered. "It's OK."

He checked his arms and legs. Everything was where it was supposed to be. "What the heck..." he began, but then he knew. That first day, when she'd started to fade in front of him and then disappeared from the girls' dorm. The reason why Mrs Terwiliger kidnapped Noodle and sent Gurl out to steal. "You can turn yourself invisible."

"Yes."

"You just turned me invisible too."

She bit her lip. "Yes."

He felt something bubbling inside him, something that made him want to jump up and up and up. "Come on," he said.

"What?"

"Do it again."

CHAPTER 11

Flyboy

"I THINK YOU BETTER CALM down," Gurl told Bug. "We're not out of here yet."

"So make us invisible and get us out!" He presented his hands as if she were about to slap handcuffs on him.

She knocked his hands away. "Cut it out."

"Please?" he begged. Gurl could see that he was trying very hard to be patient and nice about it, though he was hopping up and down like he had mosquito bites on the soles of his feet. Bug was right, though. They could escape more easily if they were invisible.

"OK," she said. Now that they were out of danger, holding

hands seemed weird – his were slightly damp – but Gurl didn't give herself time to think about it. All she thought was, *We are the walls and the floor and the air. We are everything and we are nothing. We are not here.* And then they weren't.

"Oh, man!" he said. "This is amazing."

"Shhh!"

"Aw," he grumbled, but she could hear the smile in his voice. It made her smile too, though she was glad he couldn't see it. She wasn't sure what was going to happen once they made it back to Hope House. Did he really expect she would give up Noodle without a fight? But it didn't matter right now, she told herself. Right now, all they had to do was get out of the building unnoticed. She would deal with everything else later.

"OK," she whispered. "Let's go. But be careful. It's hard to move when you can't see where you're putting your feet."

"I'll be careful – ow!"

"Or," Gurl continued, "where you're putting your head."

They stood – awkwardly, as they had to hold on to each other for them both to remain invisible. Gurl felt Bug squeeze her hand. "What?" she said.

"Nothing," he told her. "It's just weird that I can, you know, feel you and everything, but I can't see you."

"Yeah, I know," she said. "Just don't let go." As soon as she said it, she could feel herself flush. "I mean, let's go."

They went. Much to Bug's disappointment, they passed no

one in the hallways or in the lobby. The street, however, was a different story. Though it was late, the night was filled with bright, silvery light from a full moon. There were plenty of people out and about, and Bug charged after them all like a puppy, dragging Gurl along with him. He would dart in front of them and wait, as if at any moment they would swerve to avoid the two grubby children blocking their way. But, of course, they didn't; at the last second, Bug and Gurl would have to jump out of the way to avoid being trampled. And each time they weren't noticed, Bug would start leaping around so much that she had to whisper in his ear, "Will you knock it off already?"

"Why?" he said, hauling her down the street. "Don't you think this is fun?"

She didn't answer, but she had to admit to herself that it was kind of fun. As much as she loved to slip unnoticed through the city, learning all its secrets, it was nice to be with someone else. Even if that someone was a hyper bug boy.

"Come on," she told him, pulling on his arm. "We should probably get back."

"What?" he said. "Why should we go back so soon? There's got to be something else to see. What do you think about the park?"

Before Gurl could respond, Bug managed to haul her across the street towards Central Park. Stopping momentarily, they looked down the long path that wound its way inside the park and vanished over a small hill. Street lamps poured hazy light over the path itself, but the shrubs and rocks beyond them were hunched and shrouded in the deep emerald lawns, and the trees seemed to huddle together as if for warmth.

"I think I read about this," said Gurl. "Hansel and Gretel."

"You afraid?" said Bug, teasing.

What she thought: the park made her nervous because it felt like a new place every time she went. What she said: "Shut up and walk."

As they made their way down the darkened paths, she wondered if the kindly pretzel vendor was still around because she could use a pretzel. And maybe a hot dog.

Bug tugged on her hand. "Hey. Why are you so quiet all of a sudden?"

Quiet? I'm always quiet, she thought. But then again, she hadn't been quiet at all tonight. She'd probably said more to Bug than she ever had to any other person her age. "I'm not—" she began, but Bug cut her off.

"Shhh! Someone's up ahead."

Thinking of the babbling rat man who had chased her in the dark, Gurl's stomach dropped to her knees. But it was only the pretzel vendor. *"Le veo,"* he said, and she and Bug stopped walking, alarmed. But the vendor wasn't talking to them. Gurl heard a faint rustling and followed the vendor's gaze to a clump of bushes, which were swaying as if there was a strong wind. One of the bushes suddenly stood up on spindly roots and scuttled across the path, looking somewhat like a headless, neckless ostrich. Another bush followed and then another. Soon all the bushes that had been on one side of the path clustered on the other. The trees behind them waved their branches as they too shifted places, waltzing around one another before settling in different arrangements.

Even plants aren't leadfeet, thought Gurl. *Every day they make this a brand-new park.*

Bug's breath tickled her ear. "Can you believe this?"

"No," said Gurl. "Yes. I think I can."

Bug tugged at her hand and the two of them continued to walk down the path to the entrance to the Central Park zoo. Bug convinced her to climb over the gate.

"I've never been to a zoo before," Gurl said.

"It can be boring. All the animals do is sleep," Bug told her.

"Really? How do you know?"

Bug didn't answer her question. Instead, he said, "It's kind of creepy in here. Lions and tigers and bears."

"Bears anyway," said Gurl. "Look."

She lifted his hand and gestured to a large water tank. An enormous polar bear swam the length of the tank, his big body ghostly and graceful in the icy water. With his powerful limbs and ham-sized paws, he might have been intimidating, except for a red bucket that he wore over his head.

"Nice helmet," Bug said.

"Maybe he's shy," Gurl said. The plaque affixed to the tank said the big bear's name was Gus. It also said that Gus had suffered from severe depression until the zoo shipped in a couple of girl bears and installed a Jacuzzi in his exhibit.

Gus stopped swimming and broke through to the surface, the red bucket above the water, the huge white body below. He looked like an iceberg rammed into a thimble. Ida and Lily – two smaller bears watching by the side of the pool – rolled on to their backs, slapping their legs with their paws. Gurl could have sworn they were laughing.

As Gurl watched the bears, Bug wandered to the next exhibit. "Hey!" he said. "Bowling pins with feet."

"What?" said Gurl. "Oh, penguins."

Convinced that nothing in this city was as it seemed, Gurl half expected the tuxedoed birds to sing show tunes, or play tiny trumpets, or step out of penguin suits to reveal trained Chihuahuas underneath. But the penguins remained penguins. They gathered together in small groups, squawking and flapping, no different than the penguins Gurl had seen on TV.

"It's like a penguin powwow," Bug said. "Maybe they're planning to take over the world."

For some reason the penguins delighted Gurl. Especially the way their awkward, stumpy-limbed bodies turned sleek and graceful as soon as they hit the water. *They're birds*, she thought, *but they don't fly.* "Let's see what other animals are here," she said.

They moved to the arctic foxes, which looked like white, fluffy dogs. "'Arctic foxes must be very clever to escape the jaws of the polar bear'," Bug read. "'Like the bear, however, they have white coats to help them blend into their winter world.'"

"Hey, puppies," said Gurl. "Good doggies!" The foxes sniffed left and right with black button noses, trying to figure out where the voices were coming from. One of the foxes approached the bars of the enclosure, flopping on to his back right at Gurl's feet. Gurl wished she could reach it through the bars and scratch its ears and belly. Somehow, she felt – she knew – it wouldn't bite her.

Next Gurl and Bug visited the sea lions, then the red panda, then the snakes and the alligators. Bug wanted to stop in the aviary to catch all the birds, but Gurl had seen and heard enough of birds to last her a lifetime. "No," she said. "No wings."

"What have you got against wings?" Bug said.

"Nothing," she said.

"Right," said Bug. "I hope you don't have anything against snacks. Let's see if we can find that pretzel vendor and get something to eat."

They took a different route out of the zoo to the pretzel vendor, walking towards the centre of the park. Though it was darker and quieter, Gurl didn't mind. She felt like an arctic fox blending into the snow. A part of the world and yet hidden from it.

The shifting trees waved their arms as if in greeting. Through their branches she saw a splash of red. "What's that?"

"What's what?" Bug said.

What turned out to be a carousel housed under a brick canopy. Bug let go of her hand and tried the gate. "Locked," he said.

Since Bug was now visible, Gurl became visible too. "A lock shouldn't stop you."

"It won't," he said, pulling out his paper clips.

"I was just kidding!" said Gurl. "We can't go in there. What if someone sees us?"

"Nobody's looking," Bug said. "Besides, the carousel isn't even on."

In a few seconds, Bug had the lock picked. He ran through the open gate and hopped aboard the carousel; Gurl followed. They counted fifty-eight carved horses, some of them big enough to be real. Gurl patted the head of a black horse with a white mane that looked as if he wanted to charge off the platform. Bug swung himself up on to a white horse, painted red and starred white.

"What are you doing?"

"Riding," he said. "What are you doing?"

"We should probably go," Gurl said.

"Come on," he said. "Pick a horse."

"This is stupid," Gurl said, pulling herself up on to the rearing black horse. Colourful clowns decorated the hub of the carousel wheel, and Gurl frowned; she was not a clown person. "OK. Now what?"

Lights flared overhead and the carousel began to turn. "Bug, what did you do?"

"Nothing! I've been sitting right here!"

The carousel picked up the pace, the horses sliding up and down on their poles. Gurl put her hands on the horse's back as the carousel spun faster. The wood felt curiously warm under her fingers. The only sounds were the whir of the engine and the hiss of the wind as the horses cut through it. Gurl thought she smelled something sweet, like candy floss.

"Bug," she said. "How are we going to make it stop?"

"I don't know!"

The carousel spun faster still – *too* fast – and the trees beyond the brick canopy blurred. Gurl's black horse jerked up and down beneath her and she threw her arms around its neck to stay on. The carousel engine's whir turned to thunder, a thunder that thudded like hooves. She felt the horse's straining muscles, its hot breath. The flying mane tickled her cheeks. She turned away, tried to focus on the clowns, but the clowns weren't there any more. The hub was blank and white. She squinted in amazement. Where were the clowns?

She gripped the horse tighter and shouted Bug's name, but she couldn't hear her own voice over the roar. On the horse in front of her, a clown sat backwards in the saddle, facing Gurl. He wore a polka-dotted satin suit and a black hat with a daisy poking through the top. He grinned, waggling his gloved fingers.

Faster and faster they went, until Gurl couldn't see the clown any more, couldn't focus on anything but the horse beneath her, the thunder in her ears, and the belief that there was no stopping this carousel unless it wanted to stop, and it never, ever, *ever* wanted to stop.

Then it stopped.

The lights cut out and the carousel screeched to a halt, nearly catapulting Gurl into the next century. She slid from the horse to the floor, gasping.

"Gurl?" Bug said.

"Yeah?"

"Are you OK?"

"I think so."

They lay a minute, breathing hard.

"Gurl?" Bug said again.

"What?"

"I felt like I was riding a horse. A *real* horse. A *crazy* horse."

"Yeah," Gurl said. "Me too."

"And there were these... uh... clown guys." He pointed to the center of the carousel. "*Those* guys."

"Yeah."

"Oh," he said. There didn't seem much else to say. They scrambled off the carousel and ran back through the gate, clasping hands without even thinking about it.

For a while they kept glancing behind them to make sure the clowns weren't creeping up on them, but it seemed that what happened on the carousel, stayed on the carousel. Their pace and their heartbeats slowed to normal and their appetites returned. They were making their way back towards the pretzel vendor when they heard a voice coming from just beyond a small hill.

"Buenas noches."

"Thank you!" said Bug. "Now we can finally get a pretzel. And some water. And maybe a reality check."

"¡Que noche tan bella para bailar!" said another voice.

"Don't tell me the trees speak Spanish," whispered Bug.

Gurl tried to turn them both invisible before she realised that they already were. They got to the top of the hill and saw not just a few vendors, but many, assembled in a clearing near the path. There was the cheerful pretzel vendor with the white apron, a dark-haired woman in a red dress and sweater, a young man with a thin moustache, and maybe three dozen others, all laughing and greeting one another like old friends. Around them, their white carts formed a large square.

"What's going on?" whispered Bug.

"I don't know," Gurl said. "Let's get a little closer."

"Are you sure?"

"They're just vendors," Gurl said. "Just people. They're not dangerous."

"Yeah, right," said Bug. "I don't think I'll ever believe that anything is just anything ever again."

As they crept closer to the gathering, one of the vendors yelled "¡Musica, por favor!"

"¡Musica! ¡Musica!" came the cries from the others. The man with the thin moustache opened the top of an ice-cream cart and pulled from it a small set of bongo drums. Two other men pulled guitars from their carts, and several others pulled horns. The small group assembled in one corner of the square. A lively drumbeat filled the air, the guitars sang and the horns bleated in turn. Around the impromptu band, a woman began to dance, left right left, right left right, swinging her hips gently. A man took her by the hand and twirled her around as the rest of the people cheered, grabbing partners for themselves.

"They're dancing!" Gurl said.

"I know," said Bug. "It's the merengue."

Gurl looked in Bug's direction, wishing that she could see him. "How do you know what it is?"

There was a pause. "Because the cha-cha would look different."

"If you say so," said Gurl, wondering if the cha-cha was as fun as it sounded. "They look like they're having a good time. And they're not even flying."

"I guess they don't need to," Bug said. "Have you ever seen this before?"

"No."

"Look at that!" Bug cried. In the air above the dancing vendors, darting in and out of the purple shadows, a bird circled, then another, then another. Soon the air was swarming with circling birds: kestrels and grackles and gannets. Hawks and robins and goldfinches. Crows and gulls and pigeons. Even the oddly named screech owls with their little tufted ears joined the swirling tornado of birds, calling with their signature whistling whinny.

Gurl could barely take in the wonder of it all. "I think the birds are dancing too!" Watching them, she almost forgot the crazy carousel. With the music and the dancing and the fabulous swirl of birds, the carousel ride seemed like a small and not so scary part of the whole.

Bug dropped her hand, instantly becoming visible. He started an awkward, stiff-jointed jig.

"What are you doing?" Gurl asked, making herself visible too.

"What does it look like?" he said.

"Some sort of seizure," said Gurl.

"Ha!" he said. "I'm dancing. Haven't you ever danced before?"

"Not like that," said Gurl.

Bug jerked around like a marionette. "I feel great, don't you? This whole day made me forget about everything. I forgot that I forgot."

"Huh?" she said. "What are you talking about?"

Instead of answering, he jumped. Not a huge jump, but a delicate pump of the knees, seemingly effortless. He rose up like a feather caught by a breeze, up and up and up, until his feet hovered above Gurl's head. His arms waved gently back and forth, like a person treading water. "I feel," he said, "like I could fly."

"Bug," said Gurl. "You *are* flying."

Bug looked down at her. "I'm what?" His eyes widened—if that were even possible—and he moved his arms faster, kicking with his legs, propelling himself higher. "I *am* flying." He let out a triumphant whoop, darting down to Gurl and then shooting back up again. "I'm flying!" he shouted again and again. "I'm flying!" He spun in the air faster than a top, cackling like a madman, then flew up to the highest tree where he plucked at the leaves.

Standing there underneath the street lamps' wan light, far below Bug, Gurl could still see the look on Bug's face, the joy and the thrill of flying. She felt a stab of jealousy so strong that it nearly knocked her over. She knew that she never looked so happy as Bug did at that moment. She knew that she had never felt joy so deep that you couldn't keep from shouting it to the world.

Bug plucked leaves from the treetop and flew down to where Gurl was standing. "For you," he said, presenting the green, red and yellow leaves to her, his grin so big and wide that he looked like the Cheshire cat straight out of Wonderland.

"Thank you," she said.

"Whoop!" he hooted, springing into the air once more. "This is the most amazing thing. I've never felt anything like this. You have no clue how amazing this is!"

Gurl sighed, crushing one of the leaves in her fist. "No, I guess I don't."

He stopped whirling and whooping. "Hey, what's wrong?"

"Nothing," she said. "Just go on flying. I think it's great. Really." She tried to put a little enthusiasm into her voice but he wasn't buying it. He flew down to her and held out his hand.

"Come on," he said.

"What do you mean?"

"You helped me disappear. I think I can help you fly."

Gurl had never heard of anyone but a Wing being able to carry someone else. "I don't think that's a good idea."

"Trust me," he said.

She shook her head. "I'm not sure that you—"

He swooped down and grabbed her hand.

"Whoa!" she yelled as she felt her toes leaving the ground. She dropped the leaves and slapped her other hand around his wrist.

Bug smiled down at Gurl. "Hold on," he said and took off, loopy as a comet.

Gurl's breath left her lungs in a whoosh as she and Bug flew straight up, higher than the street lamps, higher than the treetops, higher and higher and higher. She screwed her eyes shut, a curious buoyancy filling her chest like a helium balloon. Bug changed direction, and it no longer felt as if she was hanging from the end of Bug's arm, but rather flying next to him, with him.

"Open your eyes!" he said.

She did, and gasped. Below them, the park spread out like a quilt. She could see the pretzel vendors twirling in their makeshift dance hall, the carousel, a pond gleaming like a dark mirror. The air, clean and chilly, tossed her hair.

"What do you think?" Bug asked her.

Think? Her mind whirled, her eyes open so wide they felt as if they might pop right from her face. She didn't want to think. All she wanted to do was feel. And what she felt was happy. Happier than she'd ever been in her life. She understood now why people wanted so desperately to fly. It was amazing! It was incredible! It was—

"Bug! Look out!"

CHAPTER 12

The Richest Man in the Universe

NOT FAR FROM GURL AND Bug, in a penthouse overlooking Central Park, Solomon Bloomington sat down at his magnificent mahogany desk and stared at the detective's report. It read:

> *All leads led to dead end. Trail is cold. It is likely that subject has either expired or has been transported to a distant, unpopulated location.*

Sol crumpled the report into a ball and threw it at the wall, where it hit an oil painting of Solomon Bloomington's great-great-great-great-grandfather, William Bloomington, known as Dandy Bill. From the picture, Bill's eyes seemed to stare reproachfully out at his many-times-great-grandson.

Sick to his stomach, Sol gazed out of the enormous floor-to-ceiling windows. Outside, in the park, someone flew, a dark puppet against a light grey sky. No, two someones, a Wing and another who dangled off the Wing's arm like a worm on a hook. As he watched, Sol frowned. The Wing was talented but unpredictable, flying and falling, then flying again. Sol knew a lot about flying. Since the first humans took flight in the mid-nineteenth century, billions of dollars had been poured into researching the phenomenon, all of it trying to answer the most basic questions. How, for example, could people fly if they didn't have wings? Why could most people fly only so high and so well? What was the cause of Leadfoot Syndrome – the total inability to fly? So far no one had come up with more than interesting theories. Sol himself hadn't been interested in theories, and poured his own energy and money into other ventures. He was on the boards of several multinational companies, including Airborne Industries, maker of the Flycycle® and Rocket Board® brand personal transportation devices (or PTDs). He had come up with the advertising slogan himself: "You don't have to be a Wing to fly like one."

His passion for flying used to consume and thrill him – after all, it had made him The Richest Man in the Universe. (Well, it had helped, anyway. Much of Solomon's fortune had been inherited from his prosperous ancestors, some honest, some, well, a bit more *creative* than honest.) But Sol Bloomington and his wife, Bunny, had suffered a loss that had broken their hearts and their spirits, leaving them ghosts of their former selves. If only he had been able to fly into the past and undo the wrong that had been done.

And for nearly thirteen years, Sol had been trying.

In his desk drawer were the solemn reports of forty-six different private detectives, ex-police officers, search firms, and high-paid mercenaries whom he had enlisted to help him scour this wretched earth for Georgie. Each one had filled him with stupid hope and each one of them had come up empty. No matter how much money he paid them or how much of a reward he'd offered if Georgie were found, the reports came back, relentless as the setting sun: gone, gone, gone, gone, gone, gone, gone.

He got up, walked around his desk and picked up the crumpled report. Smoothing it out in his hands, he opened a filing cabinet and stuffed the document in with the rest of them. It was over. He would not hire another one.

Solomon sat down at his desk. After a long moment, he reached into his pocket and pulled out a silver pen – a long, fat, ornate sort of pen that looked like no other – an artefact of another time, perhaps, or another world. Every night he'd been coming to his desk and staring at the blank sheet of paper, and every night he hadn't dared to write a word. The pen, this simple instrument, was more powerful than all the presidents of all the nations in the world. It had more impact than a meteor. It spoke louder than money. This pen could rewrite history, but it could also undo history. It could take his words and turn them upside down, twisting the world in the process. For all he knew, once he'd used it, once he'd written down the precise thing he wanted most, he might wake up a con man or a madman, a lizard or dog or mosquito. He might not exist at all.

But tonight something was different, something was in the air; he could feel it. The Wing on the wing outside maybe, dipping and lurching like a kite, reminding him of how glorious things could be. He watched the flying pair and felt the same stupid hope – the hope that kept him hiring one detective after another, the hope that kept him going – rising in his chest. The ornate pen twitched in his fingers, encouraging. *It would be so easy. All I have to do is use the simplest, plainest words possible. What could go wrong?*

He looked at the painting of his great-great-great-great-grandfather again. *He* would know what to do. *He* wouldn't hesitate.

The silver pen twitched again and this time he didn't slip it back into his pocket. This time he let himself scribble that name, the most beautiful name he knew: *Georgie.*

He dropped the pen to the desk and stared at the rich blue ink sinking into the fine linen paper. And then something brushed his ankle. What was that? He looked down to see fresh shoots growing up from the carpet under his feet, shoots that burst quickly into ripe red strawberries. He gasped, glancing up again to see broccoli bunching and cauliflower flowering around a ripe peach tree. A wave of silvery wheat danced along the wall, whispering and shushing in a mysterious wind. Not just fruits and vegetables grew; all around the room, delicate flower buds burst into perfect cups of red, yellow and pink. The scent of new roses perfumed the air.

At first, Solomon couldn't understand what was going on. He'd written a name, just a name. Then he thought: wait, every name has a meaning. What does the name Georgie mean? Solomon pulled fragrant strings of snow peas from his keyboard and monitor before typing "Names and Meanings" and then "Georgie" into his computer. *Nickname for George. Origin: Greek. Meaning: Farmer.* He'd written the name Georgie with the silver pen and grown himself a garden and who knows what else.

The Richest Man in the Universe rubbed his cheeks with his hands, not sure whether to laugh or to cry. Green vines festooned with fat purple grapes snaked up the glass of the enormous windows, but not too many to obscure the view. Sol stood up from his chair. The Wing and his companion were no longer flying in the park; they were flying across the street, high and fast and out of control.

And heading right for Sol's window.

CHAPTER 13

Turkey Burger

SOMEHOW THEY HAD FLOWN OUT of the park and were making a beeline right for the penthouse across the street. Bug pulled up hard, yanking Gurl back with him just before she crashed into the large window. As they hovered there, panting, they saw the older man standing inside, peering out at them through a tangle of vines. Behind him a peach tree dropped heavy fruit on patches of blooming tulips, sweet peas and begonias. A river of wheat swayed gently against the walls. An orange hibiscus twined itself around a desk lamp, while a single lily, with petals as thin and diaphanous as baby skin, sprang from an open desk drawer.

The man inside the indoor garden blinked, and then lifted his hand and gave a wan little wave. Gurl waved back.

Bug slapped at her hand. "What are you doing?"

"He waved at us."

"Why don't you turn us invisible or something?"

"He's already seen us," said Gurl. "What difference does it make?"

"He probably thinks we're here to steal all his flowers and whatever else he's got in his crazy house."

"He looks sad."

"Sad? You're crazier than he is. Rich people aren't sad. They're rich."

"I still think he looks sad," said Gurl. The sad rich man pressed his face closer to the window, staring at them. Suddenly, he slapped both palms against the glass, yelling something that they could not hear. One word, shouted again and again.

Before Gurl could protest, Bug yanked her away from the window.

"Bug," said Gurl, "he's talking to us."

"He's going to call the cops. Come on!" Bug said, sending them into a steep dive for the street below.

"Slow down!" Gurl shrieked as the pavement came closer and closer.

Abruptly, Bug jerked upwards, trying to set them on their feet, but he misjudged their speed. The two of them went sprawling across the sidewalk. A smartly dressed woman out with her shiny black mynah bird stepped right over Bug, clucking her tongue with disapproval.

Groaning, Bug got to his knees. "Hey, don't worry, lady," he called after the woman. "We're just fine. No need to get an ambulance or anything."

The mynah, perched on the woman's shoulder, turned to look at Bug. "Scoundrel!" it said primly. "Rapscallion!"

"Yeah," said Gurl weakly, picking tiny bits of gravel out of her palms. "What the bird said."

"Sorry," Bug told her. "I guess I have to work on the landing part." He picked up a monkey that was lying next to him on the sidewalk.

"Is that one of Mrs Terwiliger's monkeys?"

"Yeah. I swiped it from the old bat's office. It must have fallen out of my pocket when we landed."

"*Crash*-landed," said Gurl.

"Whatever."

"The monkeys all have names. Did you know that?"

"Not all of them. Unless 'What's It To You?' counts as a name." He showed Gurl the sticker on the monkey's butt.

"I wonder what that's supposed to mean."

Bug rolled his eyes (a gesture with great power when one had eyes twice the regular size). "Who knows?" he said, shoving the little monkey back in his pocket.

They half flew, half walked back to the orphanage. Bug kept grabbing her hand to lift them off the ground and whisk them away, but he seemed tired and deflated, and couldn't fly more than a block or two without having to take a rest. Still, flying was flying and Bug was thrilled.

"I guess I'm a little worn out. And I do have to work on landing," he said. "But, admit it. I'm pretty good."

"Not bad," said Gurl.

"Not bad! I'm better than anyone at Hope House, that's for sure."

"Like that's hard," said Gurl, smiling.

Bug tipped his triangular head thoughtfully as they walked. "I could never fly at Hope House, but I'm flying now. I wonder if it's because you turned me invisible."

"How would that make a difference?"

"I have no idea, but maybe it did. Up till tonight, I could barely get my feet off the ground. Then you turn me invisible, we take a ride on a crazy carousel, we watch some pretzel guys dance the merengue and all of sudden I'm flying like a Wing. Come on, it's got to be you."

Gurl thought that it might be something else; it might be Noodle. Maybe cats were more than just rare, maybe they were magic? But she didn't want to say so. She didn't want to give Bug another reason to want Noodle all for himself.

Despite being able to fly only a little, and then not very fast, they reached the orphanage much more quickly than Gurl would have on her own.

"Thanks," she said when they got to the front gate of Hope House.

Bug opened the gate. "For what?"

"For helping me. And for taking me flying with you."

"Oh. Well." Even in the dark, Gurl could see him blushing and felt herself flush too. "Uh... no problem. Thanks for the now-you-see-us, now-you-don't thing."

"You're welcome."

They stood awkwardly until Gurl said, "You better go. I've got to wait for Mrs Terwiliger and tell her that she'll be able to have another facelift after all. You don't want her to catch you too."

"I guess you're right." He walked over to the door to the dormitories. "I'll see you tomorrow."

She smiled. "Maybe you will, maybe you won't."

"Heh," he said. "Funny." He gave the brick wall one of his signature punches before he opened the door and was gone.

He did see her the next day, of course, and she saw him. As usual, no one asked Gurl how she was, no one sat with her at breakfast. And, as usual, Digger lumbered over, a mocking scowl on her blockhead head (but she skulked away when Gurl put a protective arm around her plate and glared). From his own table, Bug waved hello, but that was all. From the outside, it appeared as if nothing had changed.

But it seemed to Gurl that everything had changed. Bug had disappeared and reappeared. Gurl had flown like any Wing. Together they had discovered the city the way it really was: magical and mysterious and surprising. And because of all this, Gurl could not help but feel different.

She felt so different that instead of staying in the dorm after school so that she could daydream the evening hours away, Gurl joined the other kids in the "rec room" – a large, breeze-block room painted an unnatural shade of green and furnished with an odd combination of beanbag chairs and rows of old auditorium seats. Unnoticed, Gurl slid into a chair by the fuzzy TV set, pretending to read a book while she eavesdropped on the numerous conversations.

"You must be joking," Persnickety was saying. "Rosy B. is a terrible singer."

"That's jive, girl," Dillydally said. He pointed to the TV, which was playing Rosy B.'s latest video: "It Don't Mean Nothing If It Ain't About Love." In the video Rosy B. was wearing a baseball cap and a mink bikini. "You going to tell me you think this song ain't boss?"

"The volume isn't even on!" said Persnickety, pursing her permanently pursed lips. "You can't even hear her!"

Dillydally shrugged. "Who needs to hear her?"

"Nobody says 'jive'. Nobody says 'boss'." Persnickety grabbed the remote control and flipped the channels until she found a movie she liked. "Now, *that's* better."

"Peter Paul Allen," said Ruckus. "Why do all the girls like Peter Paul Allen? He needs a shower. And his teeth are crooked. He looks like a rabbit." Ruckus stuck his front teeth out over his bottom lip.

"You're just not normal," Persnickety told him. "Normal people do not have worms sticking out of their heads. They don't act like you."

"Oh and you're so normal," Ruckus said. "You would fold your own *hair* if you could. What do you know about normal? What do you think normal people do?"

Persnickety stuck her pointy nose in the air. "I know that normal people respect one another's opinions. They spend time with their families. They play games with their parents."

"You think parents are fun?" Ruckus grumbled.

"Oh, yes," Persnickety said. "I think it would be nice to have parents. You'd have birthday parties. And maybe get to go to the movies once in a while. And have new shoes every month."

"Aw, who cares about shoes?"

"When yours pinch you as much as mine do, you care. Anyway, I just think it would be nice, that's all."

"I don't think it would be that nice," said a familiar voice. Gurl looked up from the book she had been pretending to read and saw Bug standing near her chair. He gave her a barely perceptible nod before sitting next to the other kids. "You'd have all these rules, like when you have to get up, when you have to go to bed, when you have to take out the garbage."

"That's not much different from Hope House," said Ruckus.

"Yeah, but at Hope House, no one cares if you get B on your biology test or what you want to be when you grow up. If you have parents, they care. Like, say you wanted to be a Wing. Parents would tell you that it's more practical to be a doctor or a plumber or something. Parents always expect you to do what they did when they were kids instead of what you want to do. You can never be your own person. And if they're not yelling at you, they ignore you."

Dillydally said, "OK, homeboy. How do you know so much about parents?"

Bug paused. "I don't."

"You sound like you do," said Ruckus.

"It's just what I think, that's all," Bug told him.

"You think a lot of things," said Ruckus. "You think a lot of yourself."

Gurl could almost feel Bug's scowl. "What are you talking about?"

"All that stuff you said your first day. How you're going to be just like Nathan Johnson. Like a Wing."

"So? So what if I want to become a Wing? Are you saying I can't?"

More laughter, this time from both Dillydally and Ruckus. Even Persnickety's lips twitched. "Nobody from Hope House ever gets to be a Wing," she said.

"Maybe I'll be the first," said Bug.

"You?" said Ruckus. "We've seen you fly. I mean, we've seen you *try*."

"You talking jive, boy," Dillydally said with a lazy grin. "You a jive turkey. A *grounded* turkey! Man, you so grounded, you a *burger*!"

Ruckus fingered his braids, twirling them so they stood higher. "You're just as bad as *her*." He poked Gurl in the arm.

But Bug only smiled. "Bad as her? Well, that's OK then." He got up from his chair and winked at Gurl. "See you on the flip side," he said and swept from the room.

Gurl sleepwalked her way through her classes the next day, wondering when she and Bug would be able to get out of Hope House again. The winter holidays were now six weeks away, so some orphans were busily knitting berets and scarves with Christmas trees, menorahs and snowflakes on them, while other orphans practised their telemarketing skills: "Thank you, Mrs. Schlockenspeil, for your kind support last year! Your purchase of a handmade Hope House paperweight kept us in gruel for a week! This year we're offering holiday hats handmade by happy orphans..." In literature class, they were working on the *Hope House Holiday Newsletter*, which featured hopeful articles paired with lots of photographs of the most pathetic, hungriest-looking kids Mrs Terwiliger could find. (Gurl herself was nearly one of them, but Mrs Terwiliger decided at the last moment that while Gurl was adequately pathetic, she didn't look hungry enough.) The worst of it was that even though Gurl had managed to erase Mrs Terwiliger's entire $20,000 plastic surgery bill, Mrs Terwiliger told her that she wouldn't be able to visit Noodle for at least a week. "That," said Mrs Terwiliger, "will teach you to be less disagreeable the next time I have an errand."

At least Wingwork would be different, thought Gurl. She would be able to watch Bug fly; the whole orphanage would. And Mrs Terwiliger would have to admit that Chicken was not the right name for him. Eagle would be better or maybe Hawk.

Watching the children line up for Wing practice, however, Gurl decided that the best name for Bug was the one he gave himself. He really was one of the weirdest-looking people she had ever seen (apart from that rat man who had chased her, but who wanted to think about him?). Even though Bug resembled nothing so much as a bug, even though he was sort of rude and impatient and liked to punch things, he was growing on her. She couldn't wait to see the look on everyone's faces when he outflew them all. Like she usually did during Wingwork, she began to daydream, a new dream. A girl looks on as a boy crosses a finish line and the audience erupts into frantic applause. The boy gets a shining golden trophy and gives it to the girl, the one to whom he owes everything.

"Crouch!" Coach Bob shouted. "Spring! Up!"

Gurl smiled as she watched Bug crouch and spring. But up he did not go. Instead of rising as they had earlier, Bug's feet remained on the ground. Bug frowned and tried again, and again and again and again, but nothing worked. He wasn't going anywhere.

"That a boy, Chicken," said Coach Bob, giving Bug a friendly pat on the head. "Don't let failure bring you down." Behind him, the boys burst into mocking snickers. Bug stalked away from them, dragging his leaden feet, and began boxing with the nearest brick wall. *Wham! Wham! Wham! Wham!* Nobody dared to stop him, not even when they saw the blood tattooing his hands.

School had been terrible, Wingwork even worse and, later, Gurl's actual dreams weren't a refuge either. In them the rat man chased her, but now he was at least nine feet tall. Instead of an umbrella, he carried a large pink eraser the size of a lunch box, which she knew he would use to rub her out completely. She ran faster and faster as the rat man gibbered, "Eraaaaassssse. Erase the missssstaaaaaaake..."

Plink!

Gurl sat up with a start. All around her, orphans snored softly, some kicking and thrashing as if they, too, were being chased in their dreams.

Plink!

Something hit the window above her bed. Gurl slipped from the covers and looked out. Bug sat under the window, a couple of pebbles in his bandaged hands. *Come outside,* he mouthed. He made turning motions and she knew he'd picked the locks for her.

Gurl quickly shoved her pillows beneath her blankets to make it look as if she were still there. Then she vanished from sight. She didn't reappear until she was standing in front of Bug.

"It's three in the morning," she whispered.

"Make me invisible."

"What?"

"Please!" he said, holding out his arm.

He looked so desperate that she did what he asked. Though she couldn't see him any more than she could see herself, she could feel his movements. Crouch. Spring. Up.

"What are you doing?" she asked him.

Abruptly, he let go of her and reappeared. "I can't fly," he said, his face furrowed with disappointment. "I thought that maybe if you turned me invisible again, it would help."

Gurl reappeared too. "I'm so sorry," she said. "I don't know why you can't fly."

"Someone must know," he said. He reached out to punch the wall, but pulled at the last minute. "Wait, someone *does* know!"

"Who?" asked Gurl.

"The guy who knows everything."

Gurl was totally confused. "There's a guy who knows everything?"

"Almost everything," Bug said, his expression brightening. "I'm sure he'll be able to help me. And he probably knows about you too, the vanishing act and everything. Geez," said Bug, shaking his head. "Why didn't I remember this before? I could have been flying all this time."

"Who is this genius?" said Gurl.

"Everyone just calls him The Professor. He lives downtown, but nobody knows exactly where."

Gurl saw the gleam in Bug's eyes, the same one he got when he was picking a lock or disabling an alarm, the gleam that made him look like someone else, someone she didn't particularly like. "But you know where he lives."

"Well, yeah. I guess."

"I still don't understand how you know."

Bug was quiet for a moment, his expression inscrutable. "It's like the locks. I don't know how I know. I just do."

"Doesn't that scare you?"

"Does it scare you?"

"Me? No," Gurl told him. "Don't be stupid."

But he gave her a look that said he didn't quite believe her. Gurl didn't quite believe her either.

CHAPTER 14

The Queen Said "Ouch"

THE NEXT NIGHT GURL AND Bug headed out again. Bug picked the locked dormitory doors with no problem, but he still couldn't fly, so the trip across town was slow and mostly silent. They didn't bother with invisibility; though people were out and about everywhere, no one seemed to notice the two grubby kids trudging moodily down the sidewalk.

As if he had a map in his head, Bug found the place by feel. "Make a left," he would say or, "Two blocks more, then a right." On a dark and dingy street, in front of an old dry-cleaner's that looked as if it could use a good cleaning itself, Bug stopped. "Here," he said. "We're here."

"The guy who knows everything works for a dry cleaner's?"

"He works *under* the dry cleaner's. Let's go around the back."

They walked down the alley and around the building. An overflowing garbage can filled with empty Chinese take-out containers sat next to a rusting red door. The sign on the door said:

KEEP OUT.

DO NOT DISTURB.

GO AWAY.

FIND YOUR FORTUNES ELSEWHERE.

SHOO.

Bug looked at Gurl, shrugged and knocked on the door. In response a voice warbled, "I only take deliveries on Suesdays and Fundays!"

"Did he say 'Fundays'?"

"This is a Funday," said Bug grimly. "Don't you think?"

"Sir," shouted Gurl, "we're not delivering anything."

"Oh," said the voice. "Then go away! Fine your porpoise elsewhere!"

"Shoo," said Bug. He pulled out a paper clip and had the door unlocked in seconds. Together, Gurl and Bug pushed open the door, stepped inside and shut the door behind them. Then they walked slowly and carefully down the short flight of steps leading into a dark apartment. When they reached the bottom of the stairs, Bug felt along the wall until he found a switch. He flicked it on.

"I don't like people," said a voice that seemed to be coming from a pile of clothing on the floor. On and around the pile, and all around the apartment, were dozens and dozens of cats. Sleeping, dozing, leaning, crouching, staring cats.

"Where did he get them?" said Gurl. "There must be a hundred cats in here."

"Do you think they're friendly?" said Bug.

"They don't look mean," Gurl said as a small black cat mewled and wound itself around her legs. On the wall a large skeleton was mounted. It might have been human, except for the large wings.

"Check this out," Bug said. He peered at a hand standing upright on the lab table and jumped back as it began to gesture frantically.

"Don't touch anyfing," the pile of clothing babbled.

Gurl followed the sound of the voice. "Sir? Hello?" She turned to Bug. "Bug, this guy has grass on his head."

The pile of clothes sat up, most of them falling away to reveal a housedress. "It's not hrass," he said. "It's my gair."

"Whew!" said Gurl, waving her hand in front of her nose. "He's been drinking. A lot."

"You think?" said Bug, pointing at the massive collection of beer cans displayed on shelving all around the apartment.

The drunken man, small and wrinkled and old, said, "I don't drink beer. I drink wine. An' I hafn't drunk much. Juss a little."

He wavered and would have fallen back down again if Gurl hadn't held him up.

"Are you sure this is the guy?" she asked.

"I'm sure," said Bug. He started picking up papers and moving aside cats. "There's got to be a coffee pot around here somewhere. He needs to sober up." He searched until he found a hot plate hidden underneath a houseplant, a kettle in the kitchen and a jar of instant coffee in a file cabinet marked "Pharmaceuticals". After boiling up some water, he filled an empty beaker with hot coffee. He and Gurl took turns helping the little old man sip it.

Many, many cups later, the little man was able to sit up by himself. "This coffee tastes like dirt," he said. Over the lip of the beaker, he scowled at his guests. "What are you?"

"My name's Bug and this is Gurl."

"I didn't ask *who* you are, I asked *what* you are," said the man. He reached into the pocket of his housedress and pulled out a striped kitten. "Hold this," he said, thrusting the kitten at Bug. He reached into his pocket again and pulled out a small mirror, which he held in front of Gurl. "Look!"

"OK, I'm looking."

"Do you see yourself?"

"Yes," she said, briefly wondering if this was a trick question. "Why wouldn't I?"

"What about you?" he said, holding the mirror up for Bug.

"Let's see. Big eyes, big nose, big mouth. Yep, that's me," said Bug.

The old man nodded and slipped the mirror back in his pocket. "At least you're not vampires."

Bug laughed. "We're not vampires," he said. "We're werewolves."

The man frowned. "There are no such things as werewolves. Wherever did you get such a silly idea?"

Bug glanced at Gurl. "I was just joking."

"Joking!" said the little man. He struggled to his feet. "That's why I stopped dealing with people years ago. They're always joking." He took the kitten from Bug's arms. "Now if you will excuse me, I have a lot of work to do. I have no time for jokes. And put that down!"

Bug, who had idly picked up a letter opener, said, "OK, OK. It's no big deal."

The man put the kitten on the floor and snatched the opener from Bug's hand. "No big deal? This is an air slicer. One slip and you'll put a tear in the fabric of space-time and all the stuffing will fall out!"

Bug gaped. "Space is made of fabric?"

"Didn't I just tell you I had no time for jokes?" said the man.

"We're sorry," said Gurl, elbowing Bug in the ribs. "We won't touch any more of your things. We just want to ask you some questions. We were hoping you could help us."

"Help you?" said the man. "How?"

"Well," said Bug. "I can't fly."

The little man blinked at him. "Of course you can't."

"What do you mean?"

"What do you mean what do I mean?" said the man. "Is this another joke?"

"No," said Bug. "I really can't fly."

"No one can fly," said the little man. "Unless of course you were a vampire and we just proved that you weren't. If you were, you wouldn't have been able to see your reflection at all. Anyway, vampires can only fly when they're in bat form. You don't have a bat form, do you?"

"No."

"Well then, what are you bothering me for?"

"But I could fly yesterday," said Bug. "Lots of people can."

On the lab table, The Hand flew through a cavalcade of gestures: *I told you so.*

The little man stared first at The Hand and then at Bug. "Lots of people can fly, you say? When did this happen?"

"Only about 150 years ago."

"People? Flying?" said the little man. "Oh, my. I thought it was the honey wine. I thought I was just seeing things." He grabbed the beaker of coffee. "So that's why they were floating around so oddly," he murmured to himself. "Or at least one of them was."

"Who?" said Gurl.

"My other visitors," the little man said. "You two aren't the only ones who've decided to break into my house in the last century, you know. I'm suddenly quite popular." He sipped the coffee and grimaced.

"Did you say 'century'?" Gurl asked.

The little man stared at Gurl as if seeing her for the first time. "Who are you?"

"Me?" squeaked Gurl. "I'm nobody."

"Nobody?" said the man. "No. Body."

I told you that, too, said The Hand. *You never listen to me.*

"Why does that hand thing keep moving around like that?" said Bug.

"It has an itch," The Professor said. "This... er... flying problem isn't the only reason why you came to see me."

"No," said Bug. "We also wanted to ask you about something else."

"Yes," said the little man. "Of course you do." He sighed. "Perhaps you should sit down. There's a couch under those cats over there."

So that Gurl and Bug could sit, the cats moved obligingly, contenting themselves to curl up on the children's laps.

"Well now. Gurl, is it? You can call me The Professor. I apologise for not realising it was you. I've been expecting you."

"You have?" said Gurl.

"Of course I have. A lot of people have."

"I don't know what you mean," said Gurl.

"You're very special," The Professor said. "As I'm sure you've figured out already. When did you start to fade?"

He really does know everything, thought Gurl. "A little more than a month ago," she said.

"Something happened to scare you?"

"Yes."

"And then you seemed to blend in with your surroundings?"

"Yes."

The Professor looked very pleased with himself. "That's just the timetable I had presumed. There are a few instances of invisibility as babies and toddlers that occur mostly when someone happens to be looking for them. Difficult to say why that is. And of course it's murder on the parents. But most Walls don't start truly vanishing until they're about twelve or thirteen."

"Walls?"

"That's what you are," The Professor told her. "A Wall. Because of the way you, and other people like you, can blend into the walls as if you were a part of them."

"I didn't know that there was anyone else like me!" said Gurl.

"There were others in the past and there should be more in the future. But in your own time, you are entirely unique. According to legend – and to my calculations – there is only one Wall born every hundred years or so. As a matter of fact, you seem to be the first Wall in over 150 years. It's a rather rare and curious phenomenon really."

"I wonder how rare champion Wings are," said Bug.

"Most people believe that Walls are just a myth," continued The Professor as if Bug hadn't spoken. "Like vampires and other creatures they would rather not have to face."

"But why?" Gurl asked.

"Why what?"

"Why are Walls born every hundred years? Why are they born at all?"

"There used to be more of them," The Professor said. "And it used to be that they made no secret of their abilities. But people don't trust what they can't see. They don't like the idea that someone could be watching them, overhearing all their dirty secrets and observing all their dirty tricks. Many of the witches hanged or burned in the fourteenth, fifteenth, sixteenth, and seventeenth centuries were Walls – that is, they were hanged and burned when people could find them. After that, Walls began to keep their talents to themselves. It's a dangerous talent to have." The Professor rubbed his drink-reddened eyes. "As for your other question, why Walls are born, well, that's like asking why there are people with a clubfoot or cleft palate, or tigers that are white and not orange. It's a genetic anomaly. A trick of nature."

"Heh," said Bug. "You're a trick of nature."

Gurl scowled in response.

"Speaking of tigers, where's the cat?" asked The Professor.

"What?" said Gurl.

"The cat. I figured that she went to look for you and when Laverna wants something, she gets it. She's a crafty one. Did you know that her name means 'goddess of minor criminals'?"

Gurl and Bug glanced at each other.

"Well?" said the man.

"The cat did find me, but Mrs Terwiliger took her," Gurl said.

"Who's Mrs Terwiliger?"

"The matron of Hope House for the Homeless and Hopeless."

"Hope House?" said the little man. "An orphanage? You're orphans?"

Bug and Gurl nodded.

"I had no idea things had gotten so... complicated," said The Professor, looking, Gurl thought, a bit queasy. "This Mrs Terwiliger. She isn't a vampire, is she?"

"Define 'vampire'," said Bug.

"I don't think so," said Gurl.

"That's something at least," The Professor said. "Who's she working for?"

"Herself," Gurl told him. "She's making me steal for her."

"What?" said The Professor. "Does she know you're here?"

"No!" said Gurl. "We sneaked out."

"Hmmm," said The Professor. "Sneaking. You'll have to do more of that. I'm glad you came here. So I could warn you."

"You could have warned me sooner," said Gurl. "It would have been helpful."

"If I had told you all these things two years ago, before you learned what you were capable of, would you have believed me?"

"If it were me," said Bug, "I would have thought you were nuts." He poked at The Answer Hand and The Hand swatted him.

"Why didn't you call the number on the flyers?" The Professor was saying. "I had them posted all over the city."

"Uh..." said Gurl, blushing.

"No matter," said The Professor. "You need to find a good hiding place."

"Hide? Where?"

The Professor shrugged. "Anywhere. Keep low, stay invisible and you won't have any trouble."

"Stay invisible for how long?" Gurl asked.

"For as long as it takes."

"For as long as *what* takes?" Bug said.

The Professor tugged at a blade of grass on his head. "Listen to me. Some very scary men are out there looking for you."

"What kind of scary men?"

"*Very* scary," said The Professor, shuddering. "They already found us once."

"Us?" said Gurl.

"You can't let them find you. If they do, they will force you to do things for them."

"What kinds of things?" said Gurl.

"What do you think?" said The Professor. "Unpleasant and criminal things. Isn't it better to stay invisible than do unpleasant things for criminal people? Yes, it is." He stood up and began removing the cats from the children's laps. "So the two of you better be on your way."

"But what about Noodle?" said Gurl as The Professor pulled her to her feet and started shoving her towards the door.

"Noodle?"

"The cat."

"Oh, well, she can take care of herself, don't you worry. Cats are extraordinarily resourceful." As if to prove his point, one of the cats sauntered by with a ham sandwich clamped in his mouth.

"What about me?" Bug said.

The Professor stared. "What about you?"

"You know, flying? I'd like to fly."

"Young man, I'm sure it will pain you to hear this, but no

one was meant to fly. That people are doing it is just an accident, no more."

"What do you mean, it's just an accident?" said Bug angrily. "What are you talking about?"

"If you'd really like to fly, get yourself bitten by a vampire. They're all over the place." The Professor reached into his pocket and pulled out another kitten. "Hold this," he told Gurl. He dug around some more and found what he was looking for. "Take this subway pass. Go uptown, far away from here. Cross over on to the mainland and keep going. I hear Maine is nice this time of year."

"Professor," said Gurl. "I don't know how to take the subway. Not many people do, except when it's cold."

"Why not?"

"Um... have I mentioned all the *flying*?" said Bug, disgusted.

"Yes. Be that as it may, I'm sure the subway's still faster. I can't imagine that most people can fly very high, very fast or very well, can they?" At Bug's expression, he said, "Right. In addition to being faster, the subway is safer too."

At this, The Answer Hand began gesticulating frantically. *Safer compared to what?*

The Professor scowled at The Hand. "As long as you don't leave the subway car. Don't leave the subway car and I'm sure you'll be fine."

"It's good to be sure," said Bug.

"Professor, this isn't even a real pass." Gurl held up the white and blue card he had given her. "Park Place," it said, "Rent $35." "I think this is from a Monopoly game, see?"

"Don't worry about that. I fixed it so it will work." He took the kitten back from Gurl's arms. "You're not safe here. Leave the apartment and walk up to Fourteenth Street. The station is right there. Take the pass and go."

"But—" said Gurl.

"Go, go, go," said The Professor.

"Yeah, yeah, we know," said Bug. "Find your fortunes elsewhere. Shoo."

After the two children were rightly and properly shooed from his apartment, The Professor emptied the contents of the beaker into the sink, rinsed it and filled it with more of his homemade honey wine. His obligation fulfilled, he could drink himself into oblivion in peace.

Except that oblivion – especially oblivion induced by honey wine – is never peaceful. You keep drinking and drinking and soon you find yourself stumbling around, slurring stupidly and waking up with a pounding headache. The Professor didn't need any more headaches, as he'd already had plenty of them in the last decade. Gangsters threatening him, snotty boys demanding to fly. It was ridiculous. All he ever wanted to do was read and think and fiddle with things in his workshop. He wanted nothing to do with *people*. People were greedy. People were messy. People unzipped their faces.

Enough, he thought. The girl had been warned, end of story, finis. The Professor idly poked at several unmarked coffee cans sitting on a side table, trying to remember what he'd put inside them. He opened one and a mechanical bumblebee the size of a grape darted from it. "The queen lives! She lives!" buzzed the bee, who then flew pell-mell at the nearest window. She slammed into it and fell to the sill with a metallic clank. "Ouch," the bee chirruped. "The queen says 'ouch'."

"Ouch," agreed The Professor.

You should be ashamed of yourself, signed The Answer Hand. *You barely told them anything. You just sent them out into the cruel world to fend for themselves. They're only children. You didn't even tell her where she belongs!*

"What are you talking about? You heard the girl; she's an orphan. She doesn't belong anywhere."

Yes, she does, The Answer Hand replied. *And if you'd only take me out of that stupid drawer once in a while, if you'd only asked me, I could have told you.*

"So you keep reminding me. I don't want to get involved."

You are involved. You are completely and utterly involved. If it weren't for you, none of this would have happened. You have a chance to correct it once and for all, but instead you just get drunk on honey wine and invent wonky stuff that no one will ever use.

"I don't invent wonky stuff! And I am *not* involved," said The Professor.

Hogwash.

"Oh, what do you know?"

Everything. I'm The Answer Hand.

"You're a pain in the butt. I wish that guy from Okinawa had never put you up for sale on eBay. I wish I'd been outbid."

Well! The Answer Hand said. *I wash my hand of you!*

The Hand went silent, but its argument rattled The Professor. What if, The Professor supposed, at least some of the mess could be attributed to The Professor himself? If not for his inventions, his calculations and his maps – not to mention his tendency to poke his nose where it didn't belong – perhaps no one would have found The Wall in the first place, no one would be looking for her now, and thus The Professor wouldn't be forced to drink honey wine in an effort to forget about it all. And if *that* were true, if The Professor had played some small role in this... this... this *situation*, well then, sending The Wall and that irksome boy off with a warning wasn't quite enough to absolve him, was it? As a matter of fact, it was likely that instead of keeping them safe, he had sent them to their doom, just as The Answer Hand was trying to tell him.

And then, of course, there was the matter of the pen. Oh! The pen! He didn't like to think of it out there, taking the foolish dictates of foolish men and twisting them to its own ends. This is why he drank: to forget. Not that he'd ever, ever admit it to The Answer Hand, but the pen was definitely wonky. The wonkiest thing he ever invented, in fact. And while it was the wonkiest thing The Professor had invented, it was also, he suspected, the most powerful thing he had ever invented. If only The Wall, the last one, had never come to him for help all those many years ago. If only he hadn't refused her. If only he hadn't gone out for some fresh air to escape her begging. If only he hadn't stumbled on to Mulberry Street and got himself robbed by all those dirty gangsters. If only The Wall hadn't followed him. If only he'd thought to bring more cats for protection. If only if only if only.

The more he thought about that Wall and this Wall and the boy and the pen, the more disturbed he became. He didn't think much of people, but he didn't want to be responsible for the harm that befell them either.

Bother! he thought. *Bother!*

"All right," said The Professor to The Answer Hand. "Are you going to tell me where the girl belongs or are you going to sulk the rest of the night?"

The Answer Hand, who liked sulking but loved to display the fact that it had all the answers, told him. And when The Professor finally began to ask questions, the *right* questions, The Hand told him that much more.

The Professor sighed and put down the wine. He started to search his rooms – lifting books and cats and papers – till he unearthed the phone. Then, after finding the number he wanted in the phone book, he placed his call.

"Hello?"

"Hello," said The Professor. "I believe I've just seen someone you might be looking for. And I think you might have something that belongs to me."

CHAPTER 15

The Punk Invasion

SCARY MEN, SCARY MEN, THOUGHT Gurl as she and Bug left The Professor's apartment. The only scary man that Gurl could think of was the rat man with the umbrella who had chased her that night, the one that came up from the subway. But The Professor said that they should take the subway!

Gurl gripped the Park Place subway pass so hard that the card bit into her fingers. What if The Professor himself was one of the men she should be worried about? Bug had said he was some sort of genius, but what if he was an *evil* genius (in addition to being a crazy drunk)?

At least The Professor had one good idea and that was

hiding. There was no reason that she should hang around Hope House for the Homeless and Hopeless if she didn't have to. Why, she could run away right now! But she didn't have to leave the city, this huge and sparkling city with as many hidey-holes as a beehive. She could find somewhere to live. A homeless shelter maybe. Or an abandoned building. Or even stay in apartments where the people were on vacation. And she could get all her food from the backs of restaurants; she knew how to do it. Maybe she could even get a job somewhere. She could lie about her age. No one would care.

And she wouldn't ever have to steal anything ever again.

But then there was Noodle. She would have to go back and get Noodle. *Then* she would run away for ever.

This decided, she looked at Bug, who plodded silently beside her. She had tried to take his hand when they first left the apartment so she could make them both invisible, but he had shaken her off. Now he had a horrible scowl on his face, making him look less like a bug and more like an owl. A furious, mutant owl.

"Bug," she said.

"What do you want?"

"I'm sorry he couldn't help you."

"Whatever," he said.

"I have to go back to Hope House."

"Whatever." Bug made a fist and punched the window of a café, startling the customers within. *Wham!*

"I have to get Noodle. And when I do, I'm leaving the orphanage. For good."

Bug didn't even look at her. "OK. Bye."

"That's the thing," Gurl said. "I won't be able to find her without you. I can't open all the locks by myself."

"Then I guess you're out of luck."

At this, Gurl got mad. "I've been a leadfoot all my life, but I never acted like such a jerk about it."

"Good for you."

Gurl punched him in the arm hard enough to knock him into the closest building. *Wham!*

That made him look. "Hey! What did you do that for?" he said, rubbing his arm.

She realised at that moment that he was just as much her friend as Noodle was. More, even. She felt like screaming: You're supposed to *want* to help me. You're supposed to *want* to come with me. But she didn't say these things. What she said was: "You deserved it. And because you're being a total rock head. You thought that you could fly because I made you invisible, right? But what if it wasn't me at all? What if it was because of Noodle?"

"That doesn't make any sense," said Bug, but she could see that he was considering this.

"Cats are rare, but The Professor had a hundred of them. He even had kittens popping out of his pockets. There has to be something about her. She *must* be special in some way."

Bug nodded. "Could be."

"So you're going to help me find her, right?"

"Only if you don't punch me again."

"We have to hurry," said Gurl. "I don't want to spend another night at Hopeless House."

Bug pointed to a subway entrance. "Do you want to try it? It will be faster than walking."

"I don't know," Gurl said. "I've seen strange things come out of subways. Like rats."

"So?" Bug said.

"Really *big* rats," said Gurl and shivered. "With big teeth."

"The old guy said the subway was safe."

"Safe if we stay in the subway car."

"Why *wouldn't* we stay in the subway car?"

"All right, all right," said Gurl. "We'll take the subway. That is," she added, "if Park Place here works like it's supposed to."

The two of them trudged towards the uptown subway entrance, down the steps and into a twisting concrete tunnel. Their footsteps echoed in the cavernous hallway, and a hot, humid wind blew, a wind that stank of fuel. Gurl heard a jingling sound coming from around the next corner.

"What's that?" she whispered.

"Don't know," muttered Bug. "But whoever it is will hear our footsteps even if we're invisible, so we better stay this way for a while."

They rounded the corner. The source of the jingling was a skinny man sitting cross-legged on a flattened brown box. He wore a green quilt that he had belted around his waist with a length of rope, and a yellow canary perched on his head. In the man's dirty hands was a tin can, which he shook vigorously so that the coins inside made a tinny jangle. "Spare some change?" he said in a wavering voice. As soon as he saw them, however, he barked, "Aw, you just little. Where your mom at?"

Bug and Gurl were too surprised to answer, but that didn't seem to be a requirement.

"What she let you out so late for?" the man continued. "Where you going? Ain't no little ones belong down here." The man popped out his false teeth and sucked them back in his face just as quickly.

"We'll be fine, Mister," said Gurl, pushing at Bug's back so that he would walk faster.

"Name's not Mister, Missy. And you best watch out for them Punks."

"Sure we will," said Bug.

"I mean it," the man called after them. "Punks is bad news. The city try to flush 'em out, but it don't work. Punks just makes more Punks. Big Punks, little Punks, everywhere a Punk Punk."

"OK, thanks," said Gurl as they hurried away from the man. They kept walking, passing a woman – short and round as a grapefruit – who stood in front of a table of souvenirs.

"Empire State Building?" the woman said, holding up a replica in her fat little hand. "Statue of Liberty?"

"No thanks," said Bug.

"I can give you a great price on the Brooklyn Bridge," the woman said. After they passed the table, she yelled at their backs: "Fine! I hope the gators get you!"

"Gators?" said Gurl. "What's she talking about?"

"Wasn't there some old story about alligators living in the sewers or something?"

"Yeah, but this isn't the sewer. And that's just an urban legend."

They finally reached the gate to the tracks. "Let's hope this works," said Gurl as she swiped the Park Place card through the electronic reader.

"I'm beginning to think that it wouldn't be bad if it didn't work," said Bug.

The gate clanked and the reader beeped. "It works," said Gurl. "Your turn."

Gurl passed through the gate and handed the card to Bug so that he could follow. Gurl pocketed the Park Place card and found a map on the grimy tile wall. After they had scrutinised it for a few minutes, Bug said, "Looks like we can take the F train."

They wandered over to the tracks and looked around. A few other passengers in rumpled clothes dotted the waiting area, reading newspapers, leaning against walls or wandering aimlessly back and forth, as if their batteries were running down. A thin, high-pitched whine cut through the air, the work of an apparently tone-deaf violinist who had set up shop by a trash bin. His violin case was open and one by one the passengers came to drop dollar bills into it, a group effort to make him stop. Gurl watched them walk over to the musician and realised that most of them were probably leadfeet (or close to it), that these tunnels beneath the city were made for people like her.

The hot wind that had assaulted Bug and Gurl in the hallways now blew up again and the passengers stood to attention. A distant rumble grew louder and louder until the train squealed into the station.

"This is us," said Bug.

The car doors flew open and the two of them hopped inside, slipping into the orange bucket seats. As was traditional in the city, the other passengers did their very best to ignore the newcomers, holding their newspapers and magazines high so that they did not have to meet anyone's eyes. One man, wearing an expensive business suit, sprawled across a length of seats and snored loudly.

The doors slid shut and the train left the station, building up speed. Bug and Gurl bounced along as the train wound through the concrete guts of the city. As if a mischievous child were playing with the switch, the lights in the car went on and off. Gurl counted the first couple of stops in her head, resisting the train's attempts to lull her to sleep. At the third stop, the snoring man woke up, and he and the last of the other passengers disembarked, leaving the car to Bug and Gurl.

"Finally," said Bug. He got up from his seat, grabbed one of the metal poles and swung around and around. "You should try this."

"What? Being stupid?" she said.

"You know, the subway is OK," Bug said, still swinging. "I don't know why it has such a bad reputation."

Just then the train's wheels began to screech and the train ground to an abrupt halt. The engine died. The lights flickered, then went out.

Gurl squinted out of the blackened windows. "You were saying?"

"The engine will come on again in a minute," said Bug, feeling his way back to his seat, "and we'll be out of here."

But it didn't come on again in a minute, or two, or three. Bug and Gurl sat in a dark car in a dark tunnel and wondered what was going on.

"They should at least make an announcement," said Bug, trying to keep the nervousness out of his voice.

"Why doesn't it feel like there's a 'they' around? Why does

it seem like we're the only two people on this train?" She grabbed for Bug's hand and turned them both invisible.

"What are you doing?" said Bug. "You just said that we're the only ones here. And it's too dark for anyone to see us anyway."

"Shhh," she said. "I don't like this."

"You think I do?"

"Remember when I said that I saw rats coming out of the subway?"

"Yeah."

"Well, I wasn't lying when I said they were big. Huge. Like the size of people kind of rats. One of them chased me."

"What are you talking about? There are no people-sized rats!"

"No," said Gurl, "but then again, bushes don't scoot around on their roots and wooden horses don't run. And I'm telling you, one of the rats chased me. It tried to get Noodle."

Bug was quiet a moment while he took this in. "Why didn't you tell me this before we got on the subway?"

"I did!"

"You did not say 'rats the size of people'. If you had said 'rats the size of people', I would not have suggested we take the subway, OK?"

"It had filed its teeth to sharp points," said Gurl.

"Oh, sure. That's even better."

As if to stop the bickering, the train came to life and the doors shot open.

"What now?" Gurl whispered.

"Did you hear that?"

"What?"

"Someone's laughing."

Sure enough, the sounds of laughter echoed dimly through the tunnels outside the car.

"Did your rat man laugh?" said Bug.

"No," Gurl said. "Well, yeah. He kind of giggled."

"Giggled," Bug repeated. "Why not?"

At first the source of the sounds seemed far away and then the noise got louder and louder. It was clear that whoever – whatever – was laughing, it was coming closer. And there wasn't just one. The laughter was all around them. Shrieks, giggles, cackles and grumbles.

"The Professor's vampires?" murmured Bug in Gurl's ear.

"I thought you didn't believe in vampires," Gurl murmured back.

In response Bug squeezed her hand, pulling her out of her seat and away from the centre of the car. If a bunch of giggling bloodsuckers or giant snickering rat men were on their way, it seemed wise to tuck into a corner. They huddled together and waited.

The laughter got louder still, interspersed with whoops

and hollers and an odd hissing sound. Bug and Gurl stiffened as a black-leather-clad, maniacally pierced, Mohawk-sporting teenager jumped into their car. Corpse pale, his wild, glassy eyes smudged with black kohl and lips painted a bruised blue, the boy shook a can of spray paint and proceeded to decorate the seats and the walls with aimless scribbles. Other whooping, hollering, leather-clad creatures ran into the car, some wearing spiked dog collars, others wearing schoolgirl outfits with combat boots and ripped fishnet tights. Most had metal threaded through their ears, eyebrows, lips, noses and cheeks (and plenty of other places that Bug and Gurl couldn't see). What was somewhat disturbing was that not all of the teenagers were... um... teenagers. Several were clearly in their forties or fifties and there were also a number of leather-wearing babies being toted around. But what was *most* disturbing was that none of their eyes seemed to have irises; yawning black pupils filled their sockets, making them look both blank and wolfish.

Gurl and Bug pressed themselves closer to the wall, not understanding who or what they were seeing. But they *had* been warned by the old beggar: "watch out for them Punks". And if they had known the history of The Punks, they would have.

Once they were wily bands of street kids who found refuge in the brand-new subway systems of the early twentieth century but, over the generations, they evolved into something else. Something sneaky, nocturnal and not quite human. In the tunnels and caves under the city, they multiplied. And flourished.

Every ten years or so, the city would launch a programme to eradicate The Punks, sending in the Animal Protection Agency to round them up, tag them and send them off to Punk Reserves (mostly in England, for some reason). But The Punks always came back. And with them the people-menacing, purse-snatching, partying, begging and, of course, spray-painting.

"They tag us," said one of The Punks, a girl who was entirely bald except for a fringe, "so we tag them."

"Good one, Nancy!" said one of the boys.

"Right, Sid," replied the girl.

But Bug and Gurl were not paying attention to Sid and Nancy – actually, all male Punks were called Sid and all female Punks were called Nancy – they were watching a tall, lean Punk, a teenager about seventeen or so, who had turned in their direction. Or rather, they were watching the man's pet *bat*, which clung to a chain on the man's leather jacket. The bat's beady eyes rolled. It spread its leathery wings and let out an eerie squeal, a squeal that immediately quieted the rest of The Punks.

"The Vamp sees something," the teen said. "Something over there." He pointed at Bug and Gurl.

Vamp? thought Gurl.

Vamp? thought Bug.

The Punks dropped their spray cans and gathered around the boy, their queer, black mirror eyes searching.

The bat squealed again. "Yeah," said Nancy (one of them, anyway). "Something there all right."

"Too much light in here, though," Sid (one of them) said. "Can't see nothing."

The bat-bearing teenager tilted his head, stooped and picked up one of the cans of spray paint. Before Gurl and Bug knew what was happening, he punched the nozzle and doused them both in electric purple.

"What the bloody hell are they?" said several Sids at once.

"Whatever they are," said the Nancys, "we should tie them to the tracks and let the train dice them to ham salad."

"After we tell Sweetcheeks," said the man with the bat.

At the mention of the word "Sweetcheeks", Bug's hand tightened around Gurl's.

"Yeah," a Nancy said. "It might make him forget that we ain't delivered his cut for a while. We tell Sweetcheeks first. Wait, why don't we bring them to Sweetcheeks ourselves? Let Odd John take care of 'em!"

Abruptly, Bug let go of Gurl, grabbed the metal pole in front of them and swung around it, punching each Punk in windmill fashion: *Wham! Wham! Wham! Wham! Wham!* Gurl snatched the paint can out of the boy's hand and sprayed the Punks still standing, making them double over and cover their eyes. In unison, Bug and Gurl ducked out of the open doors of the car, running down the thin ribbon of concrete alongside the tracks. Dozens of screaming, half-blinded Punks gave chase but, luckily, they couldn't fly either. Bug and Gurl ran until their lungs and legs burned, and then they ran some more. They ran and ran until the screams of The Punks faded and there was no sound but the echo of their own footsteps in the dark.

"Stop, stop!" said Gurl, breathing heavily. "I have to stop."

"Yeah, OK," Bug said, breathing just as heavily.

Gurl sat, drawing her knees close. "The Professor told us not to leave the subway car."

"We could go back and be diced into ham salad, if you want."

"Do you think those guys were the Punks that beggar was talking about?"

"Probably," said Bug.

"I wonder why they stopped chasing us," Gurl said.

"Who knows? They probably had a graffiti schedule to keep."

"And who's Sweetcheeks? And Odd John? Do you recognise the names?"

"Sounds familiar," Bug said. "But I don't know why. Maybe I saw something on TV?"

Gurl stood and looked left and right. Nothing but rusting tracks sliding into a deep, impenetrable darkness. "What do we do now?"

Bug sighed. "Walk until we hit the next station, I guess."

"If we keep following the track in the same direction the train was moving, we should be OK, don't you think?"

"Yeah. That is, if there aren't any more Punks wandering around down here."

"Or something else," added Gurl.

They moved in single file. Though it seemed as if they marched a long time – the concrete strip was narrow, the fumes from the trains were dizzying and they were exhausted – they eventually saw a light up ahead.

"The station," said Bug, and Gurl could hear the relief in his voice.

"I thought we'd never make it."

As they approached, they heard the thin screech of an abused cello paired with a flatulent tuba.

"Music to my ears," said Gurl.

The walked a bit faster. Then they saw the metal grate that sealed off the station from the tracks, the cellist and tuba player seated on a bench behind it. "Hey!" said Gurl. "What's all this?" She pulled on the grate, but it didn't budge.

"I think it's locked from the inside," Bug said.

"Can't you pick it?"

"If I can find the lock. Do you see it anywhere?"

"No."

The cellist and tuba player played on, ignoring the two kids who rattled the metal grate and pleaded with them to open it.

"What's wrong with them?" said Gurl. "Why aren't they even looking at us?"

"Because," said Bug, "they're looking at *that*."

He pointed to one end of the station. An alligator – fifteen feet long, albino white, with a jaw full of jagged teeth – crabbed along the tile floor.

CHAPTER 16

The Face in the Mirror

"LOOK OUT!" SAID GURL. "THERE'S a gator!"

The cellist rolled his eyes, making the pouches beneath them quiver. "No!" he said, over the din. "Really?" He sawed at his cello even harder, and the resulting squeals made Bug and Gurl clap their hands over their ears. The alligator didn't seem to like it either; he hissed, working his jaws in a most threatening fashion.

"I'm glad we're on this side of the gate," said Bug.

The tuba player got off the bench and slowly approached the gator, the instrument rumbling and snorting off-key. The alligator stopped crawling, seemingly paralysed by all this terrible noise. The cellist set aside his cello, stood and reached up behind him, pulling a pole with a net at the end from inside the back of his jacket. Using the tuba player for cover, the cellist crept up on the gator. At the last moment, the tuba player threw himself aside and the cellist netted the gator. Both musicians belted the animal's mouth shut.

After the gator had been taken care of, the cellist shambled over to the gate and slid it open. "Not a good idea for you guys to be running around the tracks," he said. "Punks are out tonight." He considered them, dirty, sweaty and covered with purple paint. "Unless you guys are a couple of Punks."

The tuba player grunted. "Not pierced enough for Punks, Fred."

Bug, of course, was already over The Punks and wanted to know about the reptile. "What did you do to that gator?"

The cellist sighed. "The gators don't like music. That's why the city lets us play down here. Keeps the gators out. Mostly, anyway."

"That was great!" said Bug. "So bad it made my ears hurt!"

The cellist scowled. "What do you mean, 'bad'? What was bad about it? Are you saying our music is bad?"

Gurl elbowed Bug to shut him up. "No, we thought it was... original. Unique. Right, Bug?"

"Sure," said Bug. "That's what I meant."

"But... uh... I thought gators lived in the sewer?"

"Did you hear that, Joe?" the cellist said to the tuba player, who patted his forehead with a hanky. "These kids think that gators live in the sewer."

"That's stupid," said Joe.

"Now, if you were a gator," said the cellist, "would you hang out in the stinky sewer with a bunch of oversized, icky rats or would you come to the subway, where the nice tasty people are?"

"Well, when you put it that way," said Gurl. "I guess we should be going."

"How about a song first?" said the cellist eagerly. "Fred and I have been working on a new piece."

"Uh..." said Bug.

"Um..." said Gurl.

"Stay right there!" the cellist ran back to his cello and the tuba player picked up his tuba. "You are going to love this!"

They started to play. The trussed gator thrashed and hissed like a punctured truck tyre as the children braced themselves for one more onslaught.

It wasn't till after one in the morning that Bug and Gurl dragged themselves back to Hope House. They were too tired to hunt for Noodle and besides, they agreed, it could take a while to find her. So they decided to stay at Hope House for at least one more night. They would wash off the purple paint and then go to bed. The next day they would attend school and search for Noodle after lights-out.

With this decision made, they parted. Gurl lay in her bed and tried to sleep. But it was no use; too much had happened and too much was going to happen. *Just a while longer, she thought, just till we find Noodle and then we're out of Hope House.* She sat up and looked around the room. Digger was sprawled flat on her back, snoring, with one bare, callused foot hanging from underneath the covers. Persnickety was neatly mummified in her blankets. The other girls – some on their sides, some in balls, some with their heads under the pillows – twitched and snorted in their sleep. All these girls, and all this time, and Gurl felt no connection to them at all. Here she had lived at Hope House for most of her life and yet there was no one here who would miss her. And no one she would miss. She had been nothing more than a ghost or a dream, and she would fade in the same curious way. But instead of making her feel sad, these thoughts cheered her. To be like a dream!

Gurl fell asleep smiling.

She didn't realise, however, how poisoned the children of Hope House had become and how hard they would work against her. Hope House – formerly The Institute of the Destitute, The Home of the Friendless and The Asylum For The Poor, The Lazy, and The Wretched – hadn't stayed in existence for 200 years by letting snot-nosed little girls fade like dreams any old time they liked. By its very nature, Hope House sucked the souls from the orphans and filled them instead with hopelessness and rage. Their hearts became hard, their feet leaden and their spirits weary. Is it any wonder that none of them could fly?

Yet Bug and Gurl *had* flown and hoped to fly again. And while they didn't know it, this hope had brightened their faces and put a spring in their steps. How could the other children help but notice? How could it not make them seethe with disappointment and despair? They kept watchful eyes on Bug and Gurl as they sat down to eat their breakfast the next morning. (Or rather, *not* eat their breakfast, because sour soy milk on stale cornflakes is not very appetising.)

Ruckus was, not surprisingly, the one to start the ruckus. "Hey, Chicken," he said to Bug. "How come you're not sitting with your girlfriend?"

Bug curled his lip at the rancid smell wafting up from his cereal bowl. "Name's not Chicken," he said. "It's Bug."

"Right on, *Chicken*," Dillydally said. "Whatever you say, *Chicken*." If he was expecting a reaction from Bug, he was disappointed. And if Gurl was worried that Bug might get up and start using the other boys as personal punch bags, she was wrong. Instead, Bug fished in his cereal bowl, pulled out a black leggy thing and examined it with great interest.

Lunchmeat joined in. "Come on, why don't you go sit with your girlfriend. She misses you."

But Bug merely reached out and dropped the black leggy thing into Lunchmeat's cereal bowl. "Here," he said. "Nice and crunchy."

Ruckus pointed to Gurl, who was deliberately ignoring them all. "Look, she's lonely. She's going to cry. Boo hoo hoo!"

At this, Bug grinned. "I don't know. You look like you're the one who's crying. And I don't blame you. If I were as dumb as you, I'd be crying too."

Ruckus scowled. "At least I'm not some sort of alien!"

Bug grinned even wider. "No, you're just plain ugly." He looked like he could keep this up all morning and might have, if Mrs Terwiliger hadn't floated into the cafeteria. Immediately, she could see that the children's attention was focused on Bug, something that she didn't much like. In her book, that boy wasn't right. It was the huge shifty eyes that gave him away. Anyone with eyes like that was bound to be up to no good.

"What's going on here?" Mrs Terwiliger barked.

Ruckus, Dillydally, Lunchmeat and even Bug himself stared up at her innocently. "Nothing," they said.

Mrs Terwiliger pinned them with accusing eyes. "Nothing?"

"Nothing," they repeated.

"Hmmm," said Mrs Terwiliger. "Hmm..." She floated around

the tables until she found a more cooperative student. "Digger!" she said. "Can you please explain what these boys are up to?"

Digger shrugged her huge shoulders. "Chicken's got a girlfriend."

"What? I won't tolerate those sorts of shenanigans. Who is it?"

"The leadfoot," said Digger.

Mrs Terwiliger thought all the orphans would classify as leadfeet, really, if one was to be technical about it. "You'll have to be more specific, Digger, dear."

Digger hooked a fat thumb in Gurl's direction. "Her. She's his gurlfriend. Heh. G-u-r-l-f-r-e-n-d. Get it?"

Mrs Terwiliger was too surprised to correct Digger's spelling. Since when did Gurl have any friends? Especially ones as shifty as Chicken! That would not do *at all*. Why, the girl could get ideas about all sorts of things. And there was nothing worse than an orphan with *ideas*. But what to do, what to do? Lock Gurl up? Lock Chicken up? Threaten the cat again? It was getting so tiresome. Children never knew what was good for them.

Then Mrs Terwiliger herself got an idea. "Listen up, children!" she said. "I've got an assignment for you all. It seems that Gurl and Chicken have need of friends. So I want you to be friends with them as best you can. Digger, Persnickety and

Tot will be friends with Gurl. And Dillydally, Lunchmeat and Ruckus will be friends with Chicken. That means that you need to stick together. I don't want Gurl or Chicken to go anywhere on their own, do you understand? You need to be with them every minute of every day and night."

Digger frowned. "What are we supposed to do at night? How are we supposed to get any sleep?"

"You'll take turns staying up and keeping an eye on Gurl, that's all." Mrs Terwiliger looked right at Gurl, noting with satisfaction the dimming of hope in her eyes. "So she doesn't get lonely."

At first Digger made the most of her assignment. She ground her knuckles into Gurl's back and kicked her shins underneath the desks. She hid Gurl's schoolbooks and ate all her dinner. "We're *friends*," she boomed in Gurl's ear. "Best, best *friends*."

But by nightfall she had tired of the game. She started punching and kicking Tot instead, which, of course, made her cry. And then she pulled on one of Persnickety's neat braids, which made *her* cry. All the crying grated on Digger's nerves, so she started to yell. None of them could agree on who was supposed to stay up and watch Gurl sleep so, after crying and yelling and kicking one another for a few hours, Gurl's three "friends" finally fell into an exhausted sleep. Gurl could only hope that Bug's "friends" were equally occupied so that they could start the search for Noodle. They had to leave *now*.

Gurl didn't have long to wait. Soon after midnight there was a soft tapping at the window as Bug picked the lock.

"What happened to all your buddies?" whispered Gurl as they made their way from the dorms to the main building.

"The weirdest thing," said Bug. "All three of them came down with horrible colds. Had to spike their drinks with cough medicine. I don't think they're gonna wake up for a week."

"Good. That will give us time to find Noodle and get out of here." Gurl looked over at Bug. "We can't stay another night. They know about us." She flushed. "I mean..."

"I know what you mean," Bug said. "And you're right. But I've looked everywhere for the cat and I've never found her."

"We'll just have to look again, that's all," said Gurl. "Go over every inch of this place. She has to be somewhere."

Bug picked the locks on the main building, and he and Gurl searched the various offices and broom and supply closets, emptying cabinets and pulling files from drawers. And they left the mess they made for Mrs Terwiliger to clean up. Once they had Noodle, they didn't plan to return.

After going through the entire building, they found themselves in Mrs Terwiliger's office, surrounded by her monkeys.

"She can't be in here," said Gurl. "I've been in this room a million times. I would know."

"Maybe Mrs Terwiliger hid Noodle somewhere else and then moved her back in here," Bug said. "She could have a lot of hiding places." To the monkeys all around them Bug said "Hey, boys. How ya doin'?"

"Some of those boys are girls," said Gurl, rifling through Mrs Terwiliger's desk, digging for a key or a clue or something that might tell her where Mrs Terwiliger was keeping Noodle. "Just check the names on the butts."

"You think I'm some kind of pervert?" said Bug. He picked up one of the monkeys and flipped it over. "Darren Darren."

"That's not what it says."

"Look for yourself," said Bug, holding out the monkey. "Darren Darren."

"I can't imagine having that name," said Gurl. She opened the last drawer: an eyelash curler, an eyebrow tweezer, tooth whitening gel and a dozen shades of lipstick. "Well, there's nothing in here." She flopped down in the chair, swivelled and stuck her tongue out at herself in the full-length mirror on the wall. "I don't know where else to look." She had thought of the little grey cat as hers for so long that the idea of leaving her with Mrs Terwiliger made her feel like weeping.

"What do you think they mean?" said Bug. "The names on the monkeys?"

Gurl shrugged. "You said she was crazy. What difference does it make?"

"It has to mean something." He looked around the room. "How many do you think there are in here?"

"Two hundred?" said Gurl.

"And how many orphans do you think live at Hope House?"

"About the same." Gurl raised a pale eyebrow. "One for each of us?"

"Yeah," said Bug. "That's what I was thinking."

Gurl looked at the monkey in Bug's hand, one with a tiny set of bongo drums. "But why?"

"Do you remember the first day you came here, to Hope House?" Bug asked her.

"No. I was just a baby."

"Well, I remember when I came," said Bug. "Sort of. I remember that I forgot."

"You said that before. I still don't know what you mean."

"I remember being here, in Mrs Terwiliger's office. I remember that she put one of these in front of me. This one." He put down Darren Darren and pulled the other smaller monkey from his pocket. "I think I told it something."

"The monkey? What did you tell it?"

"I can't remember," said Bug, making a fist (but, miraculously, not punching anything). "I must have told it who I was. You know, before I came here. I know I was someone. I just don't know who."

Gurl couldn't imagine having a whole other life that you can't remember, a life that could have been good or even great. She got up from the desk and walked over to Bug. She took the monkey from his hand and flipped it over. "What's It To You? But what's that supposed to mean?"

Bug frowned, then sighed. "I don't know."

"My monkey just has the word 'Gurl' on it. That doesn't help either."

"But what could I have told it? And why don't I remember?"

Gurl thought about this. "When I was here once, Mrs Terwiliger put one of those monkeys in front of me. It started to play the cymbals. So annoying. I thought that if I told it a secret, it would stop. I have no idea why I'd think that. Why would I think that?"

"So did you?"

"What?"

"Tell it a secret?"

"I didn't have any secrets to tell it," said Gurl.

"So you think maybe I told Mr What's It To You? my secrets?"

"I guess," said Gurl. "That's if you had any secrets. And who knows if you did?"

"Maybe," said Bug. But he continued to look like he wanted to punch something and Gurl was starting to feel the same way. She had no idea what the purpose of the monkeys was.

More importantly, she had no idea where Noodle was and they'd already looked everywhere there was to look.

"If a cat meows in a cage," said Gurl, "does it make a sound?"

"What kind of nutball question is that?"

That's when the word exploded in her head: *MEOW*.

Gurl sat up in the chair. "Did you hear that?"

Bug slipped the monkey back in his pocket. "No. What?"

Meow.

"There it is again," said Gurl. "But where is that coming from?"

"Where's what coming from?"

"The meow. Noodle."

"Gurl, I didn't hear anything."

Meow.

"Maybe because there is no sound," said Gurl. "But that doesn't mean she isn't making one."

"I have *no* idea what you're talking about."

"It's hard to explain. When I pet Noodle, I get this weird riddle in my head. If a tree falls in a forest when there is nobody around, does it make a sound? I have this feeling that she's making a sound right now, but we can't really hear it."

"But we *are* around. And you just said you heard it."

"Well, I didn't exactly hear it. But the sound sort of popped into my head. I think it's Noodle."

Bug looked at her dubiously, but shrugged. "If you say so. What do you want to do?"

"Help me look around."

"But we already checked everywhere."

"There must be something we missed."

"What? Like a secret door?"

Bug was kidding, but Gurl wasn't. "Yeah. Like that. Start knocking on the walls," she said. "Maybe one of them is fake. Or look behind the pictures."

"Let's think about this for a second," said Bug. "If you had gotten $20,000 in plastic surgery so that you could look a hundred years younger, where would you put your secret door?"

Gurl and Bug spoke at the same time: "The mirror!"

Both of them ran over to the mirror on the wall and began plucking and pulling at the ornate gold frame. It didn't budge.

"That's too bad," said Bug. "I was beginning to believe that there *was* a secret door."

But Gurl wasn't ready to quit. "There's got to be some way to open it." She knelt and felt all the edges of the mirror, smiling when she came to something on the middle of the right side, tucked just behind the gold frame. "What do you know?" she said. "A combination lock."

That was all the encouragement Bug needed. He brushed Gurl aside, rubbed his fingers together to warm them, and started dialling.

"Can you open it?" said Gurl.

"Shhh!"

Bug pressed his ear to the wall next to the lock, dialling carefully this way and that. Gurl heard the tiny click as he found the right combination. He pulled on the frame of the mirror and it swung away from the wall like the not-so-secret door it was. Behind the door was a huge metal safe the size of a walk-in closet, stuffed to the brim with fur coats, shoes, scarves, neatly stacked jars of caviar, a row of champagne bottles and a very peeved cat sitting in a birdcage.

"Noodle!"

"Meow," said Noodle in a rather irritated way, as if to say, *What took you so long?*

Gurl dragged the cage out and opened the latch. Noodle leaped from the cage and gave Gurl's cheek a few quick rasps with her tongue. Then she wound herself around and around Bug's legs.

"I think she's happy to see us," said Gurl.

"I don't know about that," Bug said. "Maybe she just has to pee."

Gurl reached down and scooped up the cat, feeling like she had just reclaimed a part of herself. "Maybe we should call her Little Pee Pee."

"I think you've been in this place too long," said Bug.

Gurl grinned and held out her hand. "So what do you say we disappear?"

CHAPTER 17

Never Trust a Monkey

MRS TERWILIGER HUNG UP THE phone, her overlifted eyebrows twitching in irritation and her overwide mouth drooping down to her jawline. *Well*, she thought, *she never!* (As in: she had never been spoken to so rudely, never been so disorganised, never been taken less seriously, never felt so old.)

What Mrs Terwiliger was particularly irked about: the fact that it didn't seem to matter to anyone that her Strongbox® Alarm System had been malfunctioning for days now and that one of her prized monkeys was missing because of it. "A monkey?" said an impertinent policeman when she'd called

911. "A *fake* monkey? Lady, you need to get yourself what the kids call a *life*."

She *had* a life, thank you. A very fine life now that she had Gurl under control. She fingered the delicate silk scarf she wore, a prize from one of Gurl's errands. Yes, this was a life that she had grown extremely fond of and one that she would not readily give up. She had to find that monkey. Who knew who had it, and who knew what the monkey would reveal? Quite unpredictable, monkeys, especially fake ones. This is what her dear mother always said: Never trust a monkey.

Her mother, how she missed her mother! So regal, so youthful and so brave. But then, that wasn't surprising. Mrs Terwiliger came from a long line of brave and youthful women. (Her great-grandmother was one of the very first people to undergo a facelift. The results were questionable, as the surgeon lifted one side of her face higher than the other, but everyone agreed that she *did* look younger, if rather lopsided.).

Mrs Terwiliger sighed and set the phone back on the bedside table. She knew that she should try to get some rest, but rest seemed impossible. When she was a little girl and couldn't sleep, her mother would come to her and tell her a story, one that had been handed down from mother to daughter for generations. It was the story of the very first monkey, the monkey that began it all. She could almost hear her mother's voice as she remembered...

Go to sleep.

Tell me a story. Tell me about the monkeys, Mother.

No.

Please!

No.

Pretty pretty pretty pretty please?

Oh, all right, if you'll stop whining. A long time ago, your great-great-great-great-grandmother Barbie had a monkey.

Did the Indians give her the monkey?

What's with you and the Indians? Anyway, like I was saying, your grandmother had a monkey.

What was its name?

For pete's sake.

Its name was Pete?

Are you going to let me finish this? So about the monkey. One day, Grandma's sitting in her living room, watching TV.

They didn't have TV 150 years ago!

Have it your way. She was sitting there, not watching TV, not watching anything. She was bored, so she decided to play a little game with her monkey.

The monkey she stole.

Of course she didn't steal it, dummy. She took it from a little man who didn't need it, OK? There's nothing wrong with taking things from people who don't need them, right?

Right.

So, anyway. Your old great-great-great-great-grandma Barbie decides to play a game with her monkey. She throws it a penny. She figures that the monkey will catch the penny and maybe throw it back or something, you know? I mean, what else was there to do when there's no TV, right? The monkey catches the penny, but instead of throwing it back, he puts it in his pocket (he wore one of those monkey waistcoats). And then he starts to talk.

What does he say?

All sorts of monkey nonsense, that's what. Monkeys don't know very much. But your grandmother figures out that every time she gives the monkey a penny, he'll start talking. She thinks it's kind of fun, so she keeps doing it. Then one day one of her friends comes over. This friend notices the monkey and wants to pet it. But instead of petting it, she starts to whisper to it.

What was she whispering?

Your grandma couldn't hear. And the friend didn't seem to remember she had whispered anything after she was through, and looked at your grandma like she was crazy to suggest that people whispered to monkeys. Anyway, after the friend left, your grandma gave the monkey a penny and the monkey started to talk. Only this time he didn't talk his regular monkey nonsense; he told your grandma what the friend had whispered to her. It seems the friend had revealed all her secrets to the monkey.

What kind of secrets?

Nothing juicy. Some stuff about eating too many cookies and

thinking her husband was boring. But your grandma thought that the monkey's trick might come in handy with some more interesting people. She started bringing the monkey out with her and found that all kinds of people would tell the monkey their secrets. And some of those secrets were useful. You know, stock tips, bank account numbers, that kind of thing. It helped her make a little extra cash. And there's nothing wrong with making a little extra cash with your monkey, now is there?

No. But the monkey died.

Yeah, the monkey died. Monkeys can't last for ever. But a monkey's tricks, now, that's a different story. Tricks last. And your grandma Barbie was tricky too. She took all those pennies that the monkey had saved up in its waistcoat, went to a toy shop and bought a brand-new monkey. A mechanical one. One that wouldn't die. And she gave the new monkey the old one's pennies. And the new one worked as well as the old, better even, because a mechanical monkey doesn't eat, or yell, or hop up and down, or swing from the light fixtures, throw bananas, or have to go to the toilet in the middle of the night. A mechanical monkey is the best sort of monkey. Which is why we still have your great-great-great-great-grandma's mechanical monkey in the living room.

Yes! But it doesn't work.

Lord have mercy, I've raised an idiot. Of course it doesn't work, you knucklehead. It's a monkey. A toy. This is a bedtime story. You're such a weird little girl.

But Mrs Terwiliger knew that the monkey did work. At least halfway. Whenever you passed it, you felt the urge to talk, to spill all your innermost secrets. Mrs Terwiliger had even seen her mother whispering a bit to the monkey occasionally. But when she gave the monkey a penny, the monkey never said a word. It was like the secrets all went in, but they never quite came back out again.

And yet she hadn't given up hope that one day, she too would be able to make a little (or a lot of) extra cash with the monkey, and she bought a whole bunch of monkeys just in case. Still, her mother had always told her that the way to move up in the world is to land a wealthy man, and that's exactly what Mrs Terwiliger had planned to do. As an eighteen-year-old, she went to work for the mayor's office, thinking that she would meet men of power and riches there. And she met one and married him as soon as she could. How was she to know that James Terwiliger would give up his lucrative fur coat resale shop to become a mime artist? How was she to know that this gloomy post at Hope House, something she took only out of desperation, would become her entire life?

Oh, it was terrible the things she had been forced to do just to make ends meet! The risks she had to take!

But she always believed that she was destined for more than this orphanage, that she was destined for something grand and that any day now it would come. The monkeys, she always thought, would be the key. Dutifully, she presented a monkey to every child who came to her, watching eagerly as each child whispered in the monkey's ear, always too low for Mrs Terwiliger to hear. As in her mother's story, she gave the monkeys pennies regularly, hoping that an orphan had held the secret to a fortune and that one day a monkey would reveal it. But monkeys never made any sense. They never told her anything important. Sometimes she got a name, or maybe a phrase, but it never added up to a thing. It was as if the monkeys liked to tease her.

Then again, it was Gurl – and not the monkeys – who filled her closets with beautiful furs and her fridge with champagne and caviar. What good were the monkeys, really, except to help to... to... to... cleanse the minds of a lot of troubled children? Yes, Mrs Terwiliger thought, that's what they did. Ease the mind, soothe the soul. When she did finally escape from this place, she would have to leave at least a few monkeys with the next matron of Hope House, along with instructions on their use. It was for the children's own good that they forget their pasts, oh, yes, yes, yes! Their pasts could bring them nothing but pain.

As for Gurl, well, Gurl was now Mrs Terwiliger's monkey of fortune. And Mrs Terwiliger intended to keep her for a good long time.

With that cheerful thought, Mrs Terwiliger unknotted the silk scarf she wore, folded it carefully and tucked it into her silk scarf drawer. She changed into her nightclothes and was about to slip into bed when she heard some strange sounds. Muffled, as if they were coming from far away.

The main building! The broken alarm!

Quickly, she threw on her robe and slippers, grabbed the nearest weapon she could find (a hairbrush) and flew from her quarters to the main offices. Holding the brush high, she slipped through the front door and floated slowly down the hallways and through the offices, astonished at what she saw. Papers were strewn about the floors, the closets were emptied of their contents, files had been pulled from cabinets.

The children. Somehow, the children had managed to disable the alarm and vandalise the offices.

Her wide mouth somehow defied its collagen injections and tightened into a thin line. It was that boy, Chicken, she could feel it in her bones. He had a terrible attitude problem (never mind the fact that he was extremely violent and quite possibly brain-damaged). Their very first meeting, when she'd asked for his name, he'd given her a bunch of nonsense before snarking, "What's it to you?!" Oh! To think that she had been concerned about the pain the children were in!

Plink!

Aha, thought Mrs Terwiliger. The little leadfoot was still there! She would teach him a thing or two. Almost smiling, she drifted back into the hallway and down the corridor, listening for any sounds.

Scritch!

He was in her office! How could he have got past her locks? Her smile turned into a grimace as she remembered what else was in her office. She couldn't let that stupid boy ruin her plans.

She edged up along the wall towards the door. "Aha!" she yelled as she flew into the room brandishing the hairbrush. "Caught you!"

A figure crouched on the floor, a figure wearing a foul-looking trench coat and mismatched shoes. "Kitty?" it said, sniffing the exposed hollow behind the mirror with a nose as long as a finger.

"Who are you?" babbled Mrs Terwiliger in her shock and fright. "Why are you so filthy? What's wrong with your nose? Why are your eyes red? How did you unlock my safe? I demand an explanation!"

"I think we're the ones who deserve an explanation."

Mrs Terwiliger turned. A man, handsome as any model, stood behind her, grinning with his brilliant white teeth.

"Oh," said Mrs Terwiliger, awed. She twisted her mouth into what she hoped was an alluring smile. "Excuse me, sir. I apologise for raising my voice... er... Mr.... er... Mr...?"

The handsome man reached out and plucked the hairbrush from Mrs Terwiliger's hand. "You can call me Sweetcheeks, Sweetcheeks."

Mrs Terwiliger's eyebrows went up so high on her head they were in danger of being lost in her dyed hair for ever. "Sweetcheeks! Sweetcheeks *Grabowski*? I've read about you in the newspaper."

"We found your monkeys," said the handsome man. "I was looking for one in particular, but it seems to be missing. Among other things." He looked pointedly at the safe behind the mirror. "My friend here thought he smelled something in your not-so-secret room. Something that he's wanted a very long time."

The rat man snuffled dispiritedly. "Kitty."

Mrs Terwiliger covered her mouth with her hand. "It's gone? Well, obviously, that horrible child stole it."

"Which horrible child are you referring to?"

But Mrs Terwiliger was too distraught to notice the menace in the man's voice. Perhaps she sensed a kindred spirit. Or maybe she thought that Sweetcheeks and the rat man were some crack team of undercover policemen that had been sent to arrest her. In any case, she leaned against the wall and began to cry (or at least tried to look like she was crying; excessive eye surgery had dried up her tear ducts for good). "My life is ruined!"

"Oh, please," said Sweetcheeks. "Let's not be overly dramatic."

"That evil, ungrateful, nasty, dirty, lying—"

"Yes, yes, we get your point."

"She stole my cat!"

"*Your* cat? *She* stole it? Who's *she*?"

"Gurl!" Mrs Terwiliger said irritably. Mrs Terwiliger stopped blubbering to stare at Sweetcheeks. "Oh! Oh!" she said. "Did the animal belong to you? If I had known that it – she... er, the cat had a proper owner, I never would have kept her, never."

"Right," said Sweetcheeks. "Let's talk about this girl who stole the cat. Or rather, where she went."

"But I don't know where she went. I don't! I swear on my life!"

"Yes," said Sweetcheeks, stepping back to allow another man entry into the bathroom, a man with a glinting silver zipper like a dagger across his face. "You certainly do."

CHAPTER 18

Run

FREEDOM! ONCE GURL AND BUG travelled a few invisible blocks, an invisible cat snuggled in an invisible sling, they were drunk with it. They were free! Free from Mrs Terwiliger. Free from the hopelessness of Hope House.

Free!

Bug's hand quivered in Gurl's; she was sure she could feel his heart beating in his fingertips. As they walked, she saw notices for Flyfest, the city's annual flying festival. Even though she couldn't see Bug, she knew he was itching to fly. She wondered aloud why he wasn't.

"I want to," he told her, "but I want to wait until we're far away from Hope House and we have plenty of room. I'm going to fly as high as I possibly can. Higher than we did before. Higher," he said, "than anyone ever has."

His words were so serious that she didn't dare make a joke or question him. So they kept moving. Noodle curled up in the sling and napped, purring loudly. After a while Gurl's legs started to ache and her eyes got tired. Her mouth was dry and her stomach growled. Plus, it was cold.

"So," said Bug. "Where are we going exactly?"

The truth was, Gurl hadn't thought much about where she would go after she found Noodle. She stopped walking and looked around with bleary eyes. She lifted his hand and used it to point. "The Palace."

The Palace Hotel, fifty-four of the grandest storeys in the whole city, loomed to their left, bedecked in lights like strings of jewels.

"Wow," said Bug.

"Yup," said Gurl. "If you've got to run, why not run to the best?"

They slipped past the doormen and entered the opulent lobby, trying to keep their sneakers from squeaking on the gleaming tile floor. Chandeliers glittered way above their heads, while gold trim gleamed along the walls. Along one wall was a grand staircase carpeted in rich red paisley.

"What do you want to do?" said Gurl, whispering in Bug's ear.

"We'll sneak behind the desk and check the computers, find a room that's empty and mark it occupied. Then we'll go up to the room and get some sleep."

"Oh!" said Gurl. "Why didn't I think of that?"

"Don't know; why didn't you?"

Since it was late, only one person manned the reservations desk, and he was too busy talking about the stock market with one of the bellhops to notice that one of the computers seemed to be operating all on its own. In just a few minutes, Gurl and Bug had registered a room under the name "B. G. Noodle". Bug even knew how to make a card key for the room, though, as with his skill with alarms, he didn't seem to know *how* he knew.

They took the elevator up to Room 2305, hoping that there were no security cameras to catch the door opening by itself. When they walked into the room, Gurl gasped and dropped Bug's hand.

"Look at this!" she said, running to the bathroom, to the bed, to the chairs, to the bathroom again. "This is bigger than the whole dorm at Hope House!"

"And about four hundred thousand trillion times as nice." Bug sat on one the red velvet chairs. "I feel like a king."

"You have to see this bathroom!" said Gurl. "A family could live in here."

Gurl freed Noodle from the sling. The cat proceeded to sniff every corner of the suite before running into the bathroom and shutting the door. Gurl and Bug soon heard the shower.

Bug shrugged. "I guess she needed to freshen up."

"I wouldn't mind that either," said Gurl, "but I also wouldn't mind finding something to eat. I'm starving. There have to be some restaurants around here." She was going to suggest that they wait behind one of them for a waiter, but Bug had other ideas.

"How about room service?" Bug said. "They usually serve food late in these fancy places." He hunted around until he found a menu on one of the writing desks. "Well, we can have a lobster salad. Or how about sea bass in a potato crust? Or here's some foie gras."

"Fwa what?"

"It's goose liver. I was just kidding though. I don't like it."

"Goose liver? When did you ever have goose liver?"

"I didn't," said Bug, a strange look coming over his face. "I don't think I did. But I'm sure I wouldn't like it. That's what I mean."

"OK," said Gurl, really beginning to wonder who Bug was before Hope House. What kind of person ate goose liver and made card keys? "Don't they have anything normal on that menu?"

"Hey! They do! Hamburgers! But they don't call them hamburgers; they call them sirloin burgers. Whatever. That's what I'm having. A burger with cheese and fries."

Her growling stomach made the decision for her. "Make that two," said Gurl. Inside the bathroom, Noodle turned off the water. Gurl heard the sound of a blow-dryer. "And an order of macaroni and cheese."

With the food ordered, Gurl and Bug kicked off their shoes and sprawled out on the two beds to watch TV. Twenty minutes later, there was a knock. Gurl made herself invisible while Bug dived under the covers. Lowering his voice as best as he could, Bug bellowed, "Come in."

The waiter wheeled in a cart piled with food. "Your food... uh... sir?"

"Yes, yes," Bug growled. "Thank you. You can leave it right by the desk."

The waiter stared oddly at Bug (or what he could see of him, just a little tuft of hair above the blankets). "No problem, sir." He put the food where he was told and left without waiting for a tip. As Bug and Gurl were uncovering dishes, Noodle wandered out from the bathroom, fluffy as a poodle.

"Is that a feather duster or a cat?" said Bug. Noodle nipped at his ankle and mewled for her pasta.

Gurl took a big bite of her burger, chewing thoughtfully. "Does this seem funny to you?"

"What?"

"Being in this fancy hotel, hiding out from 'scary men'?" What she meant to ask was whether it felt funny for them to be in the fancy hotel *together*, or rather, didn't it feel funny that it didn't feel funny at all? For a minute she let her mind wander into a brief daydream: a girl goes on vacation with her family and hangs out with her cousin, no, not a cousin, but a friend of the family, no relation at all. The girl and the boy spend all their time sightseeing, flying in the park and getting great snacks from room service.

But she didn't want to tell him any of this for fear he'd think she was getting weird on him. "Think about it," she said. "Tomorrow we could be waking up at Hope House to runny eggs and lumpy oatmeal."

"Monkey chow," said Bug.

"Right. And Digger's attitude problem."

Bug nodded. "And Mrs Terwiliger's freaky trout face."

"Instead we're going to wake up here."

"It's pretty amazing," Bug agreed. "Aren't you glad I decided to take you with me?"

Gurl threw a napkin at him and he threw one back, but neither of them wanted to stop eating long enough for a serious linen fight.

Bug, Gurl and Noodle ate every morsel of food on their plates before collapsing into the huge soft beds. "I don't know about you," said Bug, "but I gotta get some sleep."

"Me too," said Gurl, through a yawn.

"Good night."

"Good night."

Bug flicked off the lights and the room was dark and still. Noodle looked from one bed to the other, unsure of who, exactly, she wanted to perch on. She settled for Gurl, curling up right beside her, so that the tip of her tail would occasionally brush against Gurl's nose and make her sneeze.

Despite the heavy food in their stomachs, despite their sore feet and their exhaustion, they were restless. They listened to the sounds of the city street far below their window: the distant wail of tyres, the tired rumbles of the buses that methodically traced their routes like ghosts. The sounds of the city were low and sad, and it made them grateful that they were not alone. All through the night, they took turns watching each other sleep.

For two weeks they switched from empty room to empty room, floor to floor. And for those two weeks, ordering cheeseburgers, omelettes and fries from room service, taking hour-long baths in the Jacuzzi, watching Noodle attack the shoelaces that Bug dragged all around the room and crashing (invisibly, of course) four elaborate weddings was enough adventure for all of them. Then Gurl and Bug grew bored. Even Noodle seemed to spend much of her time napping and heaving long, pathetic sighs.

"How long do you think we have to hide from the scary men?" said Gurl, flipping through the 846 channels on the TV.

"I wonder how we even know that there are scary men," said Bug. "I mean, this is the same guy who thought we were vampires. And the same guy who told us to take the subway. Maybe he's just crazy."

"Maybe," said Gurl. "I'm getting sick of being in here. Why don't we go out flying in the park for a while?"

"Tomorrow," Bug said. "I want to make sure that I'm rested."

"We've been resting for two weeks. And the Flyfest is coming up soon. They have an amateur race. If you practise, maybe you could sign up for that."

Bug said nothing, however. Gurl started to wonder if he wasn't scared to try for fear that even with Gurl and with Noodle, he was still a leadfoot. That the one night in the park was a fluke and would never happen again.

"I have an idea," said Bug, brightening. "Why don't we go out and see a movie?"

"A movie?" At Hope House sometimes Mrs Terwiliger would rent old movies and show them on a big screen, but she had never seen a movie in a real movie theatre. "That would be great. But Noodle comes with us. I bet she'd like to see a movie too."

"Fine," said Bug, picking up the cat and cupping her chin so that she would look him in the eye. "But you can't take that long in the bathroom, OK? I don't feel like sitting around for two hours while you blow-dry your fur."

Gurl called the hotel concierge to find out where the nearest theatre was and then they set off. They didn't bother with invisibility this time, since it seemed apparent that no one was interested in them. That was the thing about the city, thought Gurl. There were so many people doing so many things that no one person could keep track of another (at least not very well).

They had only been on the street for a few minutes when Bug stiffened.

"What?"

"How far is the theatre?" he asked.

"Around the corner, down a few blocks, why?"

"'Cause there's a police car behind us, that's why. Don't look!"

But Gurl had already glanced back and seen the black and white car driving slowly up the block. "How do you know they're looking for us?" Gurl said. "Do you think Mrs Terwiliger called them?"

"I don't know what they're looking for," said Bug. "Pretend like you don't notice anything. Once we turn the corner, grab me and turn us both invisible. Then we'll be fine."

"OK," Gurl said. She forced herself to be casual as they came up to the corner.

"Ready?" said Bug.

"Yeah." They turned left and Gurl grabbed Bug's arm. Instantly, they vanished. They looked behind them and saw the cop car round the corner and stop dead. One cop got out of the car and disappeared into a nearby smoothie shop. After a few minutes, the cop returned carrying two giant fruit smoothies. The cop got back into the car and the two men drove away.

"Whew!" said Bug once the car was gone.

"They were just hungry. Had nothing to do with us."

"We can't be sure. Mrs Terwiliger could have called the police. Maybe we shouldn't have messed up her offices so much. They could charge us with vandalism or something like that."

"They're not going to charge us with anything if they can't see us," said Gurl.

"Right," said Bug. "No one can see us and no one can find us."

Noodle made a low growl in her throat, a warning. A familiar slap-drag sound made the skin on the back of Gurl's neck ripple in alarm and her stomach drop to her feet. "Nice?" said a guttural voice and the sounds of sniffing filled the air.

This time Gurl didn't wait for the rat man to say anything else. She said it for him:

"Run!"

CHAPTER 19

What's It To You? Has His Say

THEY RAN. GURL COULD STILL hear the snuffling sounds and knew that though the rat man couldn't see them, he could *smell* them.

Bug tugged on her hand, yanking her into an alleyway where they crouched against several garbage cans. Gurl could hardly breathe for the noxious odour of the trash.

They watched anxiously as the rat man who had followed them passed the alley where they hid. He stopped, sniffing the air, but soon moved on.

"What *is* that thing?" said Bug.

"I don't know exactly," Gurl said. "And I don't want to know."

"At least the smell of the garbage confused it."

"Yeah," said Gurl. "It's confusing *me* so much I think I might throw up."

They crept up to where the alley opened on to the street and looked around. Several other dim, trench-coated shapes lurked in doorways and alleys, umbrellas lowered to hide their filed teeth.

"There's more than one," said Gurl. "What are we going to do?"

"Wait here for a few minutes. Then, when they've gone, we'll go to the theatre. It's closer than the hotel and there are always a lot of people there. All that candy and popcorn should cover up our smell too, don't you think?"

"OK. Let's do it."

They watched the rat men patrol the street, sniffing and searching. Then they took their search up the next block. When Bug and Gurl couldn't see them any more, they left the safety of the alley for the theatre.

They were just walking past the ticket booth to go inside when the man behind the glass said, "Tickets, please!"

Gurl and Bug checked to see if they were still invisible. They were.

"Yes, I'm talking to you. You do need tickets to see the movie or did you think you were special?"

Bug and Gurl moved dumbly towards the ticket booth, gaping at the man. Gurl thought the man's deep, raspy voice sounded familiar.

"I recommend the French film myself," the man said. "Très magnifique! But I can imagine that you two are going to want to see this stupid action-adventure. I can sum *that* up for you: the hero shoots all the bad guys and gets the girl. Or maybe you'll like this horrid romantic comedy. Neither romantic nor comic, if you ask me."

"Jules?" said Gurl. He looked different than he had at Harvey's months ago, his glasses plain and round, his short dark hair slightly mussed. But it was definitely him. And just like in the Harvey's changing room, he could see her. He could see them all.

"Nice cat," Jules was saying. "I won't charge extra for her since she'll probably sleep through the whole thing. Unless you see the French film, of course. That's right up her alley."

"Jules," Gurl began, but the man ignored her and kept chattering on about French films in general, how they were superior in every way to every other sort of film, except, he said, for kung-fu films, which he felt were underrated as a genre.

"Do you know this guy?" said Bug. "And how can he see us when everyone else can't?"

Jules's eyes got squinty behind the plain round lenses. "You'd be amazed at the things I've seen," he said. "That will be ten bucks."

"Ten bucks!" said Bug. "We don't have ten bucks!"

"Ten bucks *each*," said Jules. "The theatres keep jacking up the prices, just like certain monkeys I know."

"What do you know about monkeys?" Bug said.

"Oh, all right all right. I never saw you. Go on," said Jules, waving them inside. Gurl and Bug continued to stare until Jules leaned forward. "Darlings, I smell a rat. Simon says move!"

They needed no other warning. They turned and ran into the theatre, not even bothering to check which picture was being shown.

"*Regarde en haut et vois le ballon rouge*," boomed the speakers as they sat down, way at the back of the theatre. "*C'est mon coeur.*"

"How did that guy see us?" said Bug.

"I don't know. I was at Harvey's a while ago and he saw me there too, when no one else could."

"Do you think he's going to tell anyone we're here?"

"No. I don't think so. Otherwise the police would have come already," said Gurl. She sighed, sinking into her seat, cuddling Noodle close. "We shouldn't have left the hotel."

"What were we supposed to do? Hide out for ever?" said Bug. "We didn't know that Mrs Terwiliger was going to call the police."

"*Regarde en bas et vois les rats! Les rats rongent mes orteils!*"

"And I didn't think the rat man was going to find me again."

"So these are the guys that you were telling me about. When did you first see one?"

"A while ago, after I'd turned invisible once. I was at a

restaurant in Little Italy. It chased me and tried to steal Noodle." At the mention of her name, Noodle mewled softly.

"Les rats? Les rats ne sont pas si mauvais! Ils ont des coeurs aussi!"

They watched the movie for a few minutes, trying to figure out what was going on. Unfortunately, reading the subtitles didn't help much.

"And what was that about monkeys?" Bug asked. "About them jacking up their prices?"

Gurl remembered something that Mrs Terwiliger said a long time before. "Do you still have that monkey you've been carrying around."

"Ole What's It To You? Sure." Bug pulled the bedraggled monkey out of his pocket.

"And do you have a penny?"

"Uh, I think so." Bug set the monkey on his lap and dug around in his pockets and came up with two pennies, a nickel and a quarter. He held out one of the pennies. "Here."

"No, I don't want it. Give it to the monkey."

"Huh? How do I give a toy a penny?"

"Put it in his waistcoat. He has a pocket. Trust me," she added, seeing Bug's sceptical look.

Bug shrugged. "OK." He tucked the penny in the monkey's waistcoat. "Now what?"

"Wait a minute."

"Wait for what?"

"I don't know. Just wait."

They waited, staring at the monkey.

"Uh, I don't think anything's going to happen," said Bug.

"Right," said Gurl. "Of course. They jacked up their prices! Try the nickel. No, the quarter. Try the quarter."

"Whatever you say," said Bug. "You're the lunatic." He tucked the quarter into the monkey's waistcoat.

Nothing.

"How about a dollar? Do you have a dollar?"

"Be serious!" said Bug, but he was already digging in his pocket. "Here. That's it. That's all the money I have." He shoved the dollar into the monkey's waistcoat. "Are you satisfied now?"

"MONKEY CHOW!" screamed the monkey.

Noodle howled, Bug and Gurl almost jumped out of their seats and all around them people said, "SHHH!"

But the monkey had just begun. "Your real name is Sylvester Grabowski," it said, lowering its voice to a hoarse whisper. "Son of Sy 'Sweetcheeks' Grabowski, master thief and criminal. You're here to find The Wall."

Stunned, Bug and Gurl stared at the monkey. "Did it say 'Wall'?" Bug asked.

"Yes, I said The Wall," chattered the monkey. "Every century or whatever, a Wall is born. One who can disappear. A long time ago, when she was just a baby, she was kidnapped, but then the stupid goons who were supposed to watch her lost her."

"Kidnapped?" said Gurl. "I was kidnapped?" The thought astonished her. For years she thought that she was nothing, no one, invisible to the world, given up because she was unwanted – nothing more than a burden. What if she had family somewhere? Family looking for her?

"For the last three years, you have travelled through every orphanage in the city, looking for her. But you're tired of this. You don't even want to find her. You hope she ran away to Toledo so that you can get out of Hope House. It's the worst place you've ever been."

"I can't believe this," cried Bug. "The monkeys have been keeping all our thoughts. That's why she has one for each of us. Our memories are in them!"

"You've only been at Hope House for a little while and you hate it already. Mrs Terwiliger has had so much plastic surgery that she looks like a cartoon, the food tastes like monkey chow and you're so bored you feel like punching the walls."

"Monkey chow?" said Gurl, turning to look at Bug. "Punching the walls?"

Bug's face was drained of colour, and his eyes looked cloudy and troubled. He said nothing, as if his silence would keep her from saying what he knew she was going to say, what she *did* say.

"When this monkey says 'you' it means *you*. This monkey has *your* thoughts. *You* were sent to find me." Her eyes widened to nearly the size of Bug's. "You're the son of a thief! That's why you can pick all the door locks and fix the alarms! You're supposed to bring me to your father! This Sweetmeats guy! You're the *scary man*!" She sprang out of her chair.

"Sit down!" barked a man sitting a few rows behind them.

"Wait," said Bug. "Please! I don't remember any of this stuff, OK? It's not me!"

But it wasn't true. Not really. As soon as the monkey began to speak, the memories had begun to flood back: his golden-haired, black-hearted father, the lock-pick set for his ninth birthday, the endless nannies, Odd John, the armour in the round meeting room, his first taste of foie gras and caviar, loneliness, loneliness, loneliness.

And though he tried to keep the recognition off his face, Gurl could see it plain as his huge blue eyes: it was him. It was him!

Suddenly, the doors burst open and light flooded the theatre. Gurl heard Jules's fussy voice yelling, "Wait! Tickets! You don't have tickets! We're sold out of that one! Try the romantic comedy! It's hilarious, I swear!"

With Noodle cradled in her arms, Gurl whirled to run towards the exit. But she was too late. An enormous man with a zipper running across his face flew like a bat across the theatre. Just as she vanished, he grabbed her, grinning with his yellow niblet teeth.

CHAPTER 20

Ups and Downs

GURL KICKED AND THRASHED, BUT the man's grip didn't loosen and a bite on the hand only served to make him giggle. What was with all the giggling creeps around this city!

A yellow-haired man strode down the length of the theatre, followed by a dozen others – bushy-browed, heavy-muscled, scowling-faced men – a few floating, most walking.

"Son!" said the yellow-haired man, when he reached Bug.

"Shhh!" said the people all around them.

"Pardon *moi*," said Sweetcheeks Grabowski smoothly. "Let's be on our way so that these lovely folks can watch their strange little movie."

"I'm not going!" yelled Gurl, struggling with all her strength.

"Neither am I," Bug said, scowling as his father put an arm around his shoulders.

"Really, Sylvester," said Sweetcheeks, exasperated. "Was this a good time to find yourself a girlfriend?"

"I'm not his girlfriend," Gurl yelled between bites and punches.

"No, and that's a good thing too," Sweetcheeks said, "because you're not going to have time for any of that. I've got lots of stuff planned for us all." He ruffled Bug's hair. "Isn't that nice?"

Bug knocked his father's hand away. "I don't know you."

"What are you going on about? Are you feeling well?"

"Leave us alone!" shouted Bug, looking around wildly for a wall on which to bloody his knuckles.

"Will you people please be quiet!" another man in the audience said. Odd John turned and smiled at the man in a sweet and terrifying way sure to turn his guts to water.

"John, my son is delirious," Sweetcheeks said. "It must have been the shock of getting his memory back." Sweetcheeks hugged his son, ignoring the fact that the boy was frantically kicking him in the skins. "That terrible, greedy woman! Stealing memories with these absurd toys! And her face! Even John was terrified."

"Let me go!"

"But don't worry. John taught her a valuable lesson that we all should learn: acceptance. We need to accept ourselves the way we are. One doesn't fool with Mother Nature. One ages with grace, blah blah blah. Once John undid most of those nips and tucks, that woman was a brand-new person, wouldn't you say, John? She told me to tell you that she was sorry and that she wouldn't ever ever ever do it again."

"Get off me!"

Sweetcheeks rolled his eyes at the other theatre patrons – who were now staring in disbelief – as if to say, *Children! What can you do?* "Sylvester, I promise I will make it up to you," said Sweetcheeks. "But right now we must be on our way." He looked around the theatre. "My sincerest apologies. My son isn't well and his friend is obviously having hysterical fits. So sorry to interrupt. *Au revoir! Tant pis! Crème brûlée! Let's go, boys.*"

The enormous scarred man scooped up Gurl as if she were no more than a toy herself and flew out of the theatre, past the ticket booth and into their getaway vehicle: a city tour bus. The scarred man strapped Gurl into a seat on the open roof of the bus and sat down next to her to make sure she didn't go anywhere. Bug followed, dragged by his father and several of his henchmen. Gurl reappeared, squealing and slapping at the scarred man, trying to get Jules's attention. But Jules was no longer in the ticket booth; Jules was nowhere to be seen. Gurl kept slapping and squealing anyway, hoping that someone, somewhere, might see or hear her and call the police. Noodle growled like a dog in her lap.

Sweetcheeks thrust his face in Gurl's. "Stop that flailing around or John will take your kitty and turn her into a nice hat."

Gurl stopped struggling and vanished. "Oooh!" said Sweetcheeks. "That *is* impressive! But even though we can't see you, we still have you. And that is the important thing." Sweetcheeks stomped on the floor and yelled, "Driver!"

The old stinking bus lurched forward like a lumbering apatosaurus. The group drove in near silence for several blocks before Sweetcheeks spoke again, pointing up at the sky. "Do you see that?"

Despite themselves, Bug and Gurl both looked up. All around them, winking skyscrapers rose like columns that held up the heavens. "Amazing, this city. Most people see all these buildings and forget that we are surrounded by a moat of water. We can't grow out, so we grow *up*. It doesn't matter that no one can fly more than five or ten storeys. Higher, says the city! Taller, says the city! More, says the city! We'll catch up! And so up and up and up they go, like concrete beanstalks."

Gurl said nothing, glancing at Bug. He looked angry enough to launch himself at his father, but why, she had no idea.

Wasn't this the reason he came to Hope House? To find her and then get back to his father? She stroked Noodle's invisible fur, the taste of Bug's betrayal like metal in her mouth.

"Well, at least some of us went up," Sweetcheeks was saying. "Some of us, however, stayed down." He moved from his seat at the front of the bus to a seat just in front of Gurl. As he couldn't see her, his gaze settled on where he thought her face might be. "There are the people who fly and the ones who crawl. The butterflies and the cockroaches, if you will. Butterflies are beautiful, of course, and everyone loves them, but what happens to butterflies? They live for a few weeks and then they die. But the roaches? Chop their heads off and they walk! Spray them with insecticides and they laugh! Bomb them and they thrive! I," said Sweetcheeks, "am a roach." He reached out for Gurl. "And so are you."

Gurl smacked his hand. "I don't know what you're talking about. I don't *care* what you're talking about."

"Of course you do. Roaches can't fly all flitter flutter like the butterfly. But they live right under the noses of everyone else. They slip through the cracks unnoticed. They take what they need and what they want. Like you, like me."

Gurl thought of all the things she had stolen for Mrs Terwiliger – and for herself – and for a moment felt ashamed.

"Yes," said Sweetcheeks, nodding thoughtfully. "You understand what I'm saying."

"*I'm* not a roach," said Bug.

Sweetcheeks sighed. "Sylvester, Daddy's busy right now."

"I said, I am *not* a roach!" Bug punched the side of the bus. *Wham!*

"You know that everything I do, I do for you," Sweetcheeks said.

"You don't do anything for me."

"Yes, I do."

Bug folded his arms across his chest. "No."

"Yes."

"No!"

"You're trying my patience," said Sweetcheeks, in a sing-songy sort of voice.

"You're making me nauseous," said Bug, in the same sing-song.

Sweetcheeks turned to Odd John, throwing up his hands, and John shrugged. The yellow-haired man said no more; neither did his son nor any of the heavy-browed, broken-nosed men who picked at their fingernails in boredom. Gurl wondered where they were being taken and why.

The bus chugged down the wide avenues until it crossed into the downtown area, where the neat grid of streets collapsed into a haphazard pile – darker, narrower, shorter and every which way – just like wood for a campfire. The buildings were still high, but not nearly so tall as they were in midtown. Gurl recognised the cheerful awnings of Little Italy, which blended into the crowded markets of Chinatown. Cramped restaurants with glazed ducks hanging in the windows stood side by side with trinket shops displaying silk slippers, fans and tanks filled with tiny turtles sold as pets. Though it was late, people swarmed in and out of the shops, stopping only to glare at the great stinking bus as it ploughed through the choked streets like an egg swallowed by a snake.

"We're here," said Sweetcheeks as the bus finally lurched and died. "Everybody out!"

Before Gurl could make a move, Odd John deftly unlocked her restraints and carried her from the bus into the nearest trinket shop. Instead of flying, he walked all the way to the back of the shop, to a door marked with some Chinese characters and an English translation: "Employees Only". John opened the door and went inside. It seemed to Gurl that they walked for a very long time down a long sloping hallway, though it didn't seem possible that this building could go back (or down) so far. She could hear the footsteps and grunts of the rest of Sweetcheeks's men as they followed, and imagined that she saw Bug's eyes gleaming like a cat's in the dark.

Finally, they reached yet another door, this one with a red, hand-shaped panel on it. Sweetcheeks shoved aside his minions and pressed his hand on the panel. The door slid open, revealing a shimmering corridor of marble and tapestry that outdid even the Palace Hotel. Gurl gasped.

"Yes, it is wonderful, isn't it? I personally stole each and every one of these tapestries from museums all over Europe," Sweetcheeks said. "Everyone into the Armoury. Wait till you see that one, you're just going to die. Oh, but not *literally*."

The group fanned out from the corridor into the Armoury, a round room with a glass table and creepy suits of armour all around the perimeter. What was worse, far worse than the creepy suits of armour, was the thing sitting at the table. The rat man with the red eyes and filed teeth. The thing that said "Kitty" and began to sniff the air.

"Kitty! Yes, absolutely. Kitty it is!" Sweetcheeks grabbed for the cat he knew Gurl carried.

"What are you doing?" said Bug.

"No!" Gurl tried to shrink away, but Odd John just gripped her tighter, holding her still. Sweetcheeks felt along her shoulders, then down her arms, until he found Noodle in her sling.

"No!" Gurl cried again, tears springing to her eyes as Sweetcheeks pulled Noodle away.

"Stop it!" Bug yelled.

The cat, once free of Gurl's touch, became visible, which sent the rat man into spasms. "Kittykittykittykitty!" he gibbered. Gurl thought if John wasn't holding her up, she might faint.

"Don't!" screamed Bug, leaping after his father.

Sweetcheeks motioned for one of his men. "Help him get control of himself, will you, Lefty?"

Lefty grabbed Bug, holding him easily, as the boy punched and spit. "Don't give it the cat!"

"I have to," said Sweetcheeks, holding Noodle out by her armpits in front of him, as if she were a baby with a dirty diaper. "I promised Mr Sewer Rat and I do keep my word. We never really got along before, The Sewer Rats and my gang. Turf wars, blah blah blah. They can never seem to stay put in the sewers, where they belong. But as you can see, they have some sort of... *thing* for cats. It has to do with a wool coat The Sewer Rats stole more than 150 years ago. Remind me to tell you that story; it's my favourite. Anyway, they found a cat in the pocket of this wool coat and they've been gaga about cats ever since, believe me. And one day not too long ago, this guy shows up yelling about a kitty and a girl who vanished into thin air. *He* wanted the kitty and *I* wanted the girl who vanished into thin air. So we made a little bargain and here we are. Friends."

Sweetcheeks walked around the table, dangling the squirming cat in front of the rat like a worm in front of a bird, and Gurl squeezed her eyes shut.

The Sewer Rat took Noodle and cradled her as gently as a mother cradles a child, cooing nonsense at her. Gurl opened her eyes to see Noodle blink at the rat man, then bat playfully at his whiskers.

"See?" said Sweetcheeks, taking a seat at the glass table. "It's love."

CHAPTER 21

The Black Box

GURL HADN'T REALISED SHE'D BEEN holding her breath until she let it out in a whoosh. If Noodle thought that the rat man was harmless, well then, he must be, mustn't he? At least it gave Gurl time to figure out a way to get her back and get both of them out of there.

Odd John thrust Gurl into a chair, keeping one iron hand clamped around her wrist. Up close, in the light, she saw that the scar wasn't really a scar: it was a zipper. She thought of the lions at the library, how they turned out to be actors in lion suits, and wondered what was underneath Odd John's Odd John suit.

She decided she did not want to find out.

A young man hobbled into the room, one foot bandaged up. "Sweetcheeks? The pizzas are here."

"Bobby! Good to hear it! How's the foot?"

"Uh, better. Thanks."

Sweetcheeks smiled in Gurl's general direction. "Bobby The Boy lost all his toes. It happens."

Gurl looked at Bobby, trying to figure out how, exactly, a person loses their toes. Bobby frowned, trying to figure out why, exactly, his boss appeared to be talking to an empty chair.

"Bobby," said Sweetcheeks.

"What?"

"You said something about pizzas?"

"Uh... yeah," said Bobby The Boy, "I'll go get them." He hobbled from the room.

Pizzas? Gurl decided that she was sick of Sweetcheeks Grabowski, sick of rat men, sick of Odd John, sick of this whole freak show. "What do you want?" she said.

Sweetcheeks looked startled, as if he'd forgotten she was there. "I thought that we could discuss that over dinner."

"I don't want dinner. I just want to get away from all of you." At this, she glared at Bug, then remembered that she was still invisible.

"Away? You just got here," said Sweetcheeks. "Have a little something to eat."

"I'm not going to eat."

"Well, *I'm* going to eat," said Sweetcheeks as Bobby the Boy limped in with a stack of pizza boxes. He opened them one at a time. "I thought I told you half escargot and half aubergine?"

"Oh!" said Bobby The Boy, his face turning a sickly shade of grey. "I thought you said half *escarole* – as in *salad*, not *snail*! I'm sorry, Boss. It won't happen again! I swear!"

"It's all right, it's all right," said Sweetcheeks. "Don't worry about it. You're lucky I like escarole."

In Gurl's opinion, a man who lost all his toes didn't have any luck, but she didn't say anything.

"Sylvester, your favourite. Come on, have a slice."

"No!" said Bug. He tried to get up from his seat, but Lefty shoved him right back down.

"I really don't know what's gotten into you," said Sweetcheeks, folding his pizza in half and finishing it off in three large bites. "That girl must have rubbed off. You never gave me problems before."

"Maybe I'm not the same as before," said Bug. "Maybe I'm nothing like I was before." His huge eyes searched for Gurl as he spoke. "I remember everything about myself, and even about you, but it's like I'm remembering someone else."

"It'll pass," said Sweetcheeks. "Have some pizza."

Bug turned away and Sweetcheeks took another piece. "So, I hear that my son calls you Gurl. Is this actually your name?"

"It's better than 'Sweetcheeks'," said Gurl.

Sweetcheeks chuckled. "You could be right. Listen, Gurl. Have you ever heard of The Richest Man in the Universe?"

"Is there one?"

"Sure there is. And wouldn't you know, he's right here in the city. As a matter of fact, he and his wife will be judging this year's Flyfest."

Bug's head shot up at the mention of the Flyfest, and Gurl wished that she could march over and punch him. "That's nice," said Gurl.

"We're all going to be going to the Flyfest and *introducing* ourselves to this man. You see, he has something that I want. Something better than a magic wool coat. Better than a kitty cat. Better than a monkey. Better than flying. Better than invisibility." Sweetcheeks' eyes, not so large as his son's but the same deep blue, got all dreamy.

"I'm not going to steal from this guy, if that's what you have in mind."

"Oh, but just this once," said Sweetcheeks. "And then I will let you go. I promise."

"You're never going to let me go. But it doesn't matter. I'm not going to steal. I don't steal."

"Sure you do," Sweetcheeks said. "Everyone does. This whole city was founded on it. Haven't you ever heard of the twenty-four-dollar deal?"

"No," said Gurl.

"European settlers supposedly bought this island from the Indians for twenty-four dollars' worth of beads back in the 1600s. Of course, the Indians had no understanding of the concept of ownership, so they probably thought that the Europeans just had a couple of extra beads and were being extra friendly. They had no idea that they would be kicked off the land. But hey, that's the way of the world."

"Not my world."

"Especially your world. How many shoes did you steal for Mrs Terwiliger anyway? That was some slick work."

"That was different!" said Gurl.

"Oh? Why? Because she had your cat?"

"Yes!"

"You could have refused anyway. You could have called the police. You could have sacrificed what you love for the greater good. For your principles." Sweetcheeks patted his lips with his napkin. "But you didn't. No, you did what she wanted to get what *you* wanted. How is that different from anyone else?"

Confused, Gurl struggled for an answer. She *was* different, wasn't she? "I'm not going to steal again. You can't make me."

"I can't?" said Sweetcheeks.

"You can't," said Gurl as firmly as she could. And she meant it. Now that Noodle seemed OK, there was nothing they could do to change her mind.

"Wow," said Sweetcheeks. "That sounds like a challenge. I *love* a challenge. John, if you please?"

Again Gurl was lifted and hauled around like a sack of onions. Instead of the opulent room that Gurl expected, however, Sweetcheeks opened the door of a room so dark that she could not see a foot beyond the doorway. "What's in there?" she managed to say before John dumped her on the floor.

"Nothing but black, black and more pitch black," said Sweetcheeks. "This is The Black Box. We can't see you, so it's only fair that you can't see us. After a few days here, I'm sure you'll start to see things my way."

"Never," said Gurl.

"Then you won't see anyone or anything ever again."

He shut the door, closing Gurl up in a world of blackness, blackness so black that it seemed almost thick, like the room had been stuffed with wool. She crawled along the cold cement floor, feeling for the walls. The room was small, little more than a closet, but it didn't mean anything to her. So what? She had broken and entered, stolen and pilfered, flown and crashed. She had been chased by rat men and Punks and cops. They meant to drive her crazy by leaving her alone in the dark, but it wasn't going to work. Didn't they know she was an expert at being alone? Didn't they realise she'd been alone her whole life?

This, she thought, would be a piece of cake.

*

At first she slept a deep and dreamless sleep. Hours later –
or, at least, what felt like hours – she awoke, expecting at least
a little light. But The Black Box was as dark as it had been the
night before and she still couldn't see a thing. And she had to
go to the bathroom. She crawled around the perimeter of the
room until she bumped into a toilet in the corner. Well, that
was one problem taken care of.

She figured that since she was a prisoner, she should keep
herself occupied like prisoners do, so she did sit-ups until it hurt.
Then she sang songs to herself – pop songs and nursery rhymes
and made-up songs about cats and roaches and rat men with
umbrellas. That afternoon, or what she thought was afternoon,
she dozed, half asleep, half awake, her fingers and nose numb
from the chill. Her body began to ache from sitting and from lying
on the hard floor. She got bored, then hungry, then bored again.

She flipped through her file of daydreams, trying to use
them to comfort herself, but her bland, pleasant scenarios of
report cards and family vacations were invaded by albino
alligators and screaming Punks. She remembered being a
baby, looking up at a yellow budgie twittering in a cage, but
that couldn't be right because who could remember being a
baby? Then she was in a court room. A whole bunch of Indians
were there, pointing at her. "Judge," they said, "there she is.
She's the one who stole our island. She's a liar and a thief."

There was a period where she thought she dreamed that someone was screaming, someone very far away, but she woke up the next day (or the day after that?) with a sore throat. She was sleeping so much, her own thoughts come slowly and sluggishly. Was she blending into the blackness, she wondered? Was she becoming like the black around her, or was the black around her becoming more *her*?

On the third (fourth?) day, curled in the corner of The Black Box, she started to count to pass the time. She'd reached 5,692 when she heard her name.

Gurl.

She smiled in the dark. It was nice to hear her name, even if she was just imagining it. Gurl, Gurl, Gurl. It wasn't her real name, she knew that now. She'd surely been named as a baby and must have another name. She supposed she could be anybody. Cornelia. Beatrice. Stephanie. Trixie. And there would be a last name too, the name of her parents. Wasn't it so interesting that people had first and last names?

"Psst, Gurl! Can you hear me?"

Now *that* sounded like a real voice, right outside the door. Feeling her way, she crawled along the wall until she found the door hinges under her fingertips. Her tongue was too thick and dry to speak; she could only moan a little. The inside of her stomach felt tight and scrapey.

"Gurl? Are you all right? They've been watching me like hawks. I couldn't get here till now. Hey, are you there?"

It was Bug.

She hadn't cried when they put her in this box because she thought she was an expert at being alone. But in reality, she hadn't always been alone. She had Noodle. And then she had Bug. He was her friend.

Now Noodle was gone and Bug was a traitor. She huddled by the door of The Black Box and cried, just a little bit, for all the things that she had lost: her name, her family, her dreams, and the only friends she had in the world. She cried, but her body couldn't produce any tears from her dry ducts.

"Gurl! Listen, Gurl. I know you're in there. I'm sorry, OK? I'm so sorry. I didn't know who I was. I told you that and it was the truth. I really didn't know. I was sent to find you, but that monkey took my memories and I was just like everyone else. Just like you."

He paused and Gurl could hear him breathing under the door. "Sweetcheeks is my father, but he's not my dad. My mother ran off when I was three years old. My father pretended I didn't exist. Until he came up with the plan to find you. Then he paid attention. He taught me how to pick locks and do all that stuff with the alarms and the key cards. I learned it to make him happy, but I never wanted to do it. The only thing I ever wanted to do was become a Wing and get out of here."

She listened hard, searching for the lies and the tricks, but heard only Bug. The Bug she knew, the one she trusted.

"We're leadfeet," he was saying. Bug laughed then, a bitter laugh. "Sweetcheeks was right about the roaches because no one in my family has ever been able to fly. We're a bunch of roaches crawling in the walls and under the floor." He punched the door: *wham!* "The only time I could fly was when I didn't know who I was. Now that I know again, I'm grounded. Probably for ever."

She believed that he hadn't known who he was; he had looked as surprised as she was when the monkey spilled its guts. And she knew something that he didn't, something that she needed to tell him. But that something could wait.

She scratched at the door with her fingertips.

"Gurl? I hear you. What is it?"

Gurl tried to moisten her beef jerky tongue. "Bug," she rasped.

"What?"

"Bug!" she said, clearer now.

"Yeah?"

"Pick the stupid lock and get me out of here."

CHAPTER 22

The Tower

BUG PICKED THE LOCK AND opened The Black Box. Gurl was so weak with thirst and hunger that she couldn't get to her feet. He took hold of her wrists, pulled her out of the darkness and rested her on the floor of the hallway. She blinked and tried to focus, but her eyes were unused to the light, and Bug's face was a blur. Bug pressed a cup of water to her lips. She tried to gulp it back, but he slowed her down. "Just take sips or you'll make yourself sick."

After she'd got her fill of the water, she found her voice again. "What took you so long?"

"I wanted to explain," he said. "I thought if I let you out

before I told you the truth, you'd just punch me and run off if you could."

Gurl nodded. "You're probably right," she croaked. "You can see me?"

"Yes."

"I wondered. Wasn't sure if I was invisible or not in there. I couldn't figure out where I ended and the black began."

Bug nodded grimly. "Yeah, I know."

"You know? What do you mean, you know?"

"How many times do you think I've been stuck in there?"

"What? He put his own *son* in The Black Box?"

"You met the guy. I don't know why you sound surprised," Bug said. "Though he never left me in there as long as he left you. Do you think you can stand up?"

She nodded and he pulled her to her feet, grabbing her tightly when she wobbled. "Where's Noodle?"

Bug looked away. "With the rat man. He took her. I couldn't stop him. I tried, but Odd John and Lefty held me down." His hands balled up in fists.

Gurl sighed. "All right, we'll have to find her later."

"How?"

She had no idea, but she thought that they had much bigger worries at the moment. "We'll figure it out, OK? Right now I have to get out of here."

"You mean *we* have to get out of here."

She was going to ask him if he really meant it, if he really wanted to leave his father, but something in his eyes said that telling her once had been painful enough. "Right," Gurl said. "Sorry. *We* have to get out of here."

"Well!" said Sweetcheeks Grabowski, striding down the hallway. "*We* do actually have to get out of here, but I'm not sure if it's the 'we' you two are talking about."

Gurl and Bug turned to run in the other direction, but Odd John blocked their way. He slapped something on her head and strapped it on tight. A hat? A helmet? She tried to turn herself invisible, but found that she couldn't. Was the hat stopping it?

Sweetcheeks tightened the belt on his silk robe. "I see my son remembered his lock-picking lessons well enough. I suppose that's something a father can be proud of. Still, Sylvester, I do wish you would try to remember who your family is."

Bug jerked his chin in Gurl's direction. "She's the closest thing I've got."

Sweetcheeks's lip curled in disgust. "You've turned into some kind of sap. Fine. I'll take you back to Hope House, and you can empty your mind back into one of those monkeys and live happily ever after."

"Better than staying here and listening to you babble about butterflies and roaches," said Bug.

"After I gave you everything I had!"

"You didn't give me anything until I could be useful. And then you gave me a set of lock picks."

"I loved you like a son!"

"I *am* your son. But I hardly ever saw you except when you wanted something from me. And the last time was to send me off to find The Wall."

Sweetcheeks thought about this. "True," he said. "But I don't see why you're so grumpy about it. My father treated me far worse. I would have been grateful to have been spared his company."

"He should have treated you better."

"Somebody's been watching too many talk shows," said Sweetcheeks.

Gurl struggled with the hat, trying to unstrap it. "What is this thing?"

"If you really must know, it's a spaghetti strainer. With a few minor modifications," said Sweetcheeks. "Anti-invisibility modifications. I got it from eBay. Lots of interesting stuff on eBay. Anyway, I'd love to continue this illuminating discussion, but I've got work to do. Gurl, you're coming with me. I was hoping that The Black Box would make you a little more pliant, but it doesn't matter. You'll do what I say."

Gurl tried to appear strong and defiant, though she still felt as weak as a baby bird. "No way."

"Way," said Sweetcheeks cheerfully, taking hold of her arm.

His grip was even stronger than his henchman's, although Gurl hadn't thought that could be possible. "John. My son needs to learn a little respect. I don't think that a couple of toes will be enough to prove my point. What to do, what to do?" He considered Bug. "Oh, well. Take an ear."

"What?" said Gurl. "What do you mean, 'take an ear'? What are you talking about?"

Bug swallowed hard. "Don't worry about me," he said. "He isn't serious."

To Gurl, Sweetcheeks looked extremely serious. "Don't *worry* about you? Did you see the guy hobbling around the Armoury trying to serve pizza?"

"Oh, but he's right," said Sweetcheeks. "You shouldn't worry. Just one itty-bitty little ear. I swear he won't even miss it. And John is quick. When he wants to be." Odd John smiled and took a huge pair of scissors from his back pocket, scissors that looked sharp enough to cut through a telephone pole. He held the scissors against Bug's head, Bug's pink ear between the glinting silver blades.

"Wait!" said Gurl. "Will you leave him alone if I help you?"

"I'll consider it," said Sweetcheeks sweetly.

A bead of sweat formed on Bug's upper lip. "Gurl, don't believe anything he says. That's just what he wants!"

"The girl isn't dumb, boy," Sweetcheeks said. "She can see that on her own."

"I'll help you," said Gurl. "I'll help you do whatever you want to do. Let him go."

"You heard the young lady, John. Let him go." Odd John pulled the scissors away from Bug's head. "But we don't want him going too far, so I think it's The Tower for my dear son."

"What's The Tower?" Gurl demanded.

"Nothing like The Black Box," Sweetcheeks told her. "And, trust me, no one will bother him there."

Gurl didn't like the sound of The Tower. "I want him to come with us," she said. "So that I know he's OK."

"Won't be possible," Sweetcheeks said impatiently. "Now, he can stay the way he is or he can be clipped down to size. Your choice."

Gurl thought about Bug's skill with locks and couldn't imagine a room that could hold him if he didn't want to be held. "Fine. I'll come. He stays here. *With* all his body parts."

"Deal," Sweetcheeks said. "John?"

John grabbed Bug around the waist and lifted him as easily as other people lift gallons of milk. She looked at Bug, his face red and furious, and she remembered what she wanted to tell him when she was locked in The Black Box. "One second," she said, "I want to say something to Bug. In private."

"Fine, fine," said Sweetcheeks, hauling her over to Bug. "Whisper."

Gurl put her lips to Bug's – thankfully still attached – ear. "You told me that you can't fly, but you can. You have to remember that."

"Fly? He can't fly!" said Sweetcheeks.

"You weren't supposed to listen!" said Gurl.

"There are no secrets in my lair. And there's no one in my family that can fly."

"*He* can," she told Sweetcheeks. "He can fly higher than anyone." She turned to Bug. "Don't forget it. Don't let anyone tell you that you can't."

"Honey, you should write a self-help book and make a million dollars. In the mean time, we've got to get going."

"Wait!" said Bug.

"Oh, what now?" said Sweetcheeks.

"I just want to give her something. To remember me." Bug reached into his pocket and pulled out Mrs Terwiliger's monkey, handing it to Gurl.

"Ironic," Sweetcheeks said dryly. "Lefty!"

Lefty came down the hallway. "What is it, Boss?"

Sweetcheeks thrust Gurl at the moustached man. "Hang on to this for a minute."

A note about Sweetcheeks' lair: it was a small city unto itself. Besides the Armoury and The Black Box, the lair boasted a restaurant-sized kitchen, a billiard room, a banquet hall, a movie theatre, a gym (Pilates classes on Wednesdays), a recording studio (Sweetcheeks was recording a CD of jazz favourites), several dozen bedrooms (with maid and laundry service), and, last but not least, The Tower.

Unlike most towers, Sweetcheeks's tower was a concrete column with most of its considerable height hidden underground. As a matter of fact, if you were lost in Chinatown and happened to stumble upon its one dingy window, you would think that you were looking into the basement of a noodle shop, not down a long vertical shaft burrowing seven storeys beneath your feet.

"I wasn't really going to have John cut off your ear," said Sweetcheeks after Bug had been sealed inside The Tower by a barred mechanical door (no pickable locks). "I would never do something like that to you. I just needed to convince that girl to do what I wanted. You *know* that."

Bug rolled his eyes.

"Come on, no hard feelings?"

"You kidnapped my friend," said Bug flatly. "You're putting me in a cage."

"It's not a cage," said Sweetcheeks. "It's just a very tall room."

"With bars."

"It's just for a little while, Sylvester. For your own good." Sweetcheeks sighed. "I admire your determination, but you need to learn a little self-discipline. You've got to start being realistic. You can't run around freeing all my prisoners. It's not right."

"*You're* not right."

"Negative, negative. You're always so negative. That's why we don't get along."

"Yeah," said Bug. "That's why."

"Be that way," said Sweetcheeks, turning to leave. Then stopped and turned back, blue eyes twinkling as if he'd just heard the funniest joke. "Here's something you can do to kill some time. Look. Way up there. See that tiny light? That's a window, oh, seven storeys up. Your girlfriend says you can fly. Why don't you give it a shot?"

Bug punched the bars, and Sweetcheeks shook his head in wonder. "Sylvester, you're my son. Whether you want to be or not. It's time you accepted that."

Bug said nothing.

"A Flying Grabowski," Sweetcheeks said, chuckling. "Sounds like a circus act. You have to admit that it *is* funny."

"Hilarious," Bug said, rubbing his knuckles.

In exasperation, Sweetcheeks blew a lock of golden hair from his brow. "There's no talking to you. Come on, John. Let's find The Richest Man in the Universe. He owes me." He wagged a finger at Bug. "I'll see you later. I hope you can work out your priorities before I get back." Then he and Odd John left Bug in his seven-storey jail all alone.

When his father was out of earshot, Bug punched the bars and then the walls a couple of times. He looked up at the tiny window, just a faint smudge of light at the top of the world, like a distant star. He had to get up there, he had to. There was no other way out.

He moved to the centre of the room, crouched and sprang. But he knew even as he went through the motions that he couldn't do it. His head was a wrecking ball, his body a slab of stone and his feet rooted tree stumps. *Wham!* He hammered at the walls in frustration. *Wham! Wham! Wham!* It wasn't fair. Why did he get a taste of the thing he wanted most in the world if he could never do it again, if he couldn't do it when he needed to? He'd even tried to fly once in the bathroom of the Palace Hotel and couldn't get his toes off the tiles.

You are my son whether you want to be or not.

Bug slid down the wall and sat on the floor. Who did he think he was? Some kind of hero? Even the name he called himself, Bug! Roach, bug, same thing. He never got away from his father, even when a monkey made him forget who he was.

Bug put his head in his hands. Gurl had reminded him that he did fly at least one time. But how in the world did he do that? He couldn't figure it out. Was it the zoo, the dancing pretzel vendors, Noodle or even Gurl?

Or maybe, he thought, it was all of it. How that stuff crowded his head until he forgot that he was an orphan, forgot that he had a life before he was an orphan, forgot that he forgot.

Forgot that he forgot.

He sat up straighter. Could he do that all by himself? Forget his father, forget that he couldn't fly, and then forget about forgetting?

Sure, genius. That'll work.

He tugged at his fringe until it hurt. This was so stupid, like that dumb fairy tale with the girl trapped in the tower. Rapunzel. Yeah, that was it. Ole Rapunzel waiting for her prince. Except it wasn't like that at all. He wasn't good at *waiting*, he was good at *doing*. He could punch things and unlock things and find things and escape things, but he couldn't sit here waiting for some lame prince in tights to come and rescue him (even if there had been a lame prince wandering around Chinatown looking for some bug boy to save).

Plink!

Startled, Bug got to his feet. "Uh... Dad?" he said, the word "dad" sour on his tongue. He walked over to the barred door. "Who's there? Hello?"

"Hell. Oh," said the rat man. His mouth, full of filed teeth, looked like a shark's and he had something hidden underneath his trench coat.

Momentarily, Bug was overjoyed that he was behind bars, but he backed up a step, just in case Mr Ratface wanted to plunge an arm between them. "How did you get in here?"

"Heeeeeere."

"Yes, you're here. Don't tell me that *you're* my prince."

"Prince?" the rat man said. "Hell. Oh."

"Um, yeah. OK. What do you want?"

"Kitty!" the rat man said. He opened his trench coat to reveal Noodle, who yawned.

At least, thought Bug, it didn't seem as if he wanted to hurt Noodle and it didn't seem that Noodle was scared. "Yes, you've got the kitty. Good for you."

"Kitty," said the rat man, gently petting the cat. "Kittykittykitty."

Noodle mewled and the rat man made a noise, somewhere between a growl and a moan. Then, reluctantly, he put the cat down on the ground. Noodle wound herself around the rat man's legs before slipping through the bars in the door.

Bug reached down to pet the cat, who was now meowing in earnest. "What?" Bug said. "What is it?"

Noodle mewled and meowed and squeaked, plucking at Bug's trouser leg with her claws until Bug sat down. The cat crawled up into his lap and began to purr.

"That's it?" said Bug. "You wanted to take a nap?" He looked at the rat man, who was now observing them with the most sorrowful expression Bug had ever seen. "What's going on?"

"Going," said the rat man sadly.

"Okeydokey," said Bug, scratching the dozing cat behind the ears. The cat kept purring and Bug kept scratching, and the more Bug scratched the more the cat purred. The purring got louder and louder until it drowned out all of Bug's other thoughts, chased them out of his mind. Instead, odd questions without answers filled his head: *If a tree falls in a forest and no one's around, does it make a sound?*

"I don't know," murmured Bug. He closed his eyes, drawing the cat close. He began to feel sleepy himself, to feel like he was drifting off, drifting away, drifting up.

Up?

He opened his eyes and saw that he and Noodle were rising gently like a cloud on a warm breeze, and that the window in The Tower, the star at the top of the world, was getting closer. With the cat's purr buzzing in his ears, Bug reached for the light.

CHAPTER 23

Supa Dupa Fly

MARDI GRAS, NEW YEAR'S EVE, Halloween, the Olympics. Put them all together and you still wouldn't equal the sparkling city's annual Flyfest.

Gurl had never been to the Flyfest before. Despite the fact that Sweetcheeks gripped her arm like a tourniquet, despite her anger over Bug and Noodle, despite the fact that she still wore a "modified" spaghetti strainer on her head (which she was positive looked ridiculous and she wasn't wrong), she couldn't help but be just a little bit excited. The avenues all around Central Park had been blocked off and costumed people – clowns, cows, cats, cuckoos – surged freely down the sidewalks, waiting for the opening parade. In the meantime, jugglers performed complicated tricks with flying squirrels, vendors sold parrot-sized crowns and pin-on propellers, and everyone drank hot cider and Kangaroo Kola ("Puts a little spring in your step!"™). The crisp autumn air pinkened cheeks, reddened noses, and made the crowd a warm and friendly place to be.

"Excuse me, pardon me, excuse me, pardon me," said Sweetcheeks, elbowing his way through the crowds. Though the festival itself had venues all around the park, the big event, the flying, would take place right in front of the art museum, on the steps to which the main stage had been set up for the judges. Rows of seats flanked both sides of the museum steps, and Sweetcheeks approached a group of college boys sitting nearest to them. "Are these seats taken?"

One of the boys, a beefy lunk with piggy eyes said, "We're sitting in them, aren't we?"

"Not for long," said Sweetcheeks, ever so sweetly. With that, Odd John stepped in front of the college boys, snipping his shiny scissors and grinning with his baby teeth. For good measure, he reached up and flicked the silver tab on his zipper head.

Mr Beefy went grey. "We were just leaving," he said, shoving his friends out of the way.

"Oh, thank you!" said Sweetcheeks. He smiled as they scurried off. "That was awfully nice of them."

"Awfully," said Gurl.

Sweetcheeks sat, pulling Gurl down into the seat next to him. He had John stay close but waved the rest of his men off. He pulled some Twinkies from his pocket and offered them to Gurl. She didn't want to take the snack cakes, but she was too hungry to resist. She ripped open the package and stuffed one into her mouth.

"Would you like a Kangaroo Kola to go with your Twinkies?" Sweetcheeks asked.

"No."

"A pin-on propeller?"

"No."

"How about some Weightless Water?"

"It doesn't work on leadfeet," said Gurl irritably.

"I know," said Sweetcheeks. "But we can pretend."

"I don't want to pretend," said Gurl. "Why are we here?"

Sweetcheeks rubbed his fingertips along his smooth jawline. "We're waiting for someone. In the mean time, we are going to enjoy the parade. Oh, look! I can see the first float coming!"

The jugglers stopped juggling, the vendors stopped vending and the costumed crowd gasped. The first float was shaped like a wedding cake, except it was made entirely of the whitest doves whose feet had been affixed – painlessly and not permanently – to the surface of the float. The doves' beating wings carried the float slowly down the street while people dressed in sequined tuxedos walked alongside the float and made sure the whole thing didn't just fly off.

"Isn't that amazing!" said Sweetcheeks.

"Yes," said Gurl, forgetting for the moment why she was there and whom she was with. "What do you think will be next?"

Sweetcheeks' eyes sparkled. "I have no idea! Maybe some invisible dancing girls?"

"I don't like you," said Gurl. "You're a horrible person."

"Yes. But I do work at it."

After the dove wedding cake came an enormous bat balloon, followed by a balloon in the shape of a winged fairy. The bumblebee, the oldest balloon float in the parade, drifted by, his canvas hide covered with sad but somehow dignified patches.

The sounds of drums filled the air and someone shouted "The Mynahs! The Mynahs are coming!" The Mynah Bird Choir, lined up in shiny black rows on a float of red roses, started to sing. First came a solemn and eerily beautiful rendition of "The Star-Spangled Banner". But as they passed the rows of seats, the music suddenly blared into a pounding rhythm you could feel in your feet. The crowd screamed and clapped as the Mynahs rapped to "Supa Dupa Fly".

As The Mynahs' music faded, the aerobats came into view. Their float was a long, simple platform with a spring from which they would launch themselves two storeys into the air, twirling and twisting in backbreaking positions before landing in the arms of one of their comrades. With each launch, the crowd oohed and ahhed in a weird sort of unison.

"Now," said Sweetcheeks, "comes the really good part."

Somewhere behind them, someone began to chant: "Wings, Wings, Wings, Wings, Wings!" Soon everyone in the stands and packing the sidewalks had joined in, clapping their hands and stomping their feet. Gurl herself felt swept away by it and found herself mouthing the word too.

"There they are!" breathed Sweetcheeks.

Flying in a straight line, in a standing position, one hundred of the city's best Wings filed into the competition area. Each of them wore a flight suit, a fluorescent unitard with a hood, designed to cut down on wind resistance (and to make them look an awful lot like superheroes). They broke into two lines, stretching their bodies flat so that they were parallel to the ground. Still moving rather slowly, they arranged themselves into a V-formation, like a flock of brightly coloured birds.

"They're not moving very fast," said Gurl. "Bug could fly faster than that."

"Bug? Oh! You mean Sylvester? Sylvester couldn't fly if his life depended on it."

Gurl tucked her hands inside her sweatshirt and felt for the little monkey that Bug had given her. She wondered if it was the only thing she had left of Bug, if she would ever see him or Noodle again.

The Wings changed formations again, from a V to a circle. They flew around and around and around, speeding up, until watching them was like watching the spin cycle on a washing machine.

"Whoa," said Gurl.

"I told you that this was the best part," Sweetcheeks said.

The Wings spiralled upwards in a cyclone, stirring a fierce wind that whipped everyone's hair and stung their eyes. Up and up and up they went, two storeys, three storeys, four, five, ten! The crowd held a collective breath as the Wings soared higher and higher and then, suddenly, one of them, the lead, dived for the ground. This Wing hurled himself at the earth as if intent on pasting himself to the tarmac below.

"He's going to crash!" cried Gurl.

"Watch," Sweetcheeks told her.

Just as it looked like he was surely going to hit the ground, the Wing stopped, his fingertips a mere foot from the pavement. The crowd erupted in a roar that could be heard around the city as the rest of the Wings fell, all of them stopping short just feet away from their own dooms, all of them holding themselves vertical like quills in inkwells. Then they flipped to their feet and bowed.

"Wasn't that amazing!" the speakers boomed and the crowd looked up to the main stage, where the mayor, Igor "Iggy" Fleishman, stood in front of the microphone. "Fabulous work!" He waited until the clapping and stomping and screaming died down and said. "Now, for those of you who don't know me by sight, my name is Iggy Fleishman and I'm the mayor of this incredible city!"

The crowd erupted in waves of applause again, not for their mayor really, but because they were giddy from the show and overcaffeinated on Kangaroo Kola.

"While our Wings take a little rest," the mayor continued, "I want to introduce the rest of our illustrious judges. Now you know our first judge as Major Wendell Wingburn in the hit movie epic *Wingworld*. Let's give a hand to actor Peter Paul Allen." A dark-haired man with a scraggly goatee and artfully dirty hair walked on to the stage, waving at the audience.

"What do you know? I always thought he'd be taller," said Sweetcheeks.

"Thanks for coming, Peter Paul," said Mayor Fleishman as the actor sat down. "Our next judge should be no surprise. A champion Wing, he won the Golden Eagle three times, in 1991, 1992 and 1993. He remains the world record holder for fastest Wing sprint. I'm thrilled to introduce Nathan Johnson!" Nathan, a slim man with close-cropped curls and deep brown skin, flew from a second-storey window of a nearby building to the stage, much to the delight of the crowd.

"Glad to have you here, glad to have you," said the mayor, shaking his hand. Nathan grinned, his white teeth blinding (which was not surprising since Nathan Johnson was the official spokesman for Mega Blast® Tooth Gel).

"Our third judge is also no stranger to you all. She's a singer, actress, model and entrepreneur. You probably hear her tunes on the radio every day, and maybe you dance to them wearing clothes from her brand-new clothing line: Poison! Let's bring out pop sensation Rosy B.!" Girls in the audience screamed and wailed as Rosy B., wearing her own leopard-print, hoodless version of the flight suit, posed for the cameras, flipping her honey-coloured hair and looking off into the distance, as if she found all this attention rather boring.

"Last," said the mayor, "but certainly not least, I'd like to bring out a couple whose support makes this yearly event possible. Please give a warm round of applause for Sol and Bunny Bloomington, The Richest Couple in the Universe!"

Again the crowd whooped and hollered. A man, grey-haired and plain, guided a thin, exceedingly pale woman on to the stage. Both wore casual but expensive clothes and smiled at the audience, but Gurl thought that they looked distracted somehow, maybe even a little sad. She remembered what Bug had said the day they saw the rich man in his penthouse: "Rich people aren't sad. They're rich!" But that man had looked sad and this one looked sad too.

Gurl squinted. Actually, now that she thought about it, they looked an awful lot like the same man.

Sweetcheeks watched her reaction carefully. "So, do you recognise him?"

"No," said Gurl. "I don't think so."

"Are you sure? You should."

"Why? Because he's The Richest Man in the Universe?"

"No, silly," said Sweetcheeks, patting her on her absurd spaghetti strainer helmet. "Because he's your father."

CHAPTER 24

The Big Fat Hairy Fib

FIRST GURL WAS SPEECHLESS. AND then she wasn't.

"What?" she shrieked.

"It's true," said Sweetcheeks. "Sol and Bunny Bloomington are your parents."

"I don't believe it."

"Would I lie to you?"

"Yes."

"About this?"

"Yes."

Sweetcheeks had the nerve to look indignant. "Well, this time I'm not lying. Just look at them up there. Look at Bunny

Bloomington. Tell me that you don't see yourself."

Gurl looked at them up there. At the kind but worn face of Sol Bloomington, at the dishwater blonde hair and pale eyes of Bunny. She thought about how the man pounded at the window when he'd seen her and Bug hovering outside. Like he'd recognised her.

"It's true?" she said. "Really true?"

"Yes, I'm afraid it is."

"I don't understand," Gurl mumbled.

"You mean you don't understand why they're up there and you're down here with me?"

Gurl nodded glumly.

"Isn't it obvious?" said Sweetcheeks. "They didn't want you."

"They didn't—" said Gurl.

"Want you," finished Sweetcheeks.

"But—"

"But what? You're going to have to stand up and face it, Gurl. People can be terribly cruel. Just look at me and my own son. Some would say that sending him off on a mission to search a bunch of orphanages to find you wasn't very nice. But at least I didn't send him to the orphanage *for ever*. That's what the Bloomingtons did to you, you know. They never wanted children. They never needed children. You were just an unpleasant surprise. You were born in secret and then given away just as secretly."

"How do you know all this?"

"I have many sources," said Sweetcheeks. "Mrs Terwiliger was the one who gave me most of the details."

"I think you're lying," said Gurl, crossing her arms over her chest. "I think something happened. I got lost somehow. Or kidnapped! That's it. Someone kidnapped me," she said, remembering what the monkey had said to Bug back in the theatre days ago. "Why else would they look so sad?"

"Because Airborne Industries stock is down a couple of points. That means that Solomon there is just a wee bit less rich today. Makes him grumpy." When Sweetcheeks saw that Gurl looked sceptical, he said, "Why would I lie about this? I have nothing to gain."

"I still don't believe you."

"You don't want to believe me? Don't. I couldn't care less. But," he said, crouching a little so that he could look into her eyes. "Consider this: he's The Richest Man in the Universe. If you were lost or kidnapped, don't you think he would have spent every penny he had to find you? That is, if he really loved you?"

Gurl opened her mouth and closed it again, silenced by his logic. It couldn't be true, it couldn't! But then, of course, it could. People gave up children every day, why not Sol and Bunny Bloomington? Maybe they were too busy doing rich people's things – judging contests and giving parties and whatever else rich people did – to care about her. Maybe she just got in the way.

"If I were you, I'd hate his guts," Sweetcheeks was saying. "You didn't ask to be born, did you? And yet here you are, the one who gets punished for it. Left all alone with a woman with an unnatural affection for mechanical monkeys. Alone and invisible to the world. Used and abused by criminal geniuses for their dastardly deeds."

"Oh, shut up already." She was not a normal girl; she would never be a normal girl. All her stupid daydreams about ice cream and beach trips would never, ever come true. Gurl swiped at her eyes when tears threatened to fall, unwilling to let Sweetcheeks see her cry. "What dastardly deed do you want me to do?"

"That's a good girl. Take life's hits and push on." Sweetcheeks motioned to Odd John and the three of them slipped off the seats. "Gurl, your dear old dad has something that I want. A pen, a particular pen that he keeps with him at all times. It's a very special pen with very special capabilities."

"If the pen's so special, why does he keep it with him? Why doesn't he put it in a safe somewhere?"

"Mr Bloomington's a little old-fashioned. Doesn't quite trust anyone but himself. He likes to keep the pen with him so that he can be sure it doesn't get into the wrong hands."

"Like yours," said Gurl.

"Ha! Like mine! Oh, that was *funny*, Gurl."

"Sure. A hoot," Gurl said.

"Like I was saying, we're going to approach the main stage. Then I'm going to remove this helmet you've been wearing – which really does make you look *so* silly, I'm sorry to say. You'll turn yourself and me invisible. John here will create some sort of ruckus to divert the attention of Solomon's bodyguards. And then you and I will grab Solomon, reach into his jacket and steal the pen. Do you have all that? Do I need to go over it again?"

"Remind me about what you'll do if I don't do this?"

"Oh, you know. Kill you, kill a whole bunch of these people, blah blah blah. Did you happen to catch the balloons in the parade? The bat, the fairy and the bee?

"Yeah."

"They're moored over there, right by the entrance to the park, see?"

"Yeah, so?"

"So, the bee's filled with poison. All I have to do is have Odd John here pop it and I can take out half the city. Do you want to be responsible for that? Over a teeny-tiny little pen that you can steal in a second?"

Stealing! Always stealing. After all Mrs Terwiliger's errands she hated being forced to steal yet another thing. But she was so shocked and upset at the revelation that a) she had parents,

b) they were The Richest Couple in the Universe and c) they didn't want her, that she couldn't get angry enough to fight. Even if she did fight, what good would it do? Sweetcheeks would just go around killing people or at least chopping off random pieces of them, and Bug would still be stuck in The Tower, and Noodle would still be gone. Was stealing one pen such a big deal? Especially after everything she'd done before? She was already a thief. Already a liar. This wouldn't change a thing.

"OK," said Gurl, finally.

"I am so glad to hear that. Remarkably glad," said Sweetcheeks. "Let's go. The Wing races are just about to start."

The three of them – Gurl, Sweetcheeks and Odd John – melted into the crowd, so intent on the Bloomingtons that they didn't see the peculiar little man with the grass for hair following close behind.

CHAPTER 25

Bugbears and Bugaboos

BUG FLEW AS HARD AND as fast as he could through the nearly deserted city streets. If Gurl did what Sweetcheeks wanted, whatever that was, he still wouldn't let her go. He would make her his personal crime slave. He might chop off her toes or her ears and make her serve his men pizza.

His stupid father and his stupid stories! His stupid father and his stupid crimes! Bug hated it all. What a dumb accident a family was. Some people got lucky, some not so lucky – and some people got the booby prize. Grinning, golden, corrupt Sweetcheeks Grabowski had to be the biggest, boobiest prize of all.

Bug flew harder, holding on to Noodle as tightly as possible without squashing her. Even with the wind rushing in his ears, he could hear music and applause and knew he was almost there. He wondered if he should slow down, blend in with the crowd, sneak up on his father. Then he wondered if he ought to fly in full speed and whisk Gurl off like Superman.

Just as he was trying to decide which method of rescue might be more successful, something whooshed by him on his right, something that almost hit him. He veered left just in time.

In the air next to him, a man wearing a shiny pink unitard yelled, "What do you think you're doing, kid? Get out of the way!"

Another Wing flew by, this one just above him. "Move it, boy!"

Bug looked around in confusion and saw that he was surrounded by dozens of zooming Wings wearing fluorescent costumes. He'd flown right into the middle of a Wing race! The Wings were flying around a circular "track" that had been created using very tall, thin rubber bumpers, which had been placed around the centre and perimeter of the avenue in front of the museum.

"Sorry!" Bug yelled. He tucked his chin into his chest and flew even faster, jetting out in front of the pack of Wings.

"Hey!" said a voice behind him. Someone caught his ankle and Bug kicked his leg.

"Let go!" Bug shouted.

The pink-suited Wing flew up next to him, his face a mask of fury. "Get out of here!"

"I'm *trying*!" said Bug.

Up ahead, right in front of the main stage, the racecourse veered into a turn so that the racers could make another lap. Bug shifted right to get himself out of the race, but another Wing, this one wearing a silver unitard with lightning bolts on the hood, blocked his way. Stuck between the pink on the left and the silver on the right, both squeezing him between their muscled shoulders, Bug was forced to make the turn along with the rest of the pack.

Over the loudspeaker, a voice said, "Wait a minute! What's that? We seem to have a newcomer to the races today! Folks, this is the most irregular thing I've ever seen! Will we have to start the race again? Will he be disqualified? Who *is* this guy?"

At the announcement, Gurl, Sweetcheeks and Odd John whipped around just in time to see Bug trapped between a pile of Wings flying off in the other direction.

"Bugbears and bugaboos. This is an unusual development," said Sweetcheeks, clearly annoyed.

Gurl lifted her chin in triumph. "I *told* you he could fly. And don't call him a bugbear, whatever that is."

"A bugbear is an annoyance. A bugaboo is something that one is afraid of. Not something *I'm* afraid of, however, but something Sylvester certainly will be. John? When we're done here, I want you to go out there and bring me my son."

John grinned.

"But you won't hurt him!" shouted Gurl.

"Oh, he won't hurt him," said Sweetcheeks, grabbing Gurl by the shoulders. "As long as you get me that pen."

He spun Gurl around to face the main stage, laughing. "Now that I think about it, Sylvester's appearance couldn't be more perfect. It's the ideal distraction. Look at Solomon Bloomington's bodyguards!"

On stage, surrounding The Richest Man in the Universe, a dozen black-suited men – all wearing dark glasses, all with little microphones in their ears – had tensed up, focused on the strange new boy in the race. Soon, Gurl knew, Odd John would appear somewhere in the mix and the guards' attention would be even more diverted.

Sweetcheeks pushed her through the crowd towards the stairs to the main stage. Though she threw pleading looks at people in the crowd, no one paid any attention to the handsome man and the girl in the spaghetti strainer hat. When they reached the staircase, Sweetcheeks paused, glancing left and right to make sure that all eyes were on the race. Sure that they were, he put an arm around Gurl's shoulders to keep her still and then removed the hat.

"Now," said Sweetcheeks, whispering in her ear, "you're going to turn both of us invisible. We are going to climb those stairs, sneak onstage behind all the judges and slip between the bodyguards. You are going to reach into Solomon Bloomington's jacket and take the pen. John will pull us away from the bodyguards before they figure out what's happening. Do you understand? Nod if you do."

Gurl nodded, her eyes on the race. The flyers had made another lap, yet Bug still seemed to be trapped in a pack of racers.

"All right," said Sweetcheeks. "Make us disappear."

Gurl's mind raced. If she didn't do what he asked, he might kill her. And Bug. And maybe everyone here. She would never get to ask her parents why they gave her up. She would never find out who she could have been.

Sweetcheeks tightened his arm around her shoulders. "Turn us invisible. Now."

Seeing no other choice, Gurl did as she was told. Sweetcheeks's hold on her shoulders relaxed. He gripped her arm and pushed her forward.

She was about to climb the steps when she caught a deep raspy voice, a familiar voice. "I am *so* tired of him. He is *such* a fibber."

A man leaned against one of the banisters, talking on a cell phone. Thin. Dark hair. Large, square glasses and a grey wool coat. He looked like everyone and no one.

"Did you catch the last lie he told?" the man said into the phone. "Yeah. I couldn't believe it either, it was so ridiculous."

Gravelly voice. Fake Britishy accent.

Jules!

"Such. A. Fibber."

Gurl hesitated, listening. Jules wasn't looking at her at all, didn't even seem to notice her. But she knew he could see her. And she felt somehow that he was trying to send her a message. An important message.

"You can't believe anything he says about anyone."

You can't believe anything he says about anyone. He who? Gurl felt Sweetcheeks shove at her impatiently and she put her foot on the first step. Jules probably meant Sweetcheeks. Sweetcheeks was the fibber. Sweetcheeks was the one you couldn't believe. Sweetcheeks was the one who said her parents didn't want her, but what if it wasn't true?

Though she resisted as long as she could, Sweetcheeks pushed her up the steps. But not before she heard Jules say one last thing: "I, for one, won't tolerate any more of his monkeyshines. He's got a lot of explaining to do. As a matter of fact, I think he wants to spill his guts. I think he's just waiting for the right moment to do it."

Before Gurl could figure out what Jules was talking about, she was propelled across the stage. She and Sweetcheeks moved behind the bodyguards as the loudspeakers boomed: "I don't know who this kid is, but he's a heck of a flyer!"

The crowd roared. Solomon's bodyguards left the stage to get a closer look at the suspicious newcomer, while the one guard left stepped forward to watch the Wings' progress. Next to him, Gurl could see Solomon Bloomington's grey head, his back. There he was, her father, sitting there, watching a race, like it was any other day. And her mother, absently patting her hair. Did they ever think of her? For a minute she thought about running forward and hugging them, telling them who she was, warning them about Sweetcheeks – but she knew that could get them killed. Better to steal the pen. Better to save them.

Again Sweetcheeks pushed her forward, past the bodyguard. Gurl steeled herself and crept up behind Solomon. Luckily, he had removed his jacket and hung it over the back of his chair; he wouldn't even notice when she took the pen. She moved around the side of the chair, crouching between Sol and Bunny. She almost cried when she saw their faces, not because they were remarkable faces, but because they were so ordinary.

Sweetcheeks poked at her back. Carefully, Gurl reached into the pocket of the jacket. As soon as she touched the fabric, the whole thing disappeared. She hoped no one would notice. Quickly, she felt around for the pen. Nothing. Maybe she had the wrong pocket? She moved around the back of the chair and tried the other pocket. As she crouched, she could feel the monkey Bug had given her pressing against her hipbone.

Sweetcheeks couldn't wait any longer. "Do you have it?" he whispered.

Solomon and Bunny Bloomington turned and looked behind them. "Your jacket!" Bunny gasped. "Where's your jacket? What's going on? Who's there?"

The bodyguard pulled his gun, glancing around wildly but seeing no one. Nathan Johnson frowned, Peter Paul Allen yawned and Rosy B. looked about as bored as she had when she was introduced.

"Do you have it? I know you do!" Sweetcheeks said again, not caring who heard him. "Come on, give it to me!"

Gurl finally realised what Jules had been trying to tell her. "Yes," said Gurl. "I do have it." She reached into her pocket, pulled out the tiny monkey and pushed it into Sweetcheeks's hand.

CHAPTER 26

Sweetcheeks Spills

GURL DIDN'T KNOW EXACTLY WHAT happened, but she felt Sweetcheeks lunge towards the guard and managed to wrench her arm from his grasp. Instantly, the gangster appeared on the stage, holding the monkey in one hand and a gun in the other. Bunny clutched at her heart in shock and the now-disarmed bodyguard shouted, but Solomon Bloomington merely raised an eyebrow.

"Hello, there," he said, putting up a hand to stay his guard. "That's a nice monkey you have."

"What's going on?" said Peter Paul Allen. "Who is that guy with the monkey? I've only been paid to sit here for two hours, you know, so if this is going to take a long time—"

"Oh, shut up," said Nathan Johnson. "Can't you see the man's got a gun?"

The bored expression dropped off Rosy B.'s face when she saw Sweetcheeks. She jumped into Nathan's lap (much to his surprise because Rosy B. was supposed to be dating Peter Paul Allen).

Mayor Iggy Fleishman glanced behind him, concern written on his face, but betrayed none of it in his words to the crowd. "Only five more laps to go in the race, folks!" he shouted into the microphone. "Who do you think's going to win?"

The monkey shook its maracas and Sweetcheeks's eyes went dreamy. "Monkey," said Sweetcheeks, seemingly in a stupor. "My father never loved me," he boomed.

"That's too bad," said Solomon, not surprised.

"I didn't love him either," Sweetcheeks said. No whispering for Sweetcheeks; he announced these things as if he'd been waiting all his life to do so.

Solomon nodded gravely. "Yes. Anything else?"

The monkey shook his maracas encouragingly and Sweetcheeks brought the monkey close. "I could have been a supermodel," he said. "A product manager. Even a minor politician, like a mayor."

Iggy Fleishman shot a look of annoyance behind him. "Yes, it's hard to believe what's going on here today, folks!"

"But I'm bad," said Sweetcheeks. "A spoiled egg, a rotten apple, a bad seed dropped from a twisted family tree. My ancestry was riddled with crooks, gangsters, thieves and liars. With an emphasis on liars." He waved the gun and Rosy B. tightened her arms around Nathan Johnson's neck, something that Peter Paul Allen didn't seem to appreciate.

"My big problem," said Sweetcheeks, "is that I lack patience. I simply can't wait for anything. Delayed gratification? Why delay it? When I was younger, it was even worse. I had no interest in waiting for my father – Tommy 'The Trigger' Grabowski – to kick the bucket so that I would inherit the family 'business'. No, I wanted to make my own fortune, and fast. I knew all about The Wall from stories my father told me. I thought: 'What if I had The Wall all to myself? Imagine all the things I could steal! The Hope Diamond! The original Declaration of Independence! Why, I could kidnap the queen of England!'"

"Is the queen of England coming? What's he talking about?" said Peter Paul Allen. "Could someone please call the police?"

Sweetcheeks swayed a little on the stage, pointing the gun in Peter Paul's direction. "Can it, Shorty. I'm talking to the monkey."

Peter Paul opened his mouth and then shut it again, having wisely decided to can it.

"Like I was telling this monkey here, after my wife left me, I was dating this girl. She was a nanny to a rich family. Liked to tell me all sorts of stories about them. I didn't think much of her job till she told me about the weird baby she was watching. Said that the kid would disappear every once in a while. That she'd put the baby in her crib and the next time she looked in, the baby would be gone. She thought she was going crazy, but I knew what was what. That baby was The Wall. I wanted to get her while she was still young, so I could shape and mould her into a nasty – but invisible – little criminal."

"Charming," Sol said. "Go on."

"We went to the rich guy's house." He looked blearily at Sol and Bunny Bloomington. "*Your* house."

"Sol," said Bunny. "What is he talking about? What does he mean?"

But Sweetcheeks was on a roll. "I waited until you went shopping one day. We broke into the service entrance of the building, disabled all the alarms and picked the locks. I am an excellent lock picker."

"I'm sure you are," murmured Solomon, his face growing red with anger. The normally pale and mild-mannered Bunny looked as if she might leap out of her chair and choke the life out of Sweetcheeks herself. They did not, thought Gurl gratefully, seem like people who didn't want their own daughter.

"We overpowered the nanny," Sweetcheeks was saying. "Oh, not in the way you think. We overpowered her *financially*.

We gave her some bucks and sent her back to Russia. Then we brought The Wall to a safe house. She was mine for three whole hours." Sweetcheeks laughed. "Can you believe it, monkey? Three hours. We bought her a crib, put her inside it, she went down for a nap and then poof! She disappeared. My men and I got on our hands and knees and patted down every inch of the room, but we couldn't find her. We thought she'd fallen out of a window and died or something. Anyway, that was the end of my big plans."

"How tragic for you," said Solomon Bloomington through clenched teeth.

"Or so I thought. Just a few days later I heard through one of my men that a homeless woman passing by the safe house had heard a baby crying. She found the baby inside. She fed it food from the Dumpsters behind an Italian restaurant for a few days, but then she decided she couldn't keep it after all. So she brought the baby to an orphanage. By the time the cops got wind of this story, she couldn't remember which orphanage she'd brought the baby to and the cops didn't believe her anyway. My dumb luck."

"Dumb," said Solomon. "Yes."

"A few months after that, my father, Tommy 'The Trigger' Grabowski, got sick. I thought he was on his deathbed, so I told him how I'd kidnapped The Wall and how I lost her. He laughed and laughed, and told me I had feathers for brains.

That I hadn't been paying attention to the old gangster stories like I was supposed to. That I was a moron if I thought that the most valuable thing that Solomon Bloomington possessed was The Wall." Sweetcheeks shook his head sadly. "No, my father never loved me. But I showed him. I went to visit this man called The Professor. You've heard of him?"

Solomon Bloomington nodded. "I thought he was just a myth."

"No, no myth. Real. Lives in an apartment below a dry cleaner's. Lots of cats." Sweetcheeks screwed up his face in disgust. "I went to ask him about The Wall and he knew what I was talking about all right, but he was more trouble than he was worth. And the map he gave me was useless." He shook his head violently, as if reliving a particularly disturbing memory. "But none of that matters. I'm here now. I've got The Wall. And I've got the pen. I can rewrite history any way I want to. I can write my own future."

"You don't have a *pen*," said Peter Paul Allen. "You have a *monkey*."

"And a gun, fool!" snapped Nathan Johnson.

"I don't have a pen?" said Sweetcheeks. He looked at the monkey and then at Solomon Bloomington, as if unsure to whom he was telling his story. "What's going on?"

Gurl, who had remained invisible through the entire story, reappeared. "You were going to take me back to your lair, remember? Now that you have the pen and everything."

Solomon Bloomington gasped. "Georgie? Is that you?"

Georgie, thought Gurl. *Is that me?*

Sweetcheeks pouted and pointed at Peter Paul. "*He* said I didn't have a pen."

"Does anyone have a pen to give this guy?" said Nathan Johnson.

Everyone except Solomon Bloomington and Gurl frantically checked their pockets.

"No," said Peter Paul glumly. "No pen."

"Rats," said Iggy Fleishman, backing away from the microphone.

"I know," said Peter Paul. "All the guy wants is a pen and we don't have one."

"That's not what I mean," Iggy said. "I was talking about those!"

He pointed out into the street. Far below the racing Wings, in the middle of the road, a manhole cover had been pushed aside. The Sewer Rats of Satan had grown tired of hiding in the bowels of the city and sprang from the depths like a thousand hungry demons.

CHAPTER 27

Undipped

AT THE SIGHT OF THE giant rats, the crowd began to panic, screaming and flying in every direction. The rats ignored them, streaming instead towards the parade floats that had been moored alongside Central Park.

What now? thought Bug, trying to muscle his way through a pack of racers who had no intention of letting him win the race and, oddly, no intention of letting him get *out* of the race. Hot Pink Unitard, flying somewhere around Bug's ankles, viciously pinched Bug's calves. Silver Unitard elbowed Bug in the gut and earned a nip from Noodle, who did not take well to hostile elbows. Above him and below him, racers kicked and slapped, trying to get ahead.

The pack rounded another corner and flew back towards the main stage. Through the throng of flying fluorescent bodies, Bug could see Sweetcheeks on stage, brandishing a gun – and a monkey? – at several other people, including Gurl. And Bug saw something else too: The Professor, half hidden by the foot of the museum steps. What was *he* doing here?

But there was no time to think about why the rats wanted to get to the balloons so badly, and no time to think about The Professor. Bug had to get Gurl away from that stage before his stupid, horrible father did something *really* stupid and horrible.

The racers careened towards the main stage and Bug could hear Sweetcheeks's voice above the din.

"I'm tired of this monkey talk!" Sweetcheeks said. "Oooh! Who's that guy? He's got a funny zipper face!"

Just then Gurl caught Bug's eye. "Bug!" she yelled. "Look out!"

Something huge and heavy slammed into him from behind, scattering the pack of Wings every which way and sending Bug into a tumbling roll. Noodle howled as Bug tried to right himself and hang on to her at the same time.

Bug turned around to face his attacker. There he was, Odd John, looking more freakish than ever, hanging in the air like some sort of creepy, zipper-faced bat. He grinned, gnashing his teeny teeth, and took a playful swipe at Bug, which Bug barely evaded. Hissing, Noodle clawed at John's hand, erasing the terrible smile and replacing it with an angry grimace. For a moment John simply glared at Bug, but then he seemed to relax. He reached up and pulled the tab on his zipper. John unzipped his face and then his whole body.

Bug could not move, could not even make a single sound, for what emerged from the Odd John suit was the oddest thing he had ever seen. First came the head, the long spiky beak (with teeth!) and the alligator eyes – more alligatorish than an actual alligator – then, as the suit slid down like a discarded Halloween costume, the brown leathery wings that fanned out like a gargoyle's. The body, which managed to be both birdlike and manlike at the same time, ended in huge yellow feet, each capped with flesh-rending talons. The suit dropped away, falling to the ground below.

Every fairy tale, every horror story flooded Bug's mind at the sight of the creature. He was a lizard, a pterodactyl, a griffin. He was a flying museum exhibit, a nightmare.

Clicking his fearsome, tooth-ridged beak, Odd John zoomed towards Bug. Bug rocketed upward. Up and up he flew, the odd monster hot on his heels. Still cradling Noodle, unable to use his arms, Bug kicked his legs frantically, scissoring into the sky until he'd cleared the top of the nearby buildings. He glanced down and saw that he was pulling away from John, almost free, when John surged up, clamped down on one of Bug's feet with his beak and shook him like a field mouse.

Several things happened at once: Bug screamed, bit his tongue and punched himself in the nose.

It took him a few seconds to realise that he had also let go of Noodle.

His foot in a vice and blood filling his mouth, he watched in horror as the little cat plummeted, mewling, towards the earth. Bug smashed his other foot down into the bird's face, once, twice, three times, until the beast let go. Like an Olympic diver, Bug jackknifed at the waist and shot past the beast, zooming after the falling cat. He darted through the swarm of confused Wings as if he were a fish navigating through a coral reef. He could see the main stage coming up fast, Noodle a few feet beyond his fingertips, Gurl's terrified face just below. Gathering all the strength that he had, Bug thrust himself forward and dived *under* the cat. He felt all four paws land on his back, the claws sinking into his flesh and tiny needle teeth gripping the back of his neck.

"Bug! Stop!" Gurl screamed.

Bug stopped, one inch between his face and the stage.

Noodle unhooked her claws from his flesh and jumped off his back, while Bug opened eyes that he hadn't realised were screwed shut. Placing both palms on the ground, he pressed himself to his feet, while Noodle pranced around him, mewing enthusiastically to her saviour. Sweetcheeks stood before him, holding the gun. Next to him stood the large, leathery bird, which must have landed the same moment that Bug did.

Sweetcheeks blinked at Bug and at everyone else in amnesiac confusion, as if he had no idea where he was and who they all were, until the Odd John monster plucked the monkey from Sweetcheek's hand, threw back its head and swallowed.

For a moment everyone on the stage was silent, staring at the bird who had been Odd John. Sweetcheeks shook his head and his eyes cleared.

"Well. That was a clever trick," Sweetcheeks said, smiling tightly at Gurl. "You nearly made me lose my mind." He turned to Bug. "I'm impressed, Sylvester. Quite a performance. Wasn't it, John?"

John clicked his beak, staring at Noodle. Noodle licked her paw and rubbed it over her ear.

"I can see now why you want to be a Wing so badly," Sweetcheeks continued. "And that's something I'm willing to discuss as soon as we take care of business here."

"I'm not discussing anything with you!" Bug snarled.

"Sylvester, be reasonable. You are who you are. Even if you can fly. Now get over here before you get hurt."

"No," said Bug.

"Sylvester!"

"I don't think he's interested," said Solomon Bloomington. "So, what do you plan to do now? Sooner or later someone is going to notice what's going on up here."

"Who? Them?" said Sweetcheeks, flicking his gun at the people in the audience, who were buzzing about like wasps disturbed by a bear. "The Sewer Rats have scared them all away."

"You only have one gun and one... er... bird. You can't kill all of us."

"That's where you're wrong," said Sweetcheeks. "I certainly *can* kill all of you. I've got a bumblebee balloon with all of your names on it. All I have to do is tell my men to burst it. Now Mr Bloomington" – Sweetcheeks turned the gun on Gurl – "you give me that pen or you'll watch your daughter die."

"Daughter!" Bug blurted, his buggy eyes practically bugging out of his face. "What do you mean, 'daughter'?"

"Stay out of this, Sylvester," his father said.

Bunny Bloomington began to weep and Solomon patted her back. "I wish I could give you the pen." Sol looked at Gurl. "I would give you anything you wanted to get my daughter back."

"So then give it to me!"

"I can't," said Solomon. "I don't have it."

"Stop lying! You have it."

"He's not lying." A funny little man with green hair hobbled up the stairs and across the stage, walking as if his trousers chafed and shoes pinched him (which they will if you haven't worn them in fifty years).

"You!" said Sweetcheeks. Odd John shrank back against his boss.

"Me," said The Professor calmly (and soberly).

"But you don't leave your apartment!"

"Not usually, no," said The Professor, tugging at the legs of his slacks. "Solomon doesn't have the pen."

"Who has it?"

The Professor shrugged. "I do."

"Where is it? Give it to me! Or I'll kill all of these people!"

"Oh?" said The Professor. "With what? I think the bee has lost its sting." He gestured to the street behind him, to the floats. The Sewer Rats of Satan had chased off all Sweetcheeks's men and surrounded the float protectively.

Sweetcheeks's lovely face turned purple. "Those dirty rats are helping you?"

"I promised them a little something," said The Professor. "Something only I can give them."

"Great," said Sweetcheeks. "So I'll just kill *you*."

"Well, that would be stupid," said The Professor. "Since I'm the only one who knows where the pen is. Then again, people are a stupid lot."

Sweetcheeks's eyes flashed with fury. "Then I'll torture it out of you. John?"

John flapped his fearsome wings but didn't move.

"He's scared," said The Professor, hooking a thumb at Noodle.

"This time there's only one cat," said Sweetcheeks. "Why should Odd John be afraid? You're not even wearing that housedress with those big pockets."

"Who needs a housedress?" The Professor said. He reached into his trouser pocket and pulled out a white kitten.

Sweetcheeks frowned. "Fine, so now you have two."

"Really?" said The Professor. He reached into his other pocket and pulled out a black kitten. "That's three." He put the kittens on the ground.

The large bird flapped his wings harder now, whipping up a breeze on the stage.

"Calm down, John," said Sweetcheeks. "They're just babies. And you're a grown-up... dinosaur... bird... thing!"

The Professor patted his pockets. "I think there's at least one more," he said. The Professor hooked a finger into the front pocket of his shirt. "Ah. Here they are," he said. There was a loud, thundering, shuddering crack, like the sound of a dam bursting, as a wave of kittens suddenly poured from the pocket. Kitten upon kitten – black, white, striped, tortoise, grey, orange, calico, short-haired, fuzzy, fat, skinny, mean, friendly, scruffy, sweet – hundreds and hundreds and hundreds of wriggling, sharp-eyed, needle-clawed kittens. This mewling, howling tsunami leaped at the leathery bird, attaching themselves like tiny biting burrs. John tried to fly but only got a few feet into the air before the weight of the kittens sent him crashing to the stage in a great fuzzy heap.

Sweetcheeks howled with rage, pointing the gun at The Professor, then at Solomon Bloomington, then at Gurl, then at Bug. "This city is mine!" he yelled. "It belongs to me!"

"No," said Bug, his voice tired. "I don't think so."

Sweetcheeks looked around, realising that he couldn't overpower so many people (and so many kittens). He reached into his own pocket and pulled out what appeared to be a half-filled red balloon. "You'll be sorry," he said and threw the red balloon to the ground. Instantly, a cloud of black dust filled the air and everyone's eyes.

"Gurl," said Bug, coughing on the black dust. "He's going to get away. He'll disappear into the crowd."

Gurl grabbed his hand. "Come on." She pointed towards the sky. Bug shot into the air, pulling Gurl along. Gurl thought she heard Bunny Bloomington scream, "No! Don't go!"

Once they were free of the black cloud, they looked down over the masses of people. "There!" said Gurl. "I see him."

"Make sure he doesn't see us," said Bug.

"Right," said Gurl and the two of them vanished. Sweetcheeks's signature golden hair was easy to follow as it bobbed through the throngs of flying, floating and hopping people. The gangster looked over his shoulder as he ran, but as it seemed no one was on his tail, he soon slowed, moving casually and confidently through the crowd. Bug and Gurl flew after him, overshooting his position to land in front of him, popping into sight.

Sweetcheeks drew up short as Bug snatched the gun from his hand. "What?" he said. "You two again! How did you...?"

"I'm a Wall," said Gurl.

"I'm a Wing," said Bug.

"Yes," Sweetcheeks said. "Of course you are. And it looks like I was wrong about the flying." He smiled a sick and oily sort of smile, like an advertisement for smiling. "And I'm glad about that. You are one amazing flyer. I mean that, Sylvester. Do you mind if I call you by your given name or would you prefer Bug?"

Bug eyed him warily. "Bug's good."

"Bug then," Sweetcheeks said. "Listen, I know you're upset with me. And I understand that. I'd probably be upset too. But we can help one another. All three of us. Now that John is... um... indisposed, I could use a Wing like you. And we both know how useful your little friend might be," he said, tipping his golden head at Gurl. "What do you say?"

Bug took a deep breath. He crooked a finger and a Sewer Rat shambled over to Sweetcheeks.

"Hell. Oh," said the rat. Before Sweetcheeks could think to

move, the Rat took hold of Sweetcheeks's arm, clicked his sharp teeth and swayed back and forth in a sort of rat purr.

Sweetcheeks tried to tug away from the grinding, swaying Rat, but its grip was too strong. "Get it off me!" said Sweetcheeks.

"I'm sorry, Dad," said Bug. "I can't let you go."

Sweetcheeks turned to stare at Bug, a look of the utmost disdain falling like a curtain over his face. "You always were such a useless little brat. No guts at all. 'I want to be a Wing, Daddy, I want to be a Wing!' Never knew what was good for you. And look, you want nothing to do with me, but you're zipping around with this girl who isn't anything more than a thief. No better than I am."

"She's the Bloomingtons' daughter," Bug said.

"So what? How does that change what she's done?" Bug said nothing and Sweetcheeks nodded. "You know I'm right. But it doesn't matter if I'm right because you won't listen to me anyway. You're just like your mother. She wanted me to settle down and be a 'normal' person. Who wants to be a normal person? What was I supposed to do, get a job selling insurance?"

"Why not?" said Bug.

Sweetcheeks clucked his tongue. "You think the Bloomingtons are going to care about you just because you've been hanging around with their brat? You're a Grabowski! A gangster! It's in your blood!"

"It might be in my blood," said Bug. "But I can still choose who and what I want to be."

Sweetcheeks tried again. "You think that this girl won't cut you out of her life as soon as she gets into that big penthouse?"

"I'd never cut Bug out of my life," said Gurl.

"Right," Sweetcheeks said, trying to tug his arm from the Rat's paw and gnashing his teeth in frustration. "You two little fools deserve each other! You're gutless, spineless, senseless and hopeless. You're just *less*, how about that? Less than zeros."

Bug looked at Gurl, and Gurl looked at Bug. Bug cocked a fist and, for a moment, it appeared he might bloody his knuckles on his father's nose. But then the hand dropped to his side.

"Maybe I am less," Bug said. "But I'm a whole lot more than you."

CHAPTER 28

Golden

AFTER THE BLACK DUST HAD settled, the police were called in, Sweetcheeks and his gang were rounded up, the poison bumblebee was contained and a certain oddity was dispatched to the Museum of Natural History. Then Mayor Iggy Fleishman held a special press conference. Cameras were set up at the penthouse of The Richest Man in the Universe, where Bug, Gurl, the Bloomingtons, The Professor and several hundred friends gathered for the celebration of the century.

"Well, folks, this has got to have been the most exciting Flyfest ever held!" Iggy said as the press corps laughed and the cameras flashed. "We saw a monster unmasked, a twelve-year-old kidnapping solved and a notorious gangster brought to justice. We also saw," he said, "some of the most spectacular flying we've ever seen. Sylvester 'Bug' Grabowski, would you approach the podium, please?"

In the audience Bug stood immobile until Gurl punched him in the arm. "Bug, it's you! Go on!"

In a trance, Bug walked up to the podium.

"Look at this modest boy, walking instead of flying. Say 'hi' to the city," Iggy said cheerfully, waving at the TV cameras.

"Uh... hi?" Bug said.

Iggy slung an arm around Bug's broad shoulders. "We witnessed this young man," he announced, "battle a fiendish beast over *twenty* storeys in the air, all while holding on to his pet cat. Yes, I said *twenty* storeys. That's a world record, my friends! Then he dived straight down, coming to a full and complete stop just an inch before he hit the ground. An *inch*! We have never seen a feat like that before. Never. Therefore, this year's Flyfest judges – Peter Paul Allen, Rosy B., Nathan Johnson and I – are proud to award this year's Golden Eagle to the youngest Wing in the city's history. Rosy?"

Rosy B., dressed in a foil T-shirt and hot pants made of yellow feathers, sashayed to the podium carrying a dazzling gold statue. "By a unanimous decision, this year's Golden Eagle goes to Sylvester 'Bug' Grabowski." She handed the statue to

Bug, grabbed his face between her two hands and gave him a long, juicy kiss.

The reporters and cameramen whooped and hollered, the Bloomingtons' party guests clapped and The Sewer Rats of Satan — each of whom cradled a brand-new kitten in their arms — said, "Nice!" (Only Gurl seemed to find Rosy B.'s performance a little over the top.)

As Iggy chattered on and the press conference wrapped up, Gurl wandered around the Bloomingtons' lavish penthouse. Instead of being stuffed with antique furniture the way that Gurl imagined a rich person's house would be, the Bloomingtons' penthouse was huge and airy, with floor-to-ceiling windows that made the night sky a part of the décor. For the party the Bloomingtons had imported thousands of butterflies, and they fluttered about the penthouse, daubing the air with bright splashes of colour. A monarch alighted on Gurl's finger, fanning itself. As she watched the butterfly's wings open and close, Gurl tried to comprehend the events of the last few hours and found it impossible, dreamier than any daydream she'd ever had.

Bunny Bloomington hovered nervously. After the whirlwind following the Flyfest, there had been a lot of hugging and crying. Sol and Bunny had told her how much they had loved her, how much they had missed her, and how glad they were to have her back and that everything was all right. But Gurl couldn't help but think that while the Bloomingtons might have loved her as a baby, she was someone else now. A person with a history. Someone who had done things, good and bad, and would have to live with them. She knew that she and her parents were strangers, and didn't know quite what to say to one another after all these years.

"I just saw your cat go into the bathroom and shut the door," Bunny said.

"She does that," Gurl told her. "Don't be surprised if you hear the blow-dryer."

"The blow-dryer? She must be a remarkable cat. But since you are a remarkable girl, that makes sense."

Gurl flushed and looked down at her feet, at the new shoes that the Bloomingtons had given her before the party.

"Are you having a good time? Can I get anything for you?"

"Oh, no," Gurl said shyly. "I'm fine, thank you."

"All right, if you say so." Bunny tugged at her pearl necklace, clearly not sure what to say to this girl, a girl she had yearned for, a girl gone for so long. "It might take a while for us to get used to each other," she ventured. "I hope you'll be patient if I seem a little overprotective."

"I think I might like you being a little overprotective."

Bunny smiled then, a small smile that showed just a hint of the pretty woman she was before Gurl was taken away. "Thank you for saying so, Georgie. Or maybe I should call you Gurl?"

"Gurl. For now." Gurl thought that this would be a good time to hug Bunny, to tell her that she loved her or at least hoped she would one day, but she didn't know how to do it. And then the moment was gone.

"Well," said Bunny, patting her on the arm. "Here's your friend. I'm going to find Sol and let the two of you talk."

"Hey," said Bug. His face was flushed and his mouth was covered in lipstick. He had a butterfly on each shoulder.

"Maybe you ought to wipe your face," Gurl said. "Unless you plan on kissing her again."

"I didn't kiss her, she kissed me."

"You didn't stop her."

"Enough! Give the boy a little slack," said a low growling voice. "He just won a Golden Eagle, for pete's sake."

Gurl turned to find a dark-haired man in a slim-fitting pinstriped suit standing next to them sipping a pink drink. "Jules! What are you doing here? Where have you been?"

"Been? Here, there, everywhere, what do you think? But ever since I saw you at Harvey's that day, I've made it my business to keep an eye on you."

"Keep an eye on me?" Gurl laughed. "What are you? My fairy godmother or something?"

"Fairy godmother! Do you see any glass slippers or pumpkins around here? I'm no fairy godmother. The correct terminology is 'Personal Assistant', if you don't mind. Unlike fairies, we Personal Assistants can't involve ourselves directly in your affairs, we can only *assist*, you understand?"

Gurl laughed again, sure that he was only kidding, but stopped when Bug nudged her and Jules glared.

"Personal Assistant?" Gurl said incredulously. "I don't believe it."

"After all that's happened to you, you don't believe in *me*?" said an indignant Jules.

"But— but—" Gurl said. "How come you only appeared once in a while? How come you didn't come to me at Hope House? Why didn't you come to me in The Black Box or in the subway?"

"I'm not Superman," Jules said. "I'm not a bird or a plane or whatever. I have a lot of clients, OK? And they all want something. You cannot believe how many keys I have to find, how many computers I have to reboot, how many weddings I have to call off. I show up when I can and that's all there is to it. Only so much Jules to go around. Besides, if I came every single time one of you had a problem, all you'd ever grow up to be is a giant whining baby. We Personal Assistants just give a person a little push every once in a while. A little encouragement is all you need."

"But why did you have to be so weird about everything?" Bug wanted to know. "Like all that stuff about the French movies at the theatre. Why couldn't you just tell us about the monkeys?"

Jules looked genuinely perplexed. "But that would have

ruined the whole mystery for you. Where's the fun in that?" He turned and called to one of the tuxedoed food servers. "Excuse me? Hey! You! This girl needs some ice water. And can I have some of that puff pastry with the little frankfurters? Thanks!" He turned back to Gurl. "What was I saying?"

Gurl decided that since she had got everything she'd ever dreamed of, who was she to question the help that Jules had given her? "I was saying thank you," said Gurl. "For the excellent Personal Assistance."

Jules winked at her. "You're very welcome, darling."

"Does everyone have one?" Bug wanted to know. "A Personal Assistant?"

"We have our assignments, but some of us do a little freelance work when we see a worthy candidate. When I've got a few minutes, I'll be checking in with you. And your little friend there." He waggled his fingers at Bug. "He's got a unique look, but I think he's a keeper."

Bug flushed an even deeper red, red enough to match Rosy B.'s lipstick stains.

"Oh! Speaking of looks, that reminds me." Jules reached into his jacket and pulled out a slip of paper. "Here's an article I thought that you might find interesting."

Gurl read the headline out loud: "Merciless Matron Cheats Hope House out of Thousands."

"Get out!" said Bug. "Let me see that." He grabbed the

article from Gurl's hands and read further. "'Geraldine Terwiliger, matron of Hope House for the Homeless and Hopeless for over thirty years, has been charged with twenty-two counts of embezzlement. The matron, who is now sixty-nine, confessed to her crimes after a freakish plastic surgery accident left her lips blown up four times their normal size and much of her face hanging down around her chin. After a search of the orphanage premises, tens of thousands of dollars worth of name-brand fur coats, designer scarves and other merchandise was found. Detectives suspect that Terwiliger was the head of a ring of petty thieves.

"'In a bizarre twist, the orphans of Hope House seem to be suffering a collective memory loss, the cause of which is being kept under wraps. The children will remain in the care of a team of psychologists and neurologists.'"

"So what do you think we should call Mrs Terwiliger now?" asked Gurl.

"Hmmm..." said Bug. "How about 'Hangdog'?"

"I wonder if they found the monkeys?" said Gurl.

"You know, I wouldn't mind if I never saw another monkey again," Bug said.

"Now don't say that," Jules said, clicking his tongue. "You are who you are because you forgot who you were. And don't forget it." Jules frowned into his drink. "Or maybe I've simply had too many of these." He looked past Gurl's head. "Oh. My.

God," he said. "Excuse me, Gurl, but there's a serious rhinestone emergency I need to take care of. I'll be in touch." And with that, he floated off into the sea of guests.

"Well," said Gurl.

"Well," said Bug.

"Nice eagle."

"Thanks. Nice penthouse."

"Thanks." Gurl tucked her hair behind one ear and struggled, once again, for something to say. The one who thought he had a father now didn't and the one who thought she didn't have a father did. If they weren't the people they believed themselves to be, who were they?

"What are you going to do now? I mean, where are you going to live?" Gurl lowered her voice to a whisper. "If you need help hiding out, I can help you."

Bug smiled and glanced down at his trophy. "I don't think I could hide out for very long with this. Besides, I've got some offers to do some advertisements and stuff. Solomon, Mr Bloomington... uh... your dad said he would help me." Bug paused a minute. "Your dad also told me that he never once stopped looking for you. Never."

"Yeah, well," said Gurl. Her throat tightened around what had been bothering her through the whole party. "He couldn't have looked that hard."

"Are you sure about that?" said Bug.

"Look at all the money he has," Gurl blurted. "He could have hired a thousand detectives."

"Maybe he did," Bug said. "You remember what The Professor said. That sometimes Walls disappear just when people are looking for them? Maybe that's what happened with those detectives. Besides, having money doesn't guarantee that you get what you want. I speak from experience."

"Oh," said Gurl. "Right. Are you...?" She trailed off. She had found her dad, but Bug had lost his. Even if he hated the guy, that had to be harder than anything Gurl could imagine.

"I'm all right," Bug said. "I think. It's not like we ever had a normal relationship. I don't think I even know him. And I'm sure he doesn't know me."

"Yeah," said Gurl, thinking about her own parents. She could barely absorb everything that had happened, and if she thought about it for longer than three minutes, she started to get dizzy. "So. You said something about advertisements?"

"I know, it's funny. With my weird face and everything."

"Your face isn't weird!" Gurl said.

"Sure," said Bug, smiling.

"OK, it's a little weird. But in a totally good way."

"I'll take your word for it." Bug scanned the room. "Where do you think The Professor's gone?"

"I don't know. He was sulking in the corner just a few minutes ago."

"We should probably find him. He doesn't like people. And he said that his clothes were itchy and he kept scratching. In very personal places."

The two of them pushed through the crowds of revellers, but as they were stopped over and over for more kisses, congratulations and "welcome homes", it took more than forty-five minutes to search a single room. Finally, after checking the living room, the sitting room and the library, they peeked into Solomon Bloomington's office. There they saw Solomon, Bunny and The Professor chatting among the broccoli, cauliflower, daisies and dandelions that pushed themselves up through the carpet.

"Oh, sorry," said Gurl. "We didn't mean to interrupt."

"No, no!" said Solomon. "Come in, come in."

Gurl and Bug walked into the office and shut the door.

"Have a seat. We were just talking about the two of you," said Solomon. "And we wanted to give The Professor a place where he could get comfortable." Solomon was leaning against his vine-covered window, Bunny perched on top of the desk and The Professor sat in a wing chair beside the fire, now wearing his favourite housedress and holding a sleeping Noodle on his lap.

"Wait a minute!" said Bug, plucking a pea pod from the top of the desk. "I remember this place! We've seen it before. The first time we went flying. We were right outside your window. You waved at us!"

"I know," said Solomon. "I remember that day too. That was the day the garden grew, the day I knew that Georgie was alive. It was like summertime."

He gazed at Gurl with such a gentle, fatherly expression that Gurl crossed both arms and hugged herself.

"I like the garden," said Gurl, watching the butterflies flit from blossom to blossom. (Noodle loved the butterflies, but seemed too sleepy to chase them.)

"I like the room this way too," Solomon told her. "So does Bunny."

"How did you grow stuff like this?" Bug wanted to know. "In the carpet? And how do you water them?"

"You'll have to ask The Professor about that," said Solomon. "He knows everything."

"Hardly," said The Professor.

"And what about the pen?" Bug said. "Gurl told me that my... that Sweetcheeks wanted to steal a pen?"

"Yes," The Professor said. "Only he knows why. An old faulty thing really. No use to anyone now. Not that your father... I mean... *Sweetcheeks* would have known that."

"Guess not," said Bug.

But Gurl wasn't paying attention, she was watching the fond way in which The Professor petted Noodle. Her heart sank. "I suppose that you're taking your cat back now?" she said, trying, and failing, to keep her voice from cracking.

"What? No," The Professor said. "Just borrowing her for a bit. She's yours. Chose you and all that. Besides, I've got a lot more where she came from."

"More?" said Bunny. "What about all those kittens you gave to The Sewer Rats?"

The Professor scratched Noodle under the chin and the cat sighed. "Oh, Riddles are always popping up. I can't stop them. I wouldn't want to."

"Riddles?" said Solomon. "You mean the cats?"

"Yes, the cats. Cats are Riddles." He glanced up from the cat and saw that his audience was frowning at him in confusion. "There are problems," he explained, clearly trying to be patient, "and there are Riddles. Problems you can solve. Problems are my business. Riddles? Well, Riddles are fascinating to think about, but you can never find the right answer to them, can you? You can never quite figure them out. And as soon as you think you have one solved, another Riddle pops up. I won't even get into when a Riddle coughs up a hairball."

Gurl thought of the riddle that popped into her head sometimes: *If a tree falls in a forest, and no one's around, does it make a sound?* "You're not going to... uh... solve my cat, are you?" Gurl fretted aloud. "Nothing's going to happen to her, right?"

"No," said The Professor. "She'll remain a Riddle for ever. Just as you like her."

Relieved, Gurl exhaled. She idly fingered the plants that

sprouted from the floor all around her and leaned down to smell a rose. All she ever wanted was to be normal and yet she had so much more. With Noodle officially hers, she was The Richest Girl in the Universe. It didn't seem fair for one person to have so much, and she was suddenly fearful that it wasn't real, that she was dreaming it all, and that it could be taken away in a blink. That she would wake up to Mrs Terwiliger's psycho-clown face, forced to sit on the sidelines while the whole world flew away. Before she knew what was happening, a tear dropped from her cheek into the heart of the rose.

"Oh," said Bunny. "Georgie, baby, are you all right?"

It was this unfamiliar name, the word "baby", that did it. Gurl flinched. "I'm sorry. I don't know who that is," she said. An ache at the back of her throat gathered and grew until she didn't think she could keep breathing another minute. But she kept breathing. "There are things you should know. About who I am. About the things I did." She began in the beginning, with Hope House. Her name. Mrs Terwiliger. The alley, with Noodle. She told them about Harvey's and stealing the scarves. About Bug and The Professor. The Punks. The hotel and the food they ordered, but couldn't, and didn't, pay for. Sweetcheeks and his lair. The Black Box. The attempt to steal the pen.

Making up for years of watching, years of silence, she talked and talked and talked and talked. The tears streamed down her face now, but she didn't seem to feel them and she didn't wipe them away. When Gurl was done telling her tale, she looked from Sol to Bunny, wondering what they would do. Did she disgust them? Did they wish she would just disappear?

Gurl didn't know her own father and didn't know what a wise man he was. Solomon knelt in front of Gurl and gathered her tightly in his arms, drawing her head to his shoulder, but he didn't tell her it was OK because he understood that it wasn't. What was OK about a baby kidnapped from her parents? What was OK about a girl alone in the world with only a cat to call a friend? What was OK about having to steal to save the thing you loved most? What was OK about being away from your own family for so long that you can't trust them to forgive you?

Bunny knelt too and put her arms around her husband and her daughter. And the silent but accepting embrace of her parents told Gurl that though things might not be OK, one day they would be.

The reunited family crouched in Sol's strange indoor garden until Gurl's tears dried and she began wiping her face self-consciously.

"This is a lot for you to take in," Solomon said, releasing her just far enough that he could look at her. "A lot for all of us. I have a suggestion. Why don't you and Bug take a break? Go out and get some fresh air?"

"Really?" said Gurl.

Solomon squeezed her shoulders. "Really. Bunny and I will be here waiting for you."

Gurl swallowed hard. "What do you think?" she asked Bug. "Do you want to get some air?"

"I think that's the best idea I've heard all day," Bug told her.

"OK," she said, standing. "We'll be back soon."

"I know you will."

Gurl and Bug walked to the door until The Professor stopped them. "Don't forget your cat."

Gurl grinned. "Right. Come on, Noodle!"

Noodle mewled, jumped off The Professor's lap, and leaped into Gurl's waiting arms. "See you all later," she said.

Solomon and Bunny stood together. "See you."

After the children had run from the room, The Professor said, "Is that really safe to send them off like that?"

"Don't worry," Solomon told him. "I've got about one hundred guards outside. And security cameras. And satellites. Nothing will happen to her. Not again."

"They'll go flying, you know," said The Professor.

Solomon laughed. "Probably. Wouldn't you?"

"Me?" said The Professor. "Certainly not. I told you on the phone that men weren't meant to fly."

"True. But then again, a lot of things weren't meant to happen and they did anyway. Look at The Sewer Rats. I'm sure they weren't meant to worship cats either."

"Yes, that is strange," said Bunny. "Why do they like cats so much?"

The Professor sighed. "It's a long story."

"Why don't you tell it?" said Solomon. "We've got the time."

So The Professor told them the story that had been Sweetcheeks Grabowski's bane and then his favourite, the story of a robbery. How a lone little man was out walking downtown. How Billy Goat Barbie had head-butted the little man and taken off with the man's monkey. How The Sewer Rats of Satan had stolen a good umbrella and a wool coat with a few small Riddles tucked inside, how those Riddles stayed to live with the rats in the sewers and how the rats had worshipped cats ever since. How Mose The Giant had seen the footprints in the snow and discovered The Wall. How Dandy Bill had made off with a notebook and a queer silver pen. The book had lots of notes, The Professor told them, but the pen was the dangerous thing. "It never worked that well, you know."

Solomon laughed, "I'd say it worked *too* well. As the story's been told in my family, all Dandy Bill had to do was scribble on a scrap piece of paper: 'I'll be rich when pigs fly!' The next thing he knew, people were flapping around like birds outside his window and he'd made a fortune in pork bellies."

"Let me get this straight: are you saying that the *pen* is what made people fly?" said Bunny. "That Dandy Bill wrote down a joke and the joke came true?"

"That's what The Professor told me when he called a few weeks ago. I didn't believe it either."

"That's ridiculous," said Bunny. "How can a pen make us do that?"

"Anything you write down with that pen comes true, but only in the way the pen wants it to," The Professor said. "Dandy Bill wrote something about pigs flying, the pen most likely thinks people are pigs, so there you are."

"But it doesn't make any sense," Bunny said. "Not everyone can fly. Most people are terrible actually."

"That," said The Professor, "is a part of the joke. Or the point. The pen has a mind of its own and interprets words the way it likes. I never intended it to be so powerful. I made it to impress a girl." He blushed a little. "I told Dandy Bill that the pen was mightier than the sword, but he didn't listen. People never listen."

"*You* told him?" Bunny said incredulously. "The little man that was robbed all those years ago was *you*? It was your monkey and your coat? It was your pen?"

"Yes. Boaz – the monkey – was a helpful little fellow and I was sorry to lose him. I'm plagued by extra thoughts and Boaz would hang on to them for me. Now it takes me for ever to remember everything. And I'm quite sure I don't."

"But you said that the robbery was in 1845! That was more than 150 years ago!"

"People from Okinawa have been known to live well over

the century mark," said The Professor. "I don't see what's so incredible about it."

"Are you from Okinawa?" Bunny asked.

"No," The Professor said. "Why do you ask?"

Bunny sat back in her chair and stared at The Professor. "Who are you? Really?"

The Professor squirmed under her gaze. "Just an old man who has invented a lot of wonky stuff. That's all."

"I wonder what would have happened if my great-great-great-great-grandfather had listened to you," Solomon said, waving at the portrait of Dandy Bill. "But clearly my ancestor wasn't very principled. I believe I'm the descendant of a madman."

"Aren't we all?" said The Professor.

"And I guess I'm not so principled myself. I tried to use it, you know," said Solomon. "To find Georgie."

"Really?" The Professor. "How did that work out?"

"All sorts of odd things popped up."

"I see that," said The Professor, flicking a sprig of basil that sprouted from the arm of his chair.

Bunny was lost in thought. "Professor, in your story you mentioned The Wall. You said the giant saw his footsteps in the snow behind you."

"*Her* footsteps."

"Her footsteps," repeated Bunny softly. "But why was she following you?"

"Well, she had come to my apartment and asked for help," said The Professor. He looked down at the ground, not wanting to meet Bunny's eyes. "She didn't want to be a Wall. She didn't want to be invisible. To my shame, I told her I couldn't help her, then went out for a walk. Maybe she was hoping to change my mind." He sighed. "I was younger then and selfish. Only interested in my inventions."

"I can't even imagine what would have happened had Sweetcheeks Grabowski gotten hold of that pen you invented," said Solomon. "What do you think he would have written?"

"The Hand only knows," said The Professor, ignoring Bunny's perplexed frown.

"So," said Bunny. "Where is the pen now?"

"Safe," The Professor said and patted the pockets of his housedress. "As safe as anything can be."

"*She'll* be safe now, won't she?" said Bunny. "Georgie?"

Solomon pointed out of the vine-choked window. "Why don't you come see for yourself?"

Bunny and The Professor joined Solomon at the picture window, brushing aside the greenery to get a better view. Outside, over the treetops of Central Park, two silhouettes, hands clasped, danced freely in the chill evening air. They looped and twirled before the watchful eye of the moon and before the eyes of the city that loved them.

THE CHAPTER AFTER THE LAST

Ha!

AT 2 AM (WAY PAST his bedtime), The Professor trudged down the city streets, a kitten under each arm and a dozen more following close behind.

"Come," he said to the cats. "We don't know what kinds of crazies are out this late. Gangsters. Vampires. Cat-eating maniacs. Who knows?"

He walked faster, hearing the bones in his knees cracking like twigs. This was no way for an old man to travel. He should have taken a bus. Or a subway. He shouldn't have refused the car that the Bloomingtons had offered.

"Some genius," he muttered to himself. A couple floating by

stared at his housedress and at the cats loping behind. "What are you looking at?" he said irritably. "I hate people. Always staring. Haven't they ever seen an old man before?"

A chill breeze rushed through the thin fabric of his housedress and he shivered. *I wonder*, he thought to himself. He stopped walking and put the kittens on the ground. He bent his old legs into a crouch, nearly falling over in the process. Using his arms as levers, he jumped. He floated up into the air for several yards, hovered there a minute or two and then came gently back to earth. He didn't notice the silver pen fall from his pocket into the gutter.

"Well, what do you know?" he said to himself. "And I wasn't even bitten by a vampire." The Professor scooped up the two kittens. "Come!" he shouted to the rest of the cats. "Time to go home."

High in a tree branch, a black crow blinked its sharp eyes as it waited for The Professor and his feline army to march down the street, around the corner and out of sight.

When the coast was clear, the crow alighted from the tree, flew down to the ground and hopped into the gutter. Like all crows, it had a penchant for shiny things and the silver pen glinted like nothing it had ever seen before. This, thought the crow, was a most spectacular find.

"Ha! Ha! Ha!" the crow laughed. It plucked up the silver pen and launched itself into the night.

acknowledgements

This book wouldn't exist without the help of the sleepover girls: Jessica, Katie, Sam and Carly, who first gave me the idea of this vast and sparkling city. The incredible Ellen Levine, whose savvy seems to be some sort of superpower. My amazing editor, Clarissa Hutton – always tactful, always insightful, always delightful. Gillie Russell and Matthew Morgan at HarperCollins UK, who brought the book overseas and helped to add the final bit of polish. Anne Ursu, Gretchen Moran Laskas and Audrey Glassman Vernick, who pored over every page and corralled all those gangsters, rats, punks, monkeys and kittens. Linda Rasmussen, Annika Noren and Tracey George for the thousand-hour phone marathons that I crave. Reader Katy McGeehee, who whipped through the manuscript in a single night and noticed things that escaped all of us cranky old people. Those Readervillians, Pubsters and Foofs who lent kind ears, good advice and snacks when necessary. And finally, thanks always to Steve – with you I can fly.